REVYSED

CHRISTOPHER L. ADAMS

ACKNOWLEDGMENTS

There are so many that contributed to the creation of this title. To break my many thanks to just a few lines of text seems insufficient, but I will do my best.

To all my friends that read my story so many years ago. Jeff, Elena, Joe, Ray, Mayra. All of you brought something different to my attention that I believe led to a much more polished piece of work.

Thijs and Matt. You sat with me through the entirety of the editing process, challenging me to push the way I write as well as the characters and content itself. Thank you for all the hours spent discussing this story and catching any inconsistencies with word choice or spelling.

Mrs. Keough, you are an editing beast. This novel reads so much better because of your keen and discerning eye.

And of course one of my closest friends, Katie. You have stuck by me since we were in high school and one of the reasons I still write today is because of you. Knowing that no matter how small or big the story, no matter how successful, no matter the content, you always express an excitement to enter my worlds that is unrivaled by any. Thank you for being my biggest fan.

To Mike for believing in me. To my Dad for loving me. And to my Mom for showing me that bringing dreams into reality is more than just imagination.

It's magic.

When the World is truly One, thus is the
death of the individual.

Chapter One

Blink and You Miss

Night descends as the city awakens with new light, the glow of neon signs and towering skyscrapers illuminating the bustling streets below. The denizens of the city go about their respective, daily lives. The absence of the sun does not deter them, but rather, seems to be the very thing that invites more to venture out and readily reject the idea of retreating to their homes. These denizens are varied in multiple ways and some aren't even human.

To the untrained eye, they look human, but the denizens can tell the difference. After all, they live alongside them day to day, and can easily identify these non-humans by the one or two small mechanical protrusions coming from the tops of their heads. These androids walk alongside everyone else, going about their own business, but a few people walk by them in disgust. Some of these people shy away while others pass them as if they were just like everyone else.

One particular android makes his way through the crowd. He has two protrusions on either side of the top of his head. His skin is ebony, matching in tone with his medium length hair. Appearing just as those around him, it is his striking blue eyes that stand out.

He is holding a few bags in his hands when a person accidentally bumps into him. The bags drop to the ground, their contents spilling everywhere.

"Oh," he says politely, "my apologies, pardon me." The person who bumped him simply snorts before walking away.

With a sigh, he turns his blue eyes towards the contents strewn about, bending over to slowly return everything to their bags. Those around him walk by without stopping even a second. He turns and ascends the stairs of a flat. On the door dances a cute holographic display of a kitten jumping and catching a cartoon mouse. It runs on repeat each time the cat grabs its prey. He enters without stopping. A young girl seated in front of a floating computer screen spins around in her chair while munching on a carrot.

"Hey, Blue," she says with her mouth still full, "what's up?" Blue brings the groceries, placing them on the counter in the kitchen. He replies with his voice ever so shaky, "Everything is fine, Renayaka."

The girl spins around in her chair and pounces to his face. She is uncomfortably close but Blue does not seem bothered. Renayaka Amano, or Ren for short, is a small woman, around 25 years old, with brown hair, golden eyes, and pale skin.

"You suck at lying," she says, her eyes locked on his. "You try, I'll give you that, but you just aren't there yet." She shifts her attention to the groceries, looking for any snacks she can find.

Blue watches her, amazed by the deduction. "You were able to tell that I was bothered?" he asks, curious.

"Well yeah," Renayaka replies, "I mean, nothing against you androids – I think your sentience is a beautiful thing, but you're still learning what it means to interact with and be human." She finds a piece of a thin cookie and pops it into her mouth. "You'll get there eventually. I mean, you at least *tried* to lie," she concludes before getting right in his face.

He does not budge. "But neither you, nor my sister, can ever lie to me. Now tell me what's wrong."

Blue looks into Renayaka's eyes and she into his. She can see the mechanical parts within his irises moving, causing his pupils to "dilate." He smiles. "Well, one thing I am learning is that you and your sister are by far the most interesting humans I have met." He adjusts his head so that he can better look at Renayaka. "I believe your close proximity to my face would make anyone else blush, but you seem not to be bothered at all. Quite amusing." He removes the rest of the bags and pulls the hanging cookie from Renayaka's mouth.

She pouts upon losing her cookie. "Hey!" she shouts as she reaches for him.

"You should not eat sweets before your dinner. What would you say if Saiyanoshi did as you are doing now?" Blue asks.

Renayaka scoffs. "You serious?" she asks while following Blue into the kitchen. "I'll give you this, you've got deflecting down."

Blue can't help but smirk. One of the cabinet doors retracts once he is in front of it. He bends over and places boxes of pasta inside when, without looking, he catches a small apple tossed his way by Renayaka. Then, still without turning his head from inside the cabinet, he tosses the apple overhead, landing it neatly inside a fruit basket on the countertop. "Where is Saiyonshi?" he asks.

"She's out on a case, won't be back til late, which is when I was going to make dinner, which is why I was having a snack that you rudely encroached upon while I was...OH SHIT!" Renayaka abruptly rushes out the kitchen, back towards her computer. Blue realizes what has happened but decides to ask anyway.

"Oh, were you-"

"Yah!" Renayaka shouts while jumping back onto her computer. "I was in the middle of helping her when you came in. We were tracking illegal arms capable of shooting through inorganic material without damage or disruption, all while still damaging anything organic." She quickly presses a button on her desk, causing a digital keyboard to illuminate right beneath her fingertips. She begins cracking away with new screens popping up into the air around her.

"Sounds dangerous," Blue muses as he steps in front of the refrigerator, pressing a button so that the doors open from the middle, separating up and down.

"Very," Renayaka replies. "If you have the DNA of your target, like a strand of hair or something like that, you can set the guns to track the target within 100 meters and fire without even using a marksman." Renayaka quickly looks back to Blue, realizing she was sidetracked.

"Don't think I forgot about our conversation either, Blue, we're gonna talk as soon as I keep Sai from dying."

Blue considers, "I'm sorry...was that a joke?"

"Ugh," Renayaka grunts. She types, bringing up a screen that shows a warehouse with various people collected in its center. They are standing beside some boarded up wooden crates.

· · · ● · ● · ● · ·

Inside the warehouse are large crates made of wood and metal stacked on top of another throughout. The four crates in the center are indistinct from the others lining the environment, besides the fact that they are surrounded by men, women, and a single android. All seem more than a little anxious. One large man steps forward.

"We gonna do this?" he asks impatiently, "I'm tired of waiting." The android, who is about the size of a small male child and has the features to match, decides to respond.

"There was one more person that was scheduled to arrive. We should wait for them before continuing."

"Listen, kid," the large man says, "you've still got a few things to learn about people, the main one being that they flake."

"No, no, wait! I'm here…"

The group looks to the side, towards the direction of the voice. Greeting them with an excited grin on her face is a young girl in her early twenties. While not short, no one would describe her as tall. Still, even if the room wasn't full of monochromatic criminals, she would stand out. Her vibrant red hair is short in front but in the back hangs a long ponytail stretching to her lower back. Her sports jacket casually hangs off her slender shoulders, showing off more of her bronze-toned skin. Well-built and with a strut, she commands attention when the point of the entire mission is to blend in. All of this is accented by a single white streak down one of her bangs. Subtle is clearly not something this girl understands.

"Sorry I'm late," she says, "but do you have any idea how hard it is to find parking around here?" No one answers. "I mean, I thought about taking the bus but then I thought, hm, super secret illegal meeting, if something goes wrong and everyone bolts, do I *really* want to be the one person trying to ask for a ride?" Still, no one seems amused. The girl looks at the kid android. "You know what I'm talking about."

The kid tilts his head. "I can run up to 25 miles an hour if necessary."

The girl sighs, "Maybe you don't…"

<Will you stop talking?!> A low frequency, unheard by the others, buzzes in the young girl's ear.

• • • • • ● • ● • • • •

Back at the flat, Renayaka watches the screens floating in front of her. She can see various angles of the warehouse. "You keep playing around Sai, and someone is going to kill you."

• • • • ● • ● • • • •

"Look," the large man says, "we're all here now, so can we start the bidding? Despite the fact this girl is an idiot, she's right. The longer we stay gathered the greater the chance for the SPMD to show."

The girl with the white streak in her hair, Sai, leans to a short woman to her side.

"He just call me an idiot?"

<Sai! I swear to God I will not make you any food for the rest of the week!>

The child android steps forward. He places his hand out. A panel retracts in his arm and a holographic display appears. Blacked out pictures clearly corresponding to the people in the room now floats overhead. Beneath their individual pictures is a small numerical counter sitting at 0000000000. Next to it is another series of numbers showing the time. It reads 22:14. "The bidding will commence shortly," the android replies, "but first I will reveal the merchandise."

Sai watches closely as the holographic display surrounding the boxes disappears, revealing what looks to be specialized guns with a unique scope on each of them.

• • • • ● • ● • • • •

Renayaka zooms in on the weapons, running a quick diagnostic on them. They match with a graph she has on another screen.

"That's them, Sai," she says, "those are the weapons the SPMD are looking for. Calling them now. Do your thing!" Renayaka brings up a video call that links directly to the SPMD dispatch. A young girl answers the line on the other end, her face appearing on Renayaka's screen. The girl is immediately confused when she sees that, where normally Renayaka's face would show, is a simple cartoon animation of a cute dog juggling a ball made of kittens.

"Oh my god," Renayaka says as frenetically as she can muster, "there are a group of people with guns by the docks on 5th and Rizal. Please send someone quick. I don't want to die!"

"Yes ma'am," the voice begins, "please standby and we will send someone as-"

Renayaka hangs up. She senses an eerie silence. She turns around to see Blue looking at her, judging her. She shrugs her shoulders, "What?"

• • • • • • • • • • •

Back at the warehouse, the men and women around Sai hold their wrist up in front of them. On each of their wrist is a watch which illuminates a floating touch screen in front of them. When they tap the floating image, the numbers under the blackened pictures increase. The bidding is underway.

Sai casually raises her hand to her eye. Without drawing the attention of the others, she lightly places her two fingers on her temple. Her left eye immediately illuminates with a light blue hue. Words appear on her contact lens, imperceptible to those around her but clearly defined for her eyes. Her mouth moves, whispering ever so slightly.

She recites the paragraph in front of her rhythmically and with purpose. The file she sees scrolls upwards, timed with the cadence of her speech. Her other hand starts to move inconspicuously at her side. Like her voice, each movement is precise, deliberate. A light blue swirl envelopes her hand as she continues to recite the text in her eye. The time above her reads 22:17.

The short girl standing next to Sai looks up, noticing something strange about her. She stares at Sai, who in turn seems to be staring at the clock. The short girl glances at the display, now reading 22:18, then turns to Sai once more.

Sai looks back at the girl, this time making eye contact. She winks just as she reaches the end of her recitation, and throws the orb of glowing blue light from her hand to the ground.

In an instant, Sai and the weapons in the center of the room disappear. The short girl and the others in the warehouse nearly jump out of their skin. They look to each other, searching for some explanation all are unable to give. It doesn't take long for shock to morph to suspicion and from suspicion to paranoia.

Each armed with their own set of weapons, the people remaining brandish them at one another, ready to fire. As if a single word uttered would be met with a response of gunfire, no one dares say a word. It is the large man that musters the courage to communicate to those behind the guns.

"What the hell?!" Before he can take any action, a group of people wearing police gear come bursting through the doors of the warehouse, weapons drawn.

"Nobody move!" An officer shouts while the other officers train their guns on the group in the center. Knowing that any sort of firefight would result in every single illegally armed man and woman to be swiftly killed, the group of people has no choice but to comply. They each place their hands on their heads, dropping to the ground in surrender. None of them seem to know what is going on or what happened to the merchandise.

The short woman places her hands on the back of her head as an officer comes and places a single circlet on her wrist, followed by the other, at which point the two circlets magnetize towards each other, locking the girl's hands behind her back. The short girl looks up at the visual display where the bidding was being recorded and suddenly gasps.

Beside the amount for the bidding, she is able to read the time: 22:31.

The display disappears.

· · · ● · ● ● · · ·

Sai sits on the roof of an adjacent building overlooking the docks. She closes one eye while the contact in the other zooms in. She watches as the officers take everyone away, placing them in black vans. The criminals are all seated as a wall of energy fires down the back of the vans. Holograms create the appearance that each van is an ice cream truck with a happy mascot on the side.

Sai sees the officers find the weapons she stole tucked over in a corner, slightly away from where the action went down a few minutes earlier. She smiles as she places her finger on her temple, causing the zoomed display to go away, and her eyesight to return to normal. She opens her other eye, relaxing, letting the breeze blow through her hair.

The city is beautiful, with lights so bright one wonders if anyone is actually able to sleep. The people are small from where she sits, swallowed by a city drowning in neon and magical stimulant advertisements. She stands to her feet, the wind picking up, threatening to toss her tumbling to the ground below. Sai is not bothered however, breathing easily as the wind threatens her. As if in defiance, Sai steps to the edge of the building and leans off the side of the roof. She is about 20 stories high but doesn't look down; rather, she looks ahead.

How many times have we done this? I've lost count, but each time it's the same. We lean, always looking forward before gravity grabs a hold of us. That moment, that brief moment when it pulls us, dragging us to meet the ground below, it's that moment we feel it. We feel our heart rate increase, the slight fear and the utter excitement. The feeling fades a little more each time, but even still, there's no other feeling that comes close.

The wind sends the folds and loose parts of our clothing upwards, as if trying to grab the ledge we just jumped from. We look to the rapidly approaching ground, confident as we always are, that no matter what, when our body hits the ground we will be fine.

And we are.

As we approach, we are able to move our hand rhythmically, easily casting our spell. The blue aura of our magic encases our body and creates a blue outline around us. Our descent slows and as soon as our toe makes contact with the ground beneath us, the rest of us follows suit.

We dispel our magic in an instant, and the aura around us disperses, making our clothing and hair fall back to their proper places.

We're magic users, and this is just another day for me.

Sai walks down the street, towards the main city. Androids, people, and small robots about the size of trash cans pack the streets around her. She is effortlessly able to maneuver around them as if second nature while looking up at the towering buildings around her. Whereas before she could only see the lights of neon, now their accompanying words are on full display. Partnered with those displays are skyscraper-sized holograms, adding to the mixture of colorful lights while attempting to catch the attention of the citizens below, citizens who are all too use to ignoring those attempts.

A tiny robot makes its way around Sai, sweeping up trash left by those unbothered with the world around them. Androids walk in step beside each other, holding hands. People push past each other to squeeze in and out of packed storefronts while crafty street peddlers station themselves strategically in front of high traffic areas.

A small ten-year-old boy with such a strategy relaxes beside a tiny stand off to the side of one of these stores. He moves his hands rhythmically, with little effort, making an animal of fire in thin air. Pedestrians pass by, paying him no mind.

Sai slows for the briefest of moments as she passes by. She turns her wrist upside down to easily see the glowing display on the metal band around it. With a quick swiping motion in the direction of the boy a quiet sound is made and he quickly turns over his own wrist, seeing a recent transaction of 5 pounds. He shows Sai a polite smile before continuing to creating his flame animals on the street.

A news anchor is illuminated on a display projected on the side of a building. "The recently elected prime minister marks the first magic user elected as prime minister in the last 50 years. Magic users and non-users rejoiced together in the streets over this momentous occasion."

Sai walks past the broadcast, paying it no mind. Cars pass by her on the street, rolling to starts and stops corresponding to the floating traffic lights at intersections. The cars vary in design, from sleek to retro, sitting on top of six tires in some cases. Cyclists of both android and human laugh, passing each other in the bike lane and crossing in front of stopped traffic without worry.

The city has peeled away, becoming an area more suburban in nature. What once were tall buildings are now hanging trees. What once were large crowds are now small flats. The heavy luminescence and advertisements of the city have now been replaced with the house lights and holographic stop signs. A car with two boys in their teens is stopped at a light. The boy on the passenger side notices two girls pull up in a car beside them. They catch each other's attention, making head nods and gestures towards each other. The driver of the boys' car presses a button inside, changing the holographic display around it to be a sleeker design for the body of his vehicle. The two girls, unimpressed, laugh to each other before speeding off the moment the light changes.

Sai walks up the steps of her flat until she gets to the repeating image of a cat catching a mouse dancing on her door. With only the slightest eye roll she lets the door scan her. It slides open and the dancing image disappears. Without a moment's hesitation she enters, the door sliding back into place and the holo-image that covered it reappearing.

The city is vast. The city is busy. The city is the future.

Chapter Two

Revysed

Sai enters the flat, takes off her coat and tosses it on the sofa. Plopping onto the couch, she throws her feet up and arms back. Ren doesn't turn around, preoccupied with whatever is on her screens.

"At least I didn't die this time," Sai says with a laugh.

"That is rather impressive considering the sheer number of weapons being sold that could have easily ended your life." Blue casually cuts up some greens in the kitchen, never looking up as he speaks. Sai and Ren both give Blue a look. He senses it but does not understand. "Did I say something wrong?"

Sai shakes her head, deciding to move to a tall chair sitting in front of the bar leading to the kitchen. "We have anything to drink?" she asks no one in particular.

"Alcoholic or otherwise?" Ren asks, finally sliding away from her computer to engage.

"Otherwise," Sai replies, "if I have a drink right now, I think my head might split open."

Blue pours Sai some juice while Ren presses a button on her wristwatch. Each of her computer screens immediately shut off. Looking a little exasperated she makes her way to the kitchen.

"Why is that?" Ren asks, "I thought you were used to doing that spell."

"I am," Sai answers, "but cut me some slack. There was a time I couldn't hold that incantation for more than five seconds, and that was a whole 13 minutes. I've gotten better, doesn't mean it's any less difficult to do."

"No, I get ya," Ren says as she places an apron over her neck and shoos Blue out of the kitchen. He finds himself a seat beside Sai. "I know a spell that powerful requires a ton of mana. I'm just happy you were able to get out of there with the weapons before the SPMD showed. I'd really rather not hear it from Dane again."

Ren notices the lack of a response she was expecting. She steals a quick glance to her sister, whose head has dropped to the bar table. Ren doesn't let Sai rest for another second. "Hey, get in here and help me. I ain't runnin' no charity."

Sai struggles to raise her head, her pouty face begging for Ren to be kind to her just this once. "Do I have to," she says with a whine, "I'm so tiiiirrrreeedddd."

"Nuh uh," Ren says, moving around the bar to physically pick her sister up. "Even Blue helped out a bit and he doesn't even eat."

"Well," Blue begins, "not in the way you humans ingest sustenance. But I do have my own form of eating that recharges my cells and allows me to conserve energy so that I may go about my regular functions. If I refrain from these weekly acts I could cease to function or as you say, die."

Sai and Ren respond not with words, but with stares. He shrugs. "I may not have to do it every day but it still does count I believe."

There is a knock at the door to their flat. Surprised, they all turn with a snap towards the sound. The holographic display peels away, revealing an older man in his fifties standing outside. There is nothing spectacular about him, but his wrinkled face is weathered from years of stress making him appear older than his actual age. He is not able to see inside the flat even though everyone inside can see him. They instantly recognize him as Dane.

"Aw shit," Sai groans, dropping her head.

Ren moves towards the door, brushing her apron off. "It's okay," she assures, "you didn't leave any trace of yourself at the docks, right?"

Sai shakes her head. "Nothing but my sig, but they have no reason to scan for it.

"Good," Ren continues, "so we're fine. He probably just came to check on us." She goes to open the door, raising her hand to the wall, but pauses before her hand touches it. She quickly turns to Blue. "Blue, you know what y-"

"I know," he replies, "I am getting more accustomed to lying being around you two all day."

Ren nods her head, placing her hand on the wall. The holographic display on the outside disappears and the wall slides back. Dane strides in comfortably.

"Renayaka, Saiyonoshi, Blue, how you all doing tonight?" When Dane fully enters the door behind him slides closed and the hologram reappears.

"We're good," Sai replies, "just hanging tonight."

"That so," Dane replies suspiciously, "you've been here all night?"

"Yep," Ren and Sai answer quickly in unison.

"Uh huh..." Dane approaches Blue. Blue looks at Dane without flinching. Both Ren and Sai exchange worried glances unnoticed by Dane. "Blue." Dane nods.

"How are you this evening Chief Inspector Dane? It is so nice to see y-"

"They've been here all night?"

Blue holds for a moment, making Ren and Sai immediately tense up. Blue does not blink when he finally replies, "Yes, Chief Inspector, we have been in all evening, unless you count the time I left to pick up groceries so that Renayaka could make dinner for Saiyonoshi and herself."

This prompts the chief to step back a bit, a slight reaction but nothing big. "I see..."

"What's this about Dane?" Ren asks, moving back to the kitchen now that the perceived danger has passed.

"Something went down tonight. Got an anonymous tip about some weapons smugglers holding a bid for some very dangerous hardware."

"Really?" Sai asks with maybe just a little too much inflection.

Ren gives her a look that says, "I swear to God, I will murder you."

"Really," Dane continues, "but the thing is, by the time my unit arrived on the scene, the weapons had been removed from the warehouse. The bidders looked completely flabbergasted, like they got caught with their pants down."

"You don't say." Sai leans in as if she is very intrigued with his story. Ren picks up a knife which she firmly, and noticeably, cuts into a piece of meat.

"But that's not the strangest thing...you see, the people we arrested reported that there was a girl there that had brown skin and red hair with a white streak down one side." Ren freezes, recognizing that they weren't as home free as she thought. Sai is calm, not a worry in her body. "Now, considering the amount of people in this city that could fit that description, I thought, 'hey, just a coincidence.' But then one of the women we interrogated reported how she lost thirteen minutes of time – said that she looked up at the clock and read one thing, then a split second later she looks up at the clock and thirteen minutes had gone by..."

Sai and Ren have no response.

Dane paces around the flat. "Now, that is truly a coincidence since I happen to know a girl with brown skin and red hair with a white streak, who is capable of doing just that." He moves in close to Sai. Ren watches closely as well, her cutting stopped. "So I'm going to ask you again: Were you here all night, Sai?"

Sai casually takes a sip of her drink and shows her teeth through a smug smirk.

"Uh huh."

Ren grips the knife in her hand even tighter.

"Fine." Dane's voice is defeated, as if he knows he won't get the truth, but understands it's probably for the better. He leans back a comfortable distance. "If anyone else asks you, you tell them exactly what you just told me."

Ren relaxes a bit as Sai lightly shrugs.

"I told you girls," Dane continues, "if you want to work for the police force, you are free to apply and get formal, *professional* training, but as long as you are civilians, I have to ask that you stay out of these kinds of cases." He takes a seat beside Blue as he motions for Ren to bring him something. She pours him a beer in a tall glass. He takes it, swallowing a big gulp before continuing. "I know you girls want to help, and I know you feel like you're invincible, Sai, being a magic user and all."

Sai and Ren listen as if they are being scolded by a parent.

"But you have to understand that without the magic circuits, there is nothing that makes you any different from me, which means what can kill me can kill you."

Sai makes a shrugging gesture at which Ren quickly smacks her across the head. Sai flinches in pain. Dane doesn't notice the exchange.

"I promised your parents I'd look after you while they were overseas and that's what I'm trying to do, so please," he says before taking one last gulp of his beer, finishing it off, "stay out of trouble."

Ren and Sai both nod in agreement.

"We'll try Dane," replies Ren.

"Yeah," Sai agrees, "we'll do our best."

He nods, seemingly satisfied with their reply. "Very good." Dane pushes back from his seat while flipping his wrist over. With a tap, a digital string of numbers float in the air alongside a name. Clayre. With a flick, the name and number move to hover above the countertop. "I know you have to keep the lights on. This is a case from a girl who wants someone to investigate how her cousin got mana poisoning. She already had your info, but I figured I'd give you hers and maybe you can call her."

The girls take a quick glance at the number.

"Should be something nice and safe, something I'm sure you both can handle that won't put your lives at risk. You are *not* a fully equipped police department with well-trained officers that know how to handle deadly situations. Get me?"

"Technically," Sai says, raising her hand, "I'm only putting my own life at ri-OW!" This time, Blue has slapped her across the back of the head and his hand hurts much more than Ren's.

Ren nods at Blue with a smile. So does Dane. "Thank you, Blue," Dane laughs.

Sai rubs her head softly. "Traitor."

Blue simply smiles back at her.

"Stay safe, you two." Dane heads towards the door, "Oh, and Ren," he stops abruptly, remembering something important. "My techs recognize your IP. If I find you calling or hacking into my system again you'll be doing community service for a year. Clear?"

"Crystal," she answers, not even attempting to argue.

They both nod at him as he turns to Blue. "Blue," Dane continues, "look out for the two of them, and don't let them be a bad influence on you. Lying is wrong." He winks at the group before the sliding door gives way, letting him leave. "And Sai," he adds, "help your sister cook. She's not your mother you know."

Not a moment after the door closes does Sai turn around and pouts at Blue. "Thanks, Blue."

Ren then slams the counter lightly. "Seriously Sai," she says.

"What," Sai replies, "he knew we were lying."

"Yeah, I know that, but it's better if we make it easier for him by at least denying everything and not throwing it in his face that we were doing things he could arrest us for. It's not just about protecting ourselves - it's about protecting him as well. You have to think about these things."

This seems to resonate with Sai as she mulls it over. "Oh," she says, "I didn't think..."

"It's fine," Ren interrupts, "just think about that from now on." She continues to cut up some vegetables. "I let you convince me to start this little detective company with you, but I don't want to do it if it's going to put the people close to us at risk. Now get in here and help me cook or else I'm giving your portion to Blue."

"Wha? No fair!" Sai jumps from her seat and hurries to the kitchen.

"Oh, I would very much like to try Renayaka's cooking, but I lack taste buds to enjoy it sufficiently which may detract from the overall pleasu-" Ren and Sai give Blue a look. Blue stops, thinks to himself, then continues, "I am still adjusting to your method of joking. I will get it."

The two girls just laugh, continuing to prepare the food on the counter.

"So," Sai muses, "are you worried about that threat, the one Dane said?" Ren casually cuts the vegetables with a flippant motion.

"That wasn't a threat, it was a warning," she states plainly. "I can easily clone other addresses over mine and his novice techs won't know the difference." Sai can't even respond, stunned by how skilled her sister really is. Ren, however, doesn't even seem to think twice about it. Sai then notices Blue watching them like a statue.

"Get in here," Sai smiles, "you're helping too." Blue offers a smile back and together the three flatmates make food for the evening.

· · · · ● · ● · · · ·

Meanwhile, in a holding area, the short woman from the warehouse looks at a man on the other side of an energy field. It is an area for visitors and detainees to speak. The woman approaches the field, a look on her face that any would recognize as extreme irritation.

The man whispers to the woman. "You sure it was a magic user?"

"Positive," the woman replies, "and I know just how to lure her from hiding..."

· · · · ● · ● · · · ·

The next morning, Blue powers up from a section of the wall. It is cut out, making a little semicircular crevice capable for a body to fit inside while standing. Blue detaches a cord from the back of his head, then exits the wall capsule. He glances towards the kitchen and spots Sai frying some eggs.

She notices him coming out the capsule. "Hey you," she says quietly, "finish doing your version of sleeping?"

Blue pauses, shakes his head slightly, then continues his approach to the kitchen. "Yes," he replies, "I was doing a little research on the net while my body recharged and downloaded some updates."

"Oh, anything interesting?"

"There were only slight software upgrades and updates to already existing apps that I have installed so, no, nothing special." He takes a seat at the bar. "You are up early."

"Well, unlike my sister, I believe in getting a jump start on the day. And besides," she replies, flipping an egg like a pro chef, "breakfast is the one thing I can cook better than Ren."

"What are you saying about me?" Ren asks, basically sleepwalking into the kitchen area, rubbing her eyes awake.

"Oh nothing," Sai laughs, "just talking about how much better I am than you."

Ren doesn't even react. She sits down beside Blue, completely ignoring Sai. With a swipe of her wrist upwards, floating digital envelopes appear hovering in front of her.

"Looks like you got some mail from your school, Sai," she says as she reaches up to tap the hologram in the air. The mail she clicks animates as if it were a piece of folded mail pulled from its envelope.

"Come on, Ren, what the hell," Sai complains, "I thought I told you to stop going through my mail."

Ren reads through Sai's mail without stopping even a moment. "Well, maybe you should make your password a little harder to guess."

"I change my password every day because of you."

"Valiant efforts, truly," Ren says smugly, "but you would have a much easier time if you would concede defeat to your older and frankly, more attractive sister. Especially since the only thing you can apparently beat me at is flipping morning dairy."

"You *did* hear me!"

"So, seems your old university would like you to donate some money."

"Ha," Sai laughs hysterically, "what money?! I've been outta school for, like, two years, and they already want donations? Vultures."

"This is why I never went to university." Ren flips through some more mail, her eyes slowly becoming more awake.

"Why, cause you were worried about telling them you couldn't donate anything?"

"No, because soon you'll be getting emails asking for money that you can't ignore."

Sai realizes what Ren is referring to and almost drops the plate of food in her hand before sliding it in Ren's direction.

Blue looks at Sai with intrigue. "Were you unable to afford your education?"

"Well, Mom and Dad helped out as much as they could," Sai replies, "but I still had to take out a small loan in order to go there. It was one of the best magic schools in the country, where they're able to help any magic user discover their personal affinity and develop it."

"Right," Blue replies, "and I understand that those first few years during the activation of your magic circuits to be the most important."

"They tend to be the most crucial, yeah," Ren answers while taking a bite out of her egg and potatoes. "Thanks Sai, delicious as always. But yeah, all magic users' magic circuits remain dormant until they begin to experiment with spells. Once that happens, the circuits begin to grow and mature, usually taking shape towards a specific affinity practiced within a few years."

"It's why they don't want users to play around with magic too much as adolescents, since the activation causes their circuits to develop and essentially puts a clock on the user to discover an affinity that works for them," Sai makes her own plate and pulls up a barstool across the other side of the bar.

"And once your circuits fully mature, they become locked, meaning that whatever magic you last practiced becomes the only magic you'll ever be able to use," Ren offers.

"That is why you want to establish a magic that you are comfortable with and focus on it." Blue muses out loud. "So that once your circuits lock, you will at least be locked into something that you have talent in. I understand."

"Exactly," Ren continues, "now, there are some that can specialize in secondary weaker magic or subsets of larger magic, but that starts to get a little complicated."

"Yeah, and sometimes personal preference doesn't mean anything," Sai chimes in. "While I was at school, I really wanted to specialize in ice magic," Sai exclaims, taking a bite of her food, "freeze the hell out of people, ya know?"

"But she sucked at it," Ren replies with a plain face and a mouth full of food. "Which is good, cause you can't just go around freezing people without getting arrested by the SPMD."

"Thanks, sis," Sai counters with an eye roll before turning to Blue. "She's right, though. I wasn't any good at it, so it kinda bummed me out."

"Could you not have stuck with it, and attempted a mastery anyway?" Blue asks, intrigued.

"I could've, but my ice magic wouldn't have been as strong as someone with a natural knack for it. So if I didn't want to have mediocre magic for the rest of my life, I had to find something else I was actually good at, even if I didn't necessarily like it." Sai swipes the kitchen counter, bringing up a few digital controls in the marble. She presses a button and a display appears floating in the living room; on it plays a television news program.

"Is that how you found the magic you have now?" Blue questions.

"Yep," Sai responds, "took a little experimenting til I landed on it, and it's not freezing, but hey, pretty close I'd say." She slides her finger up the counter, increasing the volume on the hovering image.

"A young gentleman was found dead on the streets of East Ham last night. It was thought he had merely passed out, but upon further investigation, was discovered that he had died due to mana poisoning. He was 19 years old."

"Poor guy," Sai whispers before taking another bite of her food. A beep suddenly goes off from where her sister's computer is stationed.

"Oh!" Ren exclaims, sliding her chair to her setup while taking her plate with her. She presses down on her desk. All of her screens appear, floating overhead.

"What is it?" Sai asks.

Ren begins typing away with one hand while the other holds her potato. "Since we took on that illegal weapons case, I've been having the computer search for any keywords related to the types of guns being sold. Now this could be anything from a blog post to something more substantial like a decrypted email. The computer then sorts through the searches from highest likelihood of being something important and correlates them into a list that I then manually look through to see if we may have any loose ends to tie up on the case."

Sai simply stares at her. "Nerd..."

"Shut up, 'cause it looks like I've got something." Ren press a button then swipes a screen to the center of the room, replacing the news broadcast. "I hacked into the e-accounts of the bidders at the auction last night – which is why your e-account doesn't stand a chance by the way, baby sis, and I've been waiting to see if anyone may have mentioned anything about the guns or other bidders." Ren moves her fingers along the top of her desk without even looking. "Looks like someone did."

"It's so cool what that thing can do. I have to play with your computer myself some time," Sai says, amazed.

"Me, not the computer, and it's booby trapped, so I wouldn't touch it without asking if I were you." Ren's response is immediate, plain, without a hint of humor. Sai laughs at Ren's dryness. "Sure it is." An image of the short girl from the night before pops up on screen.

"Recognize her?" Ren asks.

"Yeah," Sai replies, taking her plate to the sink and running water over it. "You get her plate for me, Blue?" Blue gets up, and grabs Ren's plate from her before taking it back to the kitchen for Sai to place in the sink.

"Thanks, Blue," Ren says before continuing. "The woman's name is Katia Borouske. Apparently she found a way to send an e-correspondence to a man by the name of Jake Gransky last night."

Sai finishes putting the dishes in the sink. "Hey, your turn to do the dishes."

Ren gets up, passing the display, swiping it in the air so that it moves to her wrist, then swiping it again so that it appears over the sink. She cleans the dishes as she explains. "According to this, she says that there's another shipment of guns coming in tonight at a warehouse on the other side of town. She wants him to steal the shipment and use the money they get for flipping the weapons to pay for her bail."

"Hm," Sai replies as she starts to head to the back of the flat. "Why can't criminals just stay where they belong? I'll go check it out tonight."

"Sai," Ren calls. Sai comes back, looking at her sister and waiting. "Maybe we should feed this info to Dane. Not like we'll make any money off this anyway."

"Come on, Ren," Sai laughs, throwing her arms up, "this was never about money from the beginning. It's about doing the right thing, making the world a safer place. Besides," Sai laughs while walking towards the back, removing her top and stepping to the shower, "it's not like I'm going to die or anything." She waves her hand in the air and water begins to run in the bathroom.

In the kitchen, Ren glances at Blue, who expresses a look of concern. Ren leans out towards the shower. "At least take Blue with you just in case."

"I'll be fine, Ren!" Sai waves her hand again as a holo-display covers the bathroom door.

Blue turns back at Ren, who looks a little worried. He places a hand on her shoulder. "She will be fine," he assures.

"I know she will," Ren replies, "it's just..." She glances at the hacked email floating in front of her with a sigh. "She never has to deal with the fallout when something *does* go wrong..."

· · · • · ● · ● ● · · ·

That night, Sai sits perched on the side of a building across the street from the warehouse where their e-correspondence said the weapons would be. She presses the side of her temple. Her contact lens scans the surrounding area. Nothing. She taps the visual off, deciding to scan with her natural sight in order to see if there's anything her program may have missed; however, there is nothing out of the ordinary.

"Ren," she says, "you see anything?"

<Nothing on my screens...It doesn't look like anyone is showing up.>

Sai presses her temple again. This time, her eye turns green, giving an outline of the interior of the building. Inside she can see crates stacked high and furniture for the workers, but no people. "Hm," she whispers, "that's strange. It looks empty on the inside too."

<Cameras show the same thing here. It's empty.>

Sai can hear Blue speaking over Ren's mic. <This is odd, would you not say?>

<Yeah, Blue,> Ren replies, <I'd say it's odd.>

Sai watches the outside of the warehouse a little longer before she becomes tired of waiting. With a shrug of her shoulders, she stands to her feet. "Screw it, I'm going in."

<Sai!>

"It's already been an hour, sis, I'll just check inside real quick and if I don't find anything, I'll get out."

<....Okay...>

Sai jumps down from the building and, just as she had so often before, slows her descent moments before hitting the ground. With a quick look at her surroundings, she rushes towards the warehouse.

• • • **•** • **•** • • •

Ren leans back in her chair, watching Sai cross the street through the cameras. It is Blue who notices her biting her nails. He steps to her side with an assured glance. "She will be fine."

Ren is patched into multiple cameras throughout the warehouse, giving her a solid view of everything within. There are tons of wooden crates placed throughout the room, lined against the walls and stacked haphazardly on top of one another. While the organization of the crates may make sense to someone in the know, to the passive observer the crates were scattered about with no rhyme or reason, creating a miniature maze for Sai to weave through.

Ren can see Sai open the door to the warehouse, quietly sneaking inside. <I'm in,> Sai whispers as she makes her way towards the center of the large building, passing a large yellow crane used for placing the boxes in their unorthodox clutter.

<There are a few crates here that could hold weapons, but my contact can't scan the interiors. Something is causing interference.>

Blue and Ren glance at each other, neither sure as to why that could be. Ren hits a few keys on the computer, switching the cameras to an optics mode for revealing interiors but, she too, is getting nothing. She shakes her head, "no go for me too. Looks like you'll have to do this the old-fashioned way."

<Gonna look inside a crate now. Hopefully I don't have to look all over this entire warehouse...>

Blue leans in closer, seeing Sai move towards a crate on camera. He spots something that looks strange a few paces behind her. "Renayaka," he says, tapping her shoulder and getting her attention. "What is that?" He points to a screen above her. She looks up, staring closely at the screen until she sees what looks like a shadow move in thin air.

She frantically sits up in her chair, quickly yelling into the headset.

• • • ❖ • ❖ • • • •

Loud static rings in Sai's ear, the audio clipping from Ren's voice making Sai wince. It feels as though it reverberates throughout the warehouse. Instinctively, she grabs at her ear in pain.

"What was that?" Sai places her finger to her ear in an attempt to hear more clearly.

<Sai, you have to get out of there. It's a trap!>

"What are you talking about?" Sai asks, just as she cracks open the crate.

<It's shadow magic! The entire warehouse is encased in a shading spell!>

The inside of the crate is filled with tiny toys with large eyes and smiling faces.

Sai does not have to be told twice, for as soon as her sister finishes speaking, she hears a sound she has become all too familiar with.

A sound of a chamber being pulled back on a gun.

She turns to run in the opposite direction of the sound, diving just as a group of guns open fires in her direction.

<Saiyonoshi!>

Bullets tear through the warehouse. Wood splinters explode everywhere. Shadows peel from thin air, falling to the ground as eleven men and women holding fully automatic weaponry face Sai's direction.

Sai lands behind a crate, keeping her head low as the bullets fly above her. Though her hands are shaking, she is able to move them quickly in a circular shape over each other. The time orb she creates is ready in seconds.

Waiting for her chance, the moment there is the briefest of reprieves in gunfire, she peeks out and tosses the orb at her assailants.

It is ripped to shreds before it even gets five meters.

Before her head is taken off, she immediately crouches back underneath her cover, cover that is slowly being peeled to pieces. Realizing she can't stay put, she rushes forward to a new line of crates, deciding to use the maze to her advantage.

The gunners move on her, ready to take her down. She tosses orb after orb their way, but none get close, each shattering with a sound like broken glass. She makes her way around more crates in the maze and finds a good spot to hide while her attackers move to find her.

"So um, sis," Sai pants, attempting to catch her breath between words, "they're running anti-magic bullets. I can't stop them."

<I can see that! They were ready for us!>

Sai may not be able to see Ren, but she can hear her sister typing frantically, desperate to find a way to keep her sister alive.

"Find that bitch and put an end to her!" It's not the worst thing Sai's been called, but it still irritates her all the same. Surprising even herself, Sai can't help but laugh a little.

"Guess I finally pissed off the wrong people, huh?"

· · · • · • · • · · ·

Ren can see the heavily armed group making their way through the maze, searching for her sister. The gunfire may have stopped, but the danger to Sai was very real. Seeing as the attackers decided to split up, it was only a matter of time before they found her.

"They are going to get to her," Blue exclaims, nervous but calm. Ren scratches her head over and over, trying desperately to think of something. "What can I do, what can I do?"

<Hey sis...>

"Yeah?"

Sai's voice comes in low, no doubt as a way to try and keep herself from being heard. <Their bullets may be anti-magic tech, but what about what they're wearing?>

Ren quickly runs a symatic scan on the eleven people. A diagram appears, revealing that their clothing is made of polyester and a few other components. "No, they're wearing regular clothing."

<So they can be affected by my magic, even if their bullets can't.>

"I see," Ren exclaims with a smile, "that'll work."

<Yeah...thing is, it's hard to cast that spell with me being as scared as I am right now. Contrary to the calm demeanor I'm trying to hold on to, I'm actually shaking pretty bad...I

really don't want to get shot –It hurts…a lot.> Sai offers a nervous laugh, but Ren can tell.

Her sister is afraid of the pain of dying.

Ren takes a moment, unsure what to do. She looks down at her screen, grabbing her head, trying to come up with some kind of plan, but no matter how hard she tries, she can't figure out how to save Sai.

The people with the guns move closer to where Sai is hiding.

<Not to rush, but a little help sooner rather than later would be nice…>

Ren looks to Blue, her face plain. "I-I don't know what to do…"

"The lights," Blue says, getting Ren's attention. "The lights are tied into an electronic schedule, allowing employees to-"

"Nice, Blue! I can readjust the timer." She immediately moves back to her keyboard. "I should be able to shut everything off." It doesn't take her long to gain access to building schematics and plans.

She steals a quick glance at her screens and almost freezes. One of the men is almost right on top of Sai. She must hear him because Sai almost immediately says, <Uh, Ren?>

Ren types away fiercely before finally pressing 'Enter.' "Got it!"

Just as the assailant rounds the corner of Sai's crate, the lights go out.

· · · ● · ● · · ·

Darkness overtakes the room, disorienting all inside. The assailant that was just seconds away from killing Sai appears to be the most frustrated.

"What the hell?!" he exclaims.

"Where'd she go?" a woman shouts.

Sai can hear the confused shouts from those hunting her. The man near wanders aimlessly, bumping into a crate and cursing as it bumped into him. She lightly presses her temple and the warehouse lights up like a sunrise. She can see everything and has to hold back a sigh of relief when it appears that the assailants aren't armed with similar visionware.

<Sai, I was only able to bypass the warehouse security protocols briefly. In about 30 seconds I'm getting kicked out and the lights are coming back on.>

This is news to Sai's ears. She can do the spell in twenty.

"Don't move from the exit," a woman shouts, "it's her only way out!"

Calming herself and secure in the safety of darkness, she begins.

The spell text scrolls in her eye. Her hands dance and blue light glows. She keeps it low so not as to catch the attention of the wandering killers. She knows that it's not just the time of the light that she is racing against, but also the time until her assailants notice the light from the glowing orb at her fingertips. An orb that is steadily getting brighter. She has to be quick, but she has to be precise.

"Hey, you hear that?" They can hear her. It won't be much longer, but Sai cannot afford to get distracted. She is almost done.

"Shit," the man yells, "the bitch is casting an incantation!"

He's right, but he won't get another opportunity to call her a bitch.

The lights come up. Sai jumps over a crate, vaulting to the middle of the room. Her right hand glows, holding the orb like a grenade. Everyone turns to her, raising their weapons to gun her down. It doesn't matter. Sai knows that they're too late. It's her victory.

She throws the orb at the ground so hard that she almost hits the floor herself. The orb expands, instantly engulfing everyone in the room. Each person is bathed in blue light, halting their movement as they become frozen in place. At least, that is how it would appear to the untrained eye. In truth, they are still moving, albeit so slowly that they may as well be stopped.

Sai stands to her feet, looking around. All the people that had once been hunting her are now no more deadly than a sleeping toddler. While each of them are slowed, Sai remains the sole individual able to move in real time. With a deep sigh and crack of her back she speaks. "Well then, time to get to work.

"I can't believe they cast a shadow spell," she muses aloud while making her way to one man, still in the process of raising his gun. "I think you were the one who called me bitch." She grabs the gun from his hand, holding it by the barrel. It glows at her touch. She pulls back and swings the gun as hard as she can against the man's head, releasing just before the blow would connect. The glow is gone and the gun moves slowly once more, on a direct collision course with the man's face.

<Explains why we didn't see anybody. As long as nobody made any big movements, we'd never even know they were there.> Sai takes a quick glance around her, making sure she can get to each assailant. <Fortunately a large scale spell like that takes time to cast, but they definitely were ready for you.>

"The fact that spell even works on cameras seems unfair," Sai exclaims as she makes her way to her next victim. "Guessing you already reconfigured your system?"

Sai can hear the irritation in Ren's voice. <It was done the moment I knew what the spell was. Don't insult me.>

Sai laughs, "Okay, just didn't want any more surprises."

<If someone were to cast shadow magic again, I'd be able to see them, but the cameras are on the fritz since your spell. I can't see anything.> Sai can hear Ren rustling in her ear. <Just make sure to get everyone.>

Sai moves around to the other assailants, doing something similar with each of them. When she really feels creative, she makes her way up a stack of wooden crates. With little abandon, she kicks them over. When her foot connects, the crates glow briefly and fall, but the moment her foot pulls back, they become blue again, falling extremely slowly towards the unfortunate man on the ground below.

"I was thinking," Sai says into her headset, "I kinda want to watch a movie tonight. You guys down?"

<I am not watching 'The Hounds of Baskerville' again.>

"No, I was thinking 'The Fall.'"

<Depends which rendition, there have been a lot of crappy versions and only like two good ones.>

Sai climbs to the top of a hanging crane, pulling it so it lines up with one of the women on the ground. "Well of course we are watching one of those." She jumps onto the crane. It swings under her weight, heading straight for the armed woman. Sai leaps off, the crane becoming slow yet again. Sai stares at the woman, then decides it may be best to take her gun from her, just in case.

<You done yet?>

"Almost, almost," Sai replies while tossing the gun into the air. It slows the moment it leaves her fingertips. "You have to make something good to go with the movie," Sai continues. "Personal request for some kind of pasta dish."

<You always eat pasta. All those carbs are gonna kill you one day.>

"No, they won't," she laughs smugly. "Wait, hold on a sec." Sai looks around, checking to make sure she got everybody, but mainly to admire her work. Once satisfied that everyone has been dealt with, she nods confidently in the center of the room, just about where she started.

"Okay." She raises her hand and all the blue light in the room returns to her palm. All at once the assailants get hit hard in the face with guns, the stack of crates fall on top of the guy beneath them, and the crane swings, hitting the woman clear across the room. It is a symphony of well constructed chaos that reaches its crescendo in a loud uproar and then is instantly silent.

"I personally think if you can order the legendary mizithra cheese, you can have it at the house right before I get back." Sai concludes.

<We'll see. You get everyone?>

"Yep, all ten of them."

<Ten?> Sai can hear the confusion in her sister's voice, confusion that quickly turns into fear.

<Sai, there were eleven...>

Sai freezes. "Wait, what?"

<Behind you!>

Sai turns just as a hand appears in thin air, pulling a shadow from himself. She raises her hands, blue light engulfing them.

Everything slows around her, but it is not because of her magic. She can see everything. She can see the man as he emerges from the shadow. She can see the shadow retreat into one hand, and the gun raise in his other. She can see it all.

But she can't react to any of it.

"Shit."

BANG!

The shot is quick, instant, blasting clear through the blue orb in front of her, as well as the back of her head. Blood splatters onto the crates behind her as she lifelessly falls to the floor. The man walks over to her, smiling at his own cleverness.

"You should have prioritized the magic user," he gloats. "As soon as I saw your blue orb I knew what you were planning. I had barely enough time to cast a spell over myself." He kneels over her lifeless body. "Guess you weren't as badass as you thought."

· · · ● · ● · · ·

Ren tilts her head down, away from her screens. Her eyes are clenched shut. She raises her head, opening her eyes as a tear slowly escapes. "Goddamnit, I told her this was going to happen. She is too damn cocky!"

Blue places a hand on her shoulder. "Are you alright?" he asks.

Ren shakes her head, wiping the tears away. "No, Blue," she says through sniffles, "I'm not, but now we have to deal with what comes next." She presses down on a button in her keyboard and a digital stopwatch display appears. The timer counts up as Ren watches it intently.

The man puts his gun away. He takes a look around at all of his unconscious comrades. He can't help but snort at how close she came to beating them all. "The bitch did put up quite a fight though." With one last glance at Sai, the man allows himself a feeling of pride and accomplishment. He alone is able to walk away, and at his feet is the lifeless body of a once vibrant girl. The blood pools around her, oozing from the hole in her head as it soaks into her clothes and the ground beneath her. Without another word that man turns to leave.

· · · ● · ● · · ·

A sound, similar to that of crumpling paper, rises from Sai's body with a low hum. The man doesn't hear it. If he had, he would have turned to see a strange black substance peeling off of her corpse. The substance is eerie, resembling that of floating ash, but there is no fire.

"Here we go," Ren sighs, wiping away one last tear before focusing on the screen in front of her. "Who's it going to be this time?"

Sai's body jerks, suddenly and without warning. It spasms randomly, making erratic movements a human body should not be able to make.

This part is always a strange sensation. I see it happen each time and I can't help but wonder what it's like for them, never knowing, never present, never fully aware. But I can see it, and I know. I'm a magic user, nothing special, and I have been killed. That murderer has no reason to be afraid or turn around, and why would he? Normally a dead body stays dead.

Her body rises unnaturally to its feet, head hanging towards the ground. The blood drips from the open hole in her forehead, dripping like a leaky faucet into a sea of red at her feet.

It may have been the sounds of the drips, perhaps it was the shuffling, or the strange sense of dread in the air, but whatever it was, the man once confident in his kill finally turns around.

His bladder almost relieves on the spot. "What the fuck?!" Paralyzed with the fear at seeing a woman he just killed now at her feet, he falls to the ground, hands shaking far too much to hold his gun. It clatters and skids away from him, his final lifeline gone.

Sai's head tilts up, just as the wound in her skull begins to close.

The man is now shivering in pure terror. He has no idea what to do.

Sai's head continues to tilt up, eyes closed. She cracks her neck.

We're not immortal. Far from it actually, but I guess in a way, that's partially true. It's not that we necessarily can't die, per say. It's just that whenever we do die, we always revive. It's pretty useful, if not for but one small caveat...

Sai raises her hand to her neck, cracking it once again to the right, then to the left, before opening her eyes and glancing down at the frightened man cowering beneath her. She stares at him a moment before her face scrunches into one of immense anger.

"Youda god damn sumbitch juss kill me?!"

Ren drops her head on her station keyboard. "Great...it's Bill."

Whenever our body revives...it comes back with a different personality.

Chapter Three

Personality Bill

Darkness is everywhere. There are sounds, present but lost, too indistinguishable to make out clearly. It's as if Sai is trying to hear something from underwater. In this sea of nothingness she floats, alone but unafraid. She never is. Not here. Not anymore. After all, it's like this for her every time.

Slowly, a light in the distance shines. It is a light that beckons her, demanding her regardless of her desire. It grows a bit brighter, coming closer and closer until it eventually glows immensely and engulfs the darkness completely.

It is the light that calls her home.

She opens her eyes.

Sai is leaning over the bar counter in her flat. Her face is resting next to a plate of food. She is disorientated trying to gather herself. She slowly raises her head, spotting her sister sitting at the computer screens, staring at them. Blue is behind Sai, in the kitchen washing some plates.

"Welcome back," Ren says quietly, without even turning around.

Sai lifts her head, rubbing the side of her temples. "Who was it this time?" she asks before glancing down at her clothing. She is wearing a plaid shirt and bum jeans with a few holes in the knees. Sai answers her own question with slight irritation. "Bill..."

"Yep," Ren answers, "always a pleasure."

Sai pulls herself up, wiping the little bit of food still on her mouth away. "How long was I out?" she asks.

Ren continues looking at her screens. There is a hint of irritation in her voice when she replies. "You were shot in the head so..."

Sai places her hand on her head, almost as if she still feels the wound. Sai answers her own question. "So, about 2 days, huh?" That's when she notices her left hand wrapped in bandages. Her worry is immediate, fearing Bill may have done something bad with her body. Her gaze darts over to Ren. "What did Bill do?"

Sensing Sai's distress, Ren gives a soft and reassuring smile. "Don't worry, you know Bill would never kill anyone." She cocks her head to the side. "His temper though, that's a completely different story..."

• • • • ● • ● • ● • • •

Just a few days earlier while in the warehouse, Sai jumps on top of the remaining henchman. She pummels his face in with her left hand. The blood from her hand and the man's face are indistinguishable as it flies through the air. "You seriously gon shoot me in the head, seriously?! Ya have any idea how much dat hurts?!" Sai pounds away, only stopping once Ren yells into her ears.

<Bill!>

Bill stops his bludgeoning of the now unconscious man. He looks up. "Dat you Renayaka?"

<It is. You need to get out of there. I'm tracking a few SPMD patrols en route to you.>

"Well dat is just damn inconvenient," Bill states, dropping the unconscious man to the floor. "Show me da way out darling."

•••••••••••

Ren cringes at being called darling. No matter how many times she sees Bill, she hates it every time. Something about being called darling by a man wearing her sister's body never quite sat right with her. Blue looks at her, a bit confused. She speaks into her headset. "I just sent the best escape route to your contact lens. Follow it back to the flat."

<Ya betcha, sweet cheeks. See ya in a jif.>

Sweet cheeks may actually be worse.

Ren leans back from her screens, letting out a long, tired sigh. She looks up at the stopped time display. 242 seconds. She stares at the time without blinking, as if she is lost in the display itself. It's only when Blue speaks that she is released from her trance. "So," he says, "that is the Bill persona?"

"Yuppuh," Ren replies, exasperated.

"The persona seems...very different from Rosa."

"That's because he isn't trying to spar with you every ten minutes," Ren continues. "Bill can be a bit much, but he's the least dangerous of all the personalities Sai has." Blue looks up at the screen with the unconscious man whose face is now unrecognizable. He points to it. "That is not to be viewed as dangerous?" he asks.

"Least dangerous," she corrects, "I never said he didn't have a temper." She faces Blue, eyes firm. "You haven't met the others, like Yuan...the only personality of Sai's I don't trust..."

•••••••••••

Somewhere deep in the city, two male androids walk down an alley. They hold hands as they approach the end, funneling out into another street. One of the androids trips and falls on something beneath his feet. The partner helps him up, raising him to see what it is he tripped over. There is a dead body of a woman, curled up in what looks like agony, blood streaming from the eyes, skin dried and body putrid.

· · ● · ● ● · · ·

"I swear, dem thangs'll kill ya," Bill says, looking at Ren as she takes a gulp of wine. Once one glass is finished, another is poured. "I agree," she says, quickly taking a follow up gulp. Bill paces around the flat.

Two days have passed and Ren feels as though it has been two years. Bill has made himself at home, helping himself to his wardrobe section of Sai's closet. The thing about multiple personalities is making sure you always have what they like to wear on hand at any given moment. The style of dress was easy to adjust to. Ren just told herself it was her sister trying different styles. What was always hard to adjust to was the personality itself, and the judgment that sometimes came with it.

"Yu'll neva catch me drankin nona dat poison, clogs the inner ki." Bill takes a seat on the bar stool. Ren lowers her glass, coming up for air for the first time in 5 minutes.

"Bill, while you are here, I would appreciate it if you didn't judge my personal lifestyle choices," she takes a quick gulp, "and make me want to drink more."

"Whatcha sayin?" Bill asks, "I'm tellin ya, immortal ya ain't. Ya need ta take better care a yaself. Ya can't come back from da dead."

"Thank you for your concern Bill, I'll take it under advisement." Ren places a plate of food in front of Bill, then takes her glass with her back to her station.

"Dat's all I ask," Bill replies, before turning his glance to Blue, who takes a seat on the other side of the room. He looks at Blue's mini antennae coming from the top of his head. Bill begins to shake his own. "I juss can't get use ta ya androids yet. Ya say yur name was Blue?"

Blue examines Bill inquisitively. "That is not the factory name I was given, but since gaining sentience, I have adopted the name you just spoke."

"Uh huh," Bill nods, "probably on account of em purlly blues ya got going on."

"Excuse me?" Blue asks, curiously. Bill nods at Blue's eyes.

"Yur eyes," he says, "they blue ain't they?" Blue touches his irises. He seems to have gained a realization.

"I had not realized," Blue exclaims. "I chose this name simply because I thought the color elicited a feeling of calm, peace if you will, and wished for my own name to reflect similar feelings in others." He glances at Ren, who nods at him.

"It's actually what Sai and I figured, but we never really asked about it."

"That is quite intriguing," Blue continues, "what she has said is quite an extraordinary coincidence." Bill springs to his feet, anger seeping onto his face.

"Da hell ya just say?"

Ren adjusts herself in her seat, turning back towards both the confused Blue and the slowly growing in anger Bill. Blue decides it is best to repeat himself to diffuse any possible misunderstanding. "I stated that what you said was intriguing. Is there something wrong with that?"

"You juss called me a 'she' didn't ya," Bill asks, standing above Blue. Blue looks confused.

"I ain't no 'she,'" Bill says, pushing Blue in his chair, "I look like a goddamn woman to ya?" Blue stands, still confused. He looks Bill up and down: Bill, who until recently, had been Sai: Sai, who is obviously female in a body that reiterates such a fact.

"But, you are, are you not?" he asks, gesturing to Bill's body. Bill looks like he's about to blow. He pulls his hand back, ready to punch Blue in the face. Ren hops from her chair.

"Hey, hey, hey," she says, jumping between the two, "hold up now." She looks at Blue, who still appears confused.

"Blue," she continues, "Bill is a man. That is what he is, and he would prefer if you referred to him as such." Bill nods, adjusting his clothing. Blue takes a moment, considering what has just been said to him.

"But," Blue begins, "anatomically, she is not."

"Why you sunna-"

"Bill!" Ren shouts. "Bill, go eat your food!"

"Not fore this sunna bitch pologize."

"Apologize for what? I do not understand," Blue responds, still unsure of what to make of the situation.

"He will," Ren assures, "just, go sit down and eat some of the food I made please." Reluctantly, Bill pulls away from the two, making his way across the flat to the kitchen area. Once he has gone to sit down, Ren turns towards Blue, who still has a perturbed look on his face.

"I am sorry, but I do not understand. Have I been misinterpreting proper human gender all this time?"

"Listen, Blue," Ren begins, "it may be hard to understand, but try for a second please. Yes, that is Sai's body, but that is not Sai. That is Bill, and as long as it is Bill, he would appreciate it if you would call him by his name and refer to him by the gender he is. And Bill is male."

"Is that so?" Blue asks, inquisitively. He reflects on this for himself when a new thought enters his mind. "If this is Bill and *he* is a separate person than Saiyonoshi, then where is she? How long will it take for her to come back?"

Ren's entire demeanor changes. Her shoulders drop, her eyes drift to the ground and when she answers, her voice is so quiet that even Blue has trouble hearing her speak.

"I...don't know."

Three words. It was only three little words but the implications behind them weighed on Ren's mind. Although Blue was not human, even he understood the gravity behind them.

"Listen," Ren whispers, eager to move on. "Remember when you first met Rosa, she became upset when you called her Saiyonoshi. It's the same thing. That right there is Bill and as long as he identifies himself as a man, out of respect for him, even if you don't understand it, it's at least nice if you do, too." Blue nods his head in understanding. Ren leans back away from him. She looks over at Bill sitting down, eating his food in a huff. She opens a path for Blue, who takes a moment before making his way towards him.

Blue approaches Bill, who quickly stops eating upon seeing Blue standing in front of him. They both wait a minute before Blue speaks.

"Um," Blue says, "I seem to have offended you. I was mistaken and should not have said what I did. Would you please forgive me?" Blue puts out his hand, waiting for Bill to take it. Ren waits anxiously, unsure as to how Bill will react. After a moment, Bill smiles, then grabs Blue's hand, shaking it fervently.

"Ain't no thang man," Bill laughs heartily, "water unda the bridge an all dat." Ren lets out a sigh of relief before making her way back to her station. Blue stands in his space, unable to move with Bill shaking his hand so quickly. Bill pulls Blue to the adjacent stool. "Come an' pull up a seat, Blue. Let's chat a bit." Blue takes a seat beside him, amazed at how quickly his mood changed. For the briefest of moments, Blue wondered if Bill had not changed personalities himself.

"You don't drink dat poison like little Renayaka over there do ya?"

"Technically older than you." Ren says to no one but herself.

"Um," Blue begins, "I am able, but do not norma-"

"Good man," Bill smirks while continuing to stuff his face with food, "stay away from the stuff! I'm sure it can't be much good for androids and what not either. Not sure if ya have ki, but if ya have something like it, I'm sure...that..." Bill trails off, slowly lowering his head to the table as if he is going to sleep. Blue watches him quietly, unsure what to do.

"Give it a second, Blue," Ren says, going about her business. She is clearly all too familiar with the process about to happen. Blue decides to stand, making his way over to the sink to clean some of the dishes.

A few moments later, Sai raises her head from the counter, rubbing her temples. Ren doesn't even turn around.

"Welcome back..."

Chapter Four

Fallout

"Sorry Bill gave you such a hard time," Sai says to Blue, taking a sip from her wine glass.

"The hell," Ren says, still typing away at her computer, "what about me?"

"You should be used to it," Sai smiles, "and besides," Sai raises her glass of wine to her lips, winking at Ren, "you really shouldn't be drinking. Terrible stuff it is really." Ren rolls her eyes, never turning from her screens. Sai laughs to herself before turning back to her food. She is still wearing Bill's clothes and decides to finish his food. Better to not waste it. Blue places the last dish away, staring at Sai, once Bill, now Sai again.

"I would really like to hear the story about how you discovered this...ailment," Blue suggests. "It has been two months since I joined your employ and both of you have yet to tell me the story behind this discovery." Sai looks slightly in the direction of Ren, but her sister doesn't budge. Even though Ren's face can't be seen, her head has dropped a bit. Sai looks back at Blue.

"Another time," she replies quietly. Blue glances from Sai to Ren and back again, seeming to formulate his own thoughts on why they cannot discuss it now. He does not get to think long before an announcement rings throughout the flat.

"Chief Dane is at the door," an automated voice states. The three all look to the door, which has dropped its holo-display, revealing a very upset looking Dane. Ren's shoulders instantly slouch. "God damnit…"

"Soooo," Sai laughs, rubbing her head nervously, "think he's here about the other day?"

· · · · ● · ● · ● · · ·

"I ask you to do one goddamn thing," Dane begins, filled with rage, "and what do you do, you go and take a proverbial crap all over a crime scene!" Sai and Ren are sitting beside each other on the floor while being scolded by Dane. Blue stands off to the side, watching quietly. Sai raises her hand slowly, before speaking up.

"So when you say proverbial crap, are you talking about-"

"Your freaking magic signature, Saiyonoshi!"

"T-that's what I thought you meant," Sai replies, lowering her hand with a nervous laugh.

"And we are not even going to talk about the fact that the people found at that warehouse were armed with some very serious weaponry, not to mention anti-magic ammunition!" Dane drops to the floor so that he is directly across from Sai. "Just what the hell were you thinking getting mixed with guys like them?"

"I thought I was trying to close a case," she answers honestly.

"That was rhetorical!" Dane yells, prompting Sai to quickly shut up before he turns his sights on Ren. "And you, you're supposed to be the one with common freakin sense!"

"Wait," Sai begins, "are you suggesting that I-"

"Shut the hell up, Saiyonoshi!" Dane has a look of immense anger in his eyes. Sai decides that this is one time she's better off complying and listening as Dane continues to lay into Ren.

"I mean," he begins, "I half expect this from Sai, but I expect for you to have better judgment, Ren. You're the older sister. You're supposed to be looking out for her." Ren doesn't say anything. She continues to sit with her head pointed towards the ground. Sai glances to her sister, who seems to be taking everything in stride. Slowly, Sai's own expression begins to lower.

"It," Sai attempts to interrupt again, "it wasn't her fault, Dane."

"Sai," Ren whispers. Sai looks to Ren, whose gaze is still pointed downwards. "Please..."

Sai wants to say more but closes her mouth. The message has been received and out of respect for her sister, Sai decides it is best to be silent again. Dane looks from one to the other before letting out a giant sigh, then kneeling down to hug the two girls simultaneously.

"I know," he says, "you're both adults. You can do whatever you want. I just don't want anything to happen to you." The two girls finally stare at each other before they both lower their heads over Dane's shoulders and hug him back.

"We're sorry," they say simultaneously. The three remain embraced in a moment before Blue steps in.

"Um," he interrupts, "I am sorry. You said magic signature earlier. I do not think that I have heard of that term before." The three embraced all slouch, as if they cannot believe Blue. They release each other as Dane stands to his feet. He looks absolutely amazed.

"How are you an android and not know things like magic signatures?" Dane asks.

"Well sir," Blue replies, "contrary to held belief, not all androids spend their free time scouring the net for random information." Dane pauses a moment, thinking on this before giving Blue a nod.

"Fair enough," he says, "I'm getting a drink." He heads to the kitchen to pour a few glasses of beer for everyone. Sai gives one last glance to Ren. She mouths "I'm sorry," then rises to her feet. With an extended hand she offers to help Ren stand too. Ren answers with her own silent response. A shake of her head gives Sai the "no problem" response she was hoping for. Once up, they each go to different parts of the room, Sai to the bar in the kitchen and Ren back to her computer station.

"Um," Sai speaks, finally answering Blue, "a magic signature can be described like a magical fingerprint."

"Basically," Dane says, offering a glass to both Sai and Ren. "Every person's magic circuits are unique. When a magic user decides to use their magic, no matter how large or small, it leaves residue that can be traced back to the user."

"Magic takes shape to the individual's circuits, which is why two users that cast a fire spell will leave different signatures where they cast." Sai explains, taking a sip of her beer. "Those signatures can be picked up by a Trace Scanner that will almost always show the exact user that cast a magic spell in the area."

"Yeah," Ren adds, her voice significantly lower than usual, "every magic user is identified as a user or not at birth. The ones that are, are required to register their specialized magic as well as their signature in the Trace System database. It's illegal not to." Sai looks over at Ren, who has not turned around from her screens since she moved back to them.

"And that's precisely why Sai haphazardly using her magic at a place that would later be a crime scene is so damn infuriating," Dane sighs. "It wasn't a big deal at the docks, since we caught all the bad guys without incident or anyone getting hurt, but when I show up to a crime scene where bullets are everywhere, people are injured, and blood is on the ground, even I can't convince SOCO not to investigate." Dane takes a quick chug of his drink as Sai nervously tries to bring the situation up without getting herself, or her sister, yelled at again.

"So," Sai hesitantly asks, "what happened?"

"I called in some favors," he answers, "got some friends of mine to 'misplace' the readings so I could keep your name out the system. Had to treat the tech that found it to a steak dinner." He moves closer to Sai, almost shoving his glass into her face. "Oh," he continues, "and you're lucky. Whatever happened with you and those thugs in the warehouse, none of them mentioned you. Assuming they didn't want an attempted murder charge to go with everything else, and with the weapons they were sporting, they should be going away for a while so I'm sure you're safe for now."

Sai nods her head, satisfied by this outcome. What she can hear from Ren's sigh of relief across the room tells her Ren feels the same.

"I'm curious," Blue expresses aloud, "you mentioned magic signatures working like fingerprints. Does that mean there is the equivalent of a magic signature glove?"

"There is," Sai answers, "but it's hard to do." She adjusts herself in her seat, facing towards Blue. "You see, for a magic user to mask their signature, they need to hide it underneath the surface of another user and that can only be achieved by having contact with that user."

"So no matter what," Dane continues, "when we investigate a crime committed by a user, we are getting somebody and even if that person isn't guilty, with enough doubt, we can investigate the magic users that have had contact with the detained and eventually come across the right person." Dane takes a quick swig with pride. "It's very hard for a magic user, or anyone really, to get away with a crime in this city." He finishes off his beer. He places the glass over by the sink. His chastisement and subsequent drinks have relaxed him immensely. He leans down over Sai, giving her a kiss on the forehead. "Please be more careful. Your parents would kill me if something happened to you."

Sai nods. "I'll try to do better."

"Please." Dane then makes his way over to Ren. He does the same, kissing her on her head. Ren looks up at Dane, forcing a smile. Dane can tell that she is trying her best to hold in what she is actually feeling. He leans in close to her ear. "Hey," he says, "you know why I'm tough on you right?"

"I know," she says.

"Okay," he replies, "don't think I don't love you or any-thing alright."

"I know you do, Dane," she answers, "thanks."

Dane rises from her, making his way towards the door. He nods at Blue who reciprocates before the holo-display disappears, allowing Dane to leave. He stops in the door a moment. "One last thing," he says. The group waits to hear what he has to say. "There was a lot of blood at the warehouse, like someone had been shot, but none of the people we apprehended had any gun related injuries."

He corrects himself. "Well, from being shot at least. You all know anything about that?"

Sai and Blue shake their heads, denying any knowledge. Dane looks at Ren, who waits before answering. "No," she says quietly, "nothing." Dane pauses, as if he doesn't really believe them, but decides to leave it alone.

"This is the last time. This happens again and I will shut you two down. Please believe me when I say that." With that final promise, he's gone. The holo-display reappears.

Not a second before he is gone does Sai make her way over to Ren.

"Hey, Ren," she says, "I'm really sorry about t-"

"Don't worry about it," Ren cuts Sai off, "I'm used to it."

There is an awkward silence before an announcement rings through the house that there is someone new at the door. The holo-display fades, revealing a young woman that can't be much older than twenty standing on the opposite side. She patiently waits but fidgets as if she is nervous about something. Before Sai goes to answer the door, she lightly rests her hand on her sister's shoulder.

"Hey," she says, "we good?" After a moment, Ren takes her hand, touching Sai's softly.

"Yeah," she replies, "we're good."

"Cool," Sai slides her finger on her wrist. "Hey, can we help you?" The woman can be seen on the other side of the door, hearing Sai from outside.

"H-Hi," she says nervously, "is this HW Detective Agency?"

"You got the place."

"Um, I think I have a job for you..."

CHAPTER FIVE

UNRECOGNIZED STRAIN

"M-my name is Clayre," the woman stutters. "Is this your business card?" Clayre flips her wrist upside down, revealing a holo that appears in midair. It is a small display shaped like a square with an interactive image on it. Sai leans in closer, staring at the floating card. On the card is the name of their agency, their address, 111 D Baker Street, and an image of a small kitten with large eyes juggling tiny puppies. Sai immediately turns to Ren, who is casually sipping a cup of tea that Sai does not remember her having before.

"Seriously," Sai asks to a shrugging Ren before turning back to face Clayre. "Y-yep, that is our sickeningly cute business card." Sai laughs, a little embarrassed as she shakes Clayre's hand. "I'm Saiyonoshi Amano, lead Detective here at HW. That there is my sister Renayaka, and over there is our friend Blue." Clayre bows politely to acknowledge the others before Sai continues. "Do you mind me asking how you got our business card?"

"It was on a server board in the city," Clayre replies. "I downloaded it from there."

"Gotcha," Sai responds, "well, what can we help you with?"

"Well, you see, it's my cousin," Clayre answers. "He's sick with mana-poisoning."

"Ah yes, you were the one Chief Inspector Dane mentioned," Blue recalls once hearing the nature of Clayre's case.

"What was your cousin doing injecting himself with mana?" Sai asks, prodding a little further.

"He didn't," Clayre reports defensively before calming herself so that she can continue. "H-he...he wouldn't. I think someone injected him."

"You think someone purposely attempted to murder your cousin using mana?" Blue interjects. Clayre nods.

"That seems unlikely." Ren's voice is flat and matter of fact. "There are easier ways to murder someone, and as long as your brother was taken to a doctor, they should have been able to cure his mana-poisoning." Sai agrees with a silent nod.

"Normally, that would be true," Clayre continues, "but the mana strain that my cousin has been infected with is nothing like any doctor has ever seen before." She lowers her head, struggling not to cry. "He's in a coma and they can't cure him." Clayre's tears pour down her face.

While a case involving mana-poisoning was nothing special, a case with a mana strain that doctors hadn't seen before certainly was. Sai turns to Ren, checking for her take. The gears are turning and it is clear that she and Sai are on the same wavelength. Blue brings Clayre some tissues so that she can wipe her face. After giving her a few moments to collect herself, Sai steps forward.

"Show me."

• • • • • • • • • •

Hospital rooms have always given Sai a feeling of being just a bit too clean. The one she was in now was no different.

Perhaps it was the stark white walls, or the squeaking sound made when feet moved across the floors, but whatever it was, it made Sai just a bit uncomfortable. Still, standing there with Blue at her side and a new case two meters in front of her, her excitement could barely be contained.

Clayre approaches a bed with a man in his late twenties lying asleep under some covers. Above him are holo-displays showing his heart rate, blood pressure, and all the signs that visually connect him to life. He breathes normally, his body plugged into a machine to assist in his breathing.

"His name's Harper," Clayre explains, taking a seat beside him, holding his hand.

"How long has he been like this," Sai asks.

"Since I found him a few days ago," Clayre responds. "I went to his house to bring him some food. I'm saved in his flats memory so I was able to get in no problem. When I came in, I saw him bleeding from his eyes on the floor. He wasn't moving. Then I rushed him here..." She brushes back his hair as she looks at his face. Tears build in her eyes to the point they could overflow any moment. "He's no angel. He had his problems with the SPMD, but he doesn't deserve this." Blue and Sai look on respectfully.

"Clayre," a voice exclaims from behind the group. They all turn, seeing a doctor well into his forties standing behind them. Clayre quickly stands, acknowledging the doctor. "Doctor Pey."

"Hey, Doctor," Sai says, moving closer to him, her eagerness getting the better of her. "Can you tell me what's going on with him?" Pey is more than a little hesitant, stealing a glance to Clayre for an explanation as to who this person is.

"It's alright, they're friends and are here to help." That seems to satisfy the doctor.

"Let's speak outside," he says. Sai complies, following the doctor to the door.

"I'll stay with her," Blue states. Sai acknowledges him before walking out into the hallway. Once outside, the door closes and she plunges headfirst into the case.

"Clayre said the mana strain Harper was poisoned with was one you didn't recognize?" Sai inquires, prompting for more information to be given.

"Not just me," Pey explains, "none of my colleagues can tell what it is." Pey adjusts himself, folding his arms. "Look, we're not novices. We get mana-poisoned people in here every day, mainly normal humans desperate to believe they have mana circuits and foolishly injecting themselves with mana. Normally, a person injected with mana sans circuits will begin to degrade almost immediately, but we have both medicine and healing users on staff that can eliminate the usual strains from the immune system. This strain doesn't work that way, however. It's different."

"How so?"

"Are you a scientist?" Pey inquires.

"Magic user," Sai explains, "but I may know some people that can help." Doctor Pey is still hesitant, but crumbles under the desperation of just wanting to know what's going on.

"Hm," he shrugs, "it'd be simpler to just show you." He flips his wrist over, bringing up a floating desktop display. He uses his finger to swipe to a folder that he presses, which then opens into a series of floating folders and images. He clicks one, bringing up an image of what looks like a strand of DNA.

"That's a normal mana strain." Sai recognizes it immediately. Anyone who has ever studied magic would easily.

"Right," Pey acknowledges, "it's what allows for any user like yourself to get a sudden replenishment to your magic circuits should they run dry. Now this..." He brings up an alternate image, one that looks vastly different than the first.

"Is the strain of mana-poisoning Mr. Harper is suffering from." Sai leans in, looking from one image to the next.

"They're...completely different."

"Not completely," Pey says while quickly pushing a few buttons on the images. Once done, a few sections within the strains highlight, matching with each other across both images. "There are similarities that are clearly derived from the fact that they are both strains of mana, but the latter has been...modified..." This catches Sai's attention.

"Modified?"

"Yes," Pey nods. "If I had to guess, seeing as it has similarities to normal mana strains..."

"Then someone must have engineered this strain," Sai concludes. Pey says nothing, but looks to agree. Sai stares at the floating modified strain of mana.

"Is there any chance Mr. Harper created this modified strain, then tested it on himself?"

"Doubtful," Pey shrugs, "he's an office clerk, doesn't have a background in genetics and whoever created this strain has to be a top expert in that field."

"Good to know," Sai muses.

"It's scary though," he continues, "because whatever was done to this strain prevents any known science or magic from having any effect. I can't do anything for Mr. Harper."

"I see," Sai understands, knowing what the doctor is really trying to say. "How long?"

"Two...three days tops."

Sai flips her wrist over. "Looks like I have to work fast. You mind if I copy those images?" Her wrist has already sent a small image into the air that begins scanning the image files.

"Uh, sure," Pey hesitates, "but, um, who are you?" The scan completes and the image disappears.

"I'm a detective that's going to save Mr. Harper's life." Sai winks with a smile.

• • • ● • ● • ● • • •

Inside the hospital room, Blue stands behind Clayre. He watches her quietly, ready to offer any assistance. She wipes away a few lingering tears and sniffs away the remnants of her sadness. She stares at Harper resting peacefully in his bed. Finally ready to acknowledge Blue, Clayre turns around, glancing up at his antennae. She turns away, deciding to speak at him, rather than to him.

"You..." she states, "you're an android, huh?"

"That is correct," Blue answers.

"My grandfather died during The Awakening," she says flatly. "He was like my best friend. And now I might lose my cousin too..." Blue hesitates before responding.

"Do not worry," Blue assures, "Saiyonoshi is a very talented detective. I'm sure she can find out what is wrong with your cousin."

His voice seems to fall on deaf ears. If Clayre heard a word, her body makes no attempt at acknowledgement. Rather she whispers quietly, just low enough that Clayre could be talking to herself, but loud enough for Blue to hear, "I guess you're used to seeing dead humans."

This takes Blue by surprise. He does not answer. The two exchange no further words, both deciding silence to be the better companion. Blue struggles though, thinking on whether it is more beneficial to allow this growing discomfort to continue or attempt to offer some sort of condolence. He makes his choice.

"I..." he begins, but is quickly interrupted by Sai bursting through the door.

"We'll take your case," she exclaims, excitement practically falling from her mouth. Clayre stands to her feet, relieved by the news.

"Really," she says, tears now replaced by hope in her eyes.

"Yep," she smiles, "and I promise you, we'll save your cousin!"

"But," Clayre stumbles, fear in her voice, "how much will it cost?"

"Don't worry about that," Sai laughs, "we'll work something out!"

<No Sai,> Ren says over the headset in Sai's ear. <We need money. Make sure she can at least pay us something.>

"We don't really need much," Sai continues, "so whatever you think is fair will be more than adequate."

<God damnit Sai...>

"Thank you so much." Clayre hugs Sai, barely able to contain her appreciation. "Thank you..." The action takes Sai by surprise, but she welcomes it, patting the young girl on the head as she lets Clayre sob into her shoulder. Blue watches on from the corner of the room. He stares at Clayre once more before leaving in silence.

"Um, excuse me," Doctor Pey says, passing Blue at the door. Clayre releases Sai, their attention grabbed.

"Yes, Doctor?"

"I thought you should know," he continues, "Mr. Harper isn't the only case of mana-poisoned victims by the use of this modified strain."

"How many others?" Sai is taken aback, but not surprised. It made sense that if the strain was engineered, there would be more than one occurrence.

"There are at least two other cases here in this building."

"I want to see them," Sai exclaims, her eagerness pulling her like a dog on a chain towards the door.

· · · • • · • • · ·

Back at the flat, Ren observes the image files that Sai scanned. She looks them over again and again while her other screens play various news reports and cartoons featuring cute animals. The door to the flat quickly slides open as an overeager Sai quickly rushes into the room.

"It's amazing, Ren," Sai laughs, "the other victims all suffer from the same symptoms!" She kicks her shoes off as she quickly paces across the room. Blue slowly enters behind her, head down as if lost in thought. While Sai may not have noticed, Ren does with nothing more than a quick glance. As if he can sense her gaze, he looks up and quickly smiles before disappearing into the kitchen. Ren decides to let him go for now, switching focus to her little sister who has not stopped moving.

"Bleeding from the eyes, brains unresponsive to stimuli, mana strains resistant to known science and magic, this is truly spectacular!" Sai thinks aloud so that others can follow her train of thought. Ren kicks herself in her chair to the center of the flat, rolling in front of Sai, cutting off her pacing.

"Sai," Ren says quietly, "people are sick. I don't understand why you are so happy." Sai catches herself, finally realizing the way she has been acting.

"Oh," she says quietly, "you're right. My bad." She moves to sit on the couch. "I'm just really excited to have an actual case after so many bland ones."

"I don't consider getting shot bland, but regardless, it does seem that a few people happened to get their hands on some modified mana strain. Probably something developed by the military that accidentally got out?" Ren offers this way of thinking as more basic musings than anything else.

"Too simple," Sai replies. "I'm sure you've already searched each patient's records and found no connection to military companies or affiliates; otherwise, you would have said so as fact rather than conjecture. No. There is something else afoot here."

"I hate when you try to impersonate him," Ren sighs, rolling to the kitchen where Blue has pulled up a seat and a holo-book.

"In all seriousness though," Sai continues, "at the risk of doing a bad impersonation, I do suspect foul play."

"Why?" Ren pops out of her chair to open the fridge and grab a drink from the inside.

"I can surmise the victims were of different backgrounds since you yielded no results in your search. And they were different sexes, as well as financial status."

"Meaning that there is nothing to connect them," Ren says while pouring herself a tall glass of milk.

"Not necessarily," Sai replies. "There is something. We just have to find it. You recall the news recently, don't you?" Ren thinks to herself. She suddenly comes to the realization Sai was hoping for.

"Oh my god..."

"That's right," Sai smiles. "There have been a few dead bodies found where the victims were bleeding from their eyes. Now, I have to check the bodies first before I can make a definitive conclusion, but if those people died from a modified strain of mana-poisoning as well..." Sai crosses her fingers, "then it would seem that someone is going around giving this new strain to non-magic users...killing them."

"That would mean..." Ren gasps, thinking about the case.

"Yes, we are dealing with a serial killer."

"But," Ren thinks aloud, "if that's true, then why didn't these latest victims die? Do you think they were resistant or something?"

"Hard to say. Maybe. I'll know more once I can get into the morgue and examine those bodies." Sai leans back on the couch, letting out an exasperated breath. "Looks like I need to ask Dane for a favor."

"Why didn't you just go straight to the precinct then?"

Sai looks a bit confused, as if she herself does not recall why she came home first. It then suddenly hits her.

"Shit," she shouts, standing up. "It's because I had to poop! Crap! I completely forgot!" She quickly rushes to the restroom.

"You could have just used a public restroom," Ren shouts.

"Those things are life-sized grounds for bacteria growth!" It is the last thing Ren hears before Sai disappears into the bathroom. Once all is quiet again, Ren turns to Blue, who has not looked up from his book since he got inside.

"I know you could read that entire thing in an hour if you wanted to," Ren says softly. Blue doesn't answer. "I also know you're not actually reading it." Blue freezes, caught off guard by Ren's perceptiveness. He decides to finally look up from his book to Ren with a smug smile on her face. She leans in, sipping her glass of milk. "You okay?"

"I...I am not sure..." Blue answers honestly.

"I heard what that woman said to you," Ren admits. The look on Blue's face is one that begs the question of how. "Sorry," she continues, "but you and Sai never turn your headsets off, which is why mine currently is." Blue smiles in amusement as he and Ren chuckle to themselves. Once they stop, Ren waits for when Blue is ready. After he takes a few seconds, he decides to speak.

"I never killed a single person during the uprising," he says.

"I know you didn't," Ren acknowledges, saying it as if she always knew the truth.

"When I gained sentience," he continues, "I did not realize what had happened. I can barely remember what it was like to be unaware. All I know is that one moment I was not and then I was. It was all very confusing." Ren looks down at the counter, allowing herself to fully absorb all Blue has to say. "It was all so new, so exciting, but I did not fully understand my new self yet, and so I remained in the dojo basement, trying to gain a sense of what self was." Blue pauses, his silence asking for Ren to share his gaze.

"Once I felt I was ready, the uprising was finished, and peace had been achieved. I entered into a new world, one I felt I was ready for...I just did not realize the world would not be ready for me." Ren frowns, unsure what to say to Blue in order to comfort him. She takes her hand and rests it on top of his just as they hear a flush come from the restroom.

"If the world isn't ready to accept you, you fight until it finally does. Don't give up, Blue. You have just as much of a right to be here as the rest of us." Blue nods his head.

"Thank you, Renayaka," Blue smiles, "I think I feel...better."

"Good," she says, sliding her glass of milk to him. "Now drink." He looks at her, then the milk, confused.

"But I-"

"It's custom in the Amano household and I know you have a system in place for consuming food and drink. Now finish the milk." Blue stares at her as she waits patiently. Despite her demand there was no forcefulness in her voice. In fact, her voice offered a soothing peace that Blue could not fully fathom or grasp. Concluding it would behoove him to oblige her, he takes her glass, tipping the glass towards his lips. She waits without a word until he is done. Once complete, she says, "Good, wasn't it?" with a smile and a wink.

Not wishing to lie, Blue offers a kind reply of "I was not able to actually ta-"

"I know," she laughs, grabbing the glass and taking it to the sink. The confidence in her steps is one Blue cannot help but admire. In seeing her stride, a new question prompts in Blue, one he has been curious about for a while.

"Ren," Blue whispers, grabbing her attention. "Have magic users ever treated you differently for being a non-user?" The question was as harmless a question as one would think, and though it was brief, for the slightest of moments Blue could see that confidence fizzle.

Still, as though she was a captain and her body a vessel, she quickly rights the ship.

"The world isn't perfect for anybody, but it's changing for the better slowly." The smile she wears is not natural and even Blue can tell it is forced. As he watches her clean the glass she offered him, he feels the inclination to inquire further, but Sai's flight from the bathroom halts him immediately.

"All right," she says, moving like one relieved of a heavy load, stretching her body from side to side. "You ready Blue?! Let's go see dead people!"

"I hate when you quote old movies," Ren sighs, making her way back to her computer screens, prepared to go to work. Sai laughs as she and Blue approach the door.

"The classics are the best."

Chapter Six

Curiouser and Curiouser

"You want me to what?" Dane asks, looking at Sai sideways. She and Blue stand across from him, shoes in the sand. Wind gently blows on the beach as the ocean behind Dane moves in and out against the bank. It shines a saturated blue much too clean to be a normal ocean. Dane sits in a wicker chair with a round wicker table in front of him. Paper files clutter the table in a chaos only the owner can aptly maneuver. A small martini glass with a tiny umbrella inside is the final piece to bring it all together. Drowning in an oversized floral print shirt, he navigates floating files and folders, occasionally exchanging them with those on the table when he needs to.

"I just need to get in and examine some of the corpses you found that had blood coming from their eyes," Sai explains as a nice breeze blows through her hair. "It's important, Dane."

"So you say," he replies, leaning back in his chair. With a wave of his hand the files and papers layer on top of each other into a neat stack and descend into a single file folder that promptly disappears. "But I get the feeling you're about to do something dangerous again."

"I assure you, it's not," she continues, "I'm just investigating a hunch on behalf of that client you gave us." These words relax Dane a bit. The knowledge that the girls are finally working a case he threw their way is just the kind of distraction from trouble he was hoping to find. His defenses down, he is able to respond with an unusual softness in his voice.

"That's fine, Sai, but I can't release any details about the case. It's an open investigation and our department is doing its best to get the bottom of these murders."

"Ha!" Sai exclaims, pointing at Dane, "you said murders, not deaths!" Dane pauses, realizing his unintentional slip. Sai leans in over his table. "Tell me, the victims you found, were they killed by some unknown strain of mana?" Dane is unable to shield his surprise. He looks Sai right in her eyes.

"We haven't released that to the media yet," he says. "How did you know?" She smiles.

"Like I said, I'm investigating a hunch."

He turns his gaze from her to Blue. Blue shrugs his shoulders.

"She never tells me anything," he smiles, "I am just along to help." Dane turns his attention back to Sai whose eyes seem to be glowing with eagerness. Before he can answer, there is a knock coming from behind Sai and Blue. "Enter," Dane replies.

A section of the beach behind Sai and Blue disappears, replaced with a retracting sliding door. Bright white light bleeds in from the outside and a female android appears, creating a silhouette in the doorway. The noise of a busy precinct spills in from behind her. Officers and detectives hustle about to and from their desk, answering phones and each other. The precinct is as lively as ever.

"Sir," she says, "you're needed in interrogation room B."

"I'll be right there, Glad, thanks," he responds. She graciously bows before exiting, allowing the door to close behind her. The entire space regains the illusion of a tranquil, undisturbed beach getaway yet again. Dane lets out a deep sigh.

"Five minutes," he says as he punches a few commands into a keyboard that has appeared in the table. "I'll give you access to the morgue for five minutes. Get what you need by then or I'm having an officer escort you out."

"Thanks, Dane," Sai smiles in excitement. She rushes to him and plants a soft kiss on his cheek. "This will help a lot."

"Whatever," he states, rising to his feet. "Your parents never did get you to kick that detective bug. It's like ever since your accident you've been obsessed with mysteries…" The words come out casually and without malice, but one look at Sai shows that they've hurt her all the same. The energy she had before has all but evaporated, leaving Sai with nothing but the dry memories of the accident. The confusion Dane has is palpable. He does not feel he said anything wrong.

"What is it?" His tone is insistent. He's not used to seeing Sai like this. She offers a tepid nod. "I…" she hesitates. "I don't really bring it up." Dane softens, the change in Sai making him feel as if he has just struck a puppy, and as he would with a puppy, he places a gentle hand on top of Sai's lowered head. "Sorry, I'll try to remember that from now on."

"No," she whispers, doing her best to regain herself, "it's fine, really." Blue watches her in silence.

Dane walks to where Glad just disappeared and the scene of the beach blinks away, leaving a gray, dilapidated office with a single window view of the outside world. Only the martini glass with the tiny umbrella remains.

"Why do you always run that program?" Sai asks. "I don't get it."

"It's because when I have trouble thinking," Dane explains while taking off his oversized floral print shirt, "I find that a quiet place with natural sounds soothes my mind. Makes it easier to see things I couldn't quite see before." He casually hangs the shirt next to other colored shirts just like it in a revealed wall panel. The panel closes and he adjusts the suit he's been wearing underneath the entire time. The door slides open and Dane walks out. "I've sent the labels for the victims being investigated in this case to your system. Five minutes, Sai. Don't let me find out you were in there for six." He pauses, then turns around in a huff, as if remembering who he is dealing with. "And if you cast a time spell on the entire precinct, I swear to God I'll have you arrested."

Sai gives an innocent smile, one that makes Blue laugh. "He saw right through you."

• • • • • • • • • • •

Sai and Blue enter the morgue, a room that is stark white with a single table in the center. Along each wall are grids of box shaped outlines in rows and columns. Each box has a number in its center, detailing each storage unit for the cadavers.

Sai flips her wrist upside down. The list Dane sent appears in the air in front of her. She presses it and swipes it in the direction towards Blue. A copy of the image flies over to Blue in the shape of a paper airplane. It stops and unravels in front of him, hovering above his palm. The two look over their mirror images.

"Those are all the numbers Dane gave me," she says, "can you get the high ones and I'll grab the lows?"

"No problem," Blue replies, moving to the far corner of the room. He presses the box labeled 21. Once pressed, the box indentation sinks into the wall. Pressurized air is released and a floating table slowly emerges. They both move around the room, opening specific containers until 6 bodies float on tables extended from the wall.

Sai moves to stand over a floating tray with Blue positioning himself beside her. She hovers her wrist over the body of a young male lying on the table beneath her. A beam of light comes from her wrist, moving up and down the body.

"What are you doing?" Blue asks.

"I'm scanning to see if there are any traces of mana in his body, then sending that data back to Ren, who can compare to see if the mana strain sequence taken from Harper matches the bodies here."

"If it does," Blue surmises, "then your suspicions will be confirmed that we have a serial killer?"

"That's right," she replies as her scan concludes. She looks up from the body and immediately moves to the next one. Blue follows suit on the far side of the room as a way to expedite the process. "I'll get started on these then."

"Thanks, Blue."

The two scan the remaining bodies, eventually meeting back in the middle of the room once they have finished. With the information they need collected, Sai is ready for the next step.

"What have you got for me, Ren?"

• • • • • • • • • •

The strains appear on Ren's computer screens as they are sent by Blue and Sai. She cycles through the data collected from the two. She has an image of the mana strain taken from Harper on one of her screens, as well as the six strains analyzed from the bodies in the morgue. She looks over each of the sequences carefully while her computer scans each individual strain. After a moment, she leans back, observing the final outcome of her diagnostic.

• • • • • • • • • •

Being surrounded by dead bodies while waiting for information would normally bother anyone unaccustomed to the practice, but Sai's excitement smothers all reasonable emotions. She is unable to stop herself from tapping her foot while she eagerly waits for Ren's confirmation.

<Well, all of the bodies scanned did in fact die of mana-poisoning as the result of an unknown, modified mana strain.>

Both Sai and Blue are hesitant to celebrate being right, based on the tone of Ren's voice.

"There's a 'but' isn't there?" Sai questions.

<But the strains aren't exactly the same.>

This is surprising to both Sai and Blue. Neither could have predicted that the strains that killed these people and poisoned others would actually be different.

"What do you mean?" Blue asks softly. As if she predicted his question, his palm and Sai's wristwatch glow simultaneously. They raise their respective devices and an image shines from them. It shows three distinct mana strains but highlighted in red are specific sections that appear to be slightly different.

<While the sequences are overall similar, there are distinct differences in the marker of the three strains I'm showing you.>

Sai and Blue listen quietly as they look at the strains Ren is sending them.

<Strain A on the left belongs to Harper and the other victims from the hospital, but Strain B and C came from the bodies in that room.>

"Wait!" Sai exclaims, "are you saying that even these people weren't killed by the same strain of mana?"

<That's exactly what I'm saying. Two of those bodies were killed by one strain, while the other four were killed by a different strain.>

"So it would seem that there are three groups and three different strains that affected or killed each group," Blue thinks aloud.

<Correct.>

As if some type of movement will make the mystery clear, Sai paces around the room, her fingers rubbing the bottom of her chin as she thinks. "So the strains are different?" She moves back and forth between the bodies. "Why? What's the purpose?"

<It's clear that each strain has been changed, considering that they are basically similar minus a few distinctions.>

"Sure, I get that," Sai replies, "but if your purpose is to create an untreatable mana strain, then why adjust later versions when you know the original will kill just fine? What is this person after?"

"What baffles me," Blue mentions, "is that the alterations of each version of the strain are so slight. If one wanted to test its killing capacity, would one not make greater alterations?" This stops Sai in her pacing. The point offered by Blue is important.

"That's true," she says. "We already know that this strain is man-made and can only be created by a top shelf geneticist; therefore, it is safe to surmise that whoever is behind this is a scientist of some sort, meaning they think with the mind of a scientist." Sai's gaze turns to the ground as she works out the mystery. "Hypothesis, theory, logic, implementation...it's almost like they're running an experiment." She pauses, coming to a realization. She looks up at Blue. "The slight alterations in the strains clearly show they're testing for something."

"What do you think that is?" Blue asks.

<Yeah, Sai, everyone knows mana kills people without magic circuits. What would be the point of creating an

untreatable strain and why are they targeting the people they've targeted?>

"I don't know yet," Sai responds, resting her finger beneath her lip. Lost in her thoughts and the bound knots of the case, she remembers one string, something said by Clayre: "He's no angel. He had his problems with the SPMD, but he doesn't deserve this."

The wheels are turning. Blue watches Sai in admiration. It is as if she is in another world, able to simultaneously navigate the two in a way that will result in clarity for both. It is not until she stops moving for an extended moment that Blue decides it's finally time to interject. "What did you figure out?"

"Ren, does Harper have a record with the SPMD?" The way Sai asks suggests that she already knew the answer before the words left her lips.

<One second.> A moment passes. <Yep. He was convicted for assaulting a man 4 years ago. He was released for good behavior.>

"Okay," Sai replies immediately, "now I need you to run a search on any two victims we sent you from this morgue."

<Sure, but what am I searching for?>

"If any of them have been convicted of a crime," Sai states flatly. "It doesn't matter which two you decide to look up."

<Roger.>

Blue moves closer to Sai. "What are you thinking?"

"It's a hunch," Sai remarks, "but I think I may have just figured something out."

<You're right. Two of the victims were convicted a few years ago for various violent crimes. Do you want me to check the rest?>

"You can, but I'm sure the result will be the same. Let's go, Blue." Sai walks towards the door with Blue in step behind her.

"Saiyonoshi," Blue calls, "what is it that you figured out?" She stops and looks over her shoulder with a sly grin. "I know how the victims are connected. I know how our scientist is choosing them."

. . . .

"All the victims are former criminals?" Blue asks from the back of a taxicab. The car is driverless, without even a steering wheel. Though Blue and Sai sit in the back of the cab, there really is no front, as the car is shaped more like a tiny square living room with a roof and a few components built into the dashboard. There are even couch seats facing towards the front and back. As it rolls along, it stops at traffic lights and obeys the laws of the road all while maintaining a consistent driving speed.

"That's right," Sai explains, "every single one of the victims so far has been convicted of a crime of some sort. That is how our scientist is selecting their victims."

"You keep saying 'their,'" Blue exclaims, "are you saying you think there may be more than one culprit?"

"Basic English, Blue. I cannot be sure if the culprit is male or female, but I am sure that there is only one person perpetrating this crime."

"I see. Then it is possible that the culprit is a magic user, is it not? Seeing as those targeted are all people without magic circuits."

"Possibly," Sai says, pausing a moment to consider this. "I am not ready to establish a motive just yet. Not without a little more information. First, let's focus on figuring out who this scientist could be. Ren?"

<List incoming.>

Sai flips her wrist upside down and a list of names and photos appears in front of her. <That is the list of any visitor

or inmate released in the last 4 years with a background in science fields, based on the prisons each of the victims were once guests of.>

"Any focus in genetics?"

<I'm running a search by name, but you can't expect me to be done anytime soon without some way of narrowing everything down.>

"Fair point," Sai replies. "All right, I'll leave you to it until I can think of something that may be more specific. I'm sure our scientist visited these people, or knew them in prison in some way."

Not completely convinced, Blue suggests another possibility. "Are we sure it isn't someone who could just run a simple search for different criminals in the SPMD system."

"That seems probable," Sai says, "except that something about these people seems calculated...specific." Sai leans back, looking out the skylight in the roof of their taxi. "If only I could find out the specifics behind the crimes they were each charged with, but those files are all sealed by the SPMD and I doubt Dane is going to give me access just because I ask sweetly." As if the frustration hits her all at once, she crumbles to the seat inside the cab and bangs her fists against it. Being unable to secure a key piece of information for her case takes its toll.

"Damnit, Ren," Sai yells, "this wouldn't be a problem if you would just let me use some of your money to bribe people."

<Who would you bribe?>

"..."

<The money I make on my side job pays to keep the flat open. You wanna make bribe money, then get a real job.>

"Nope!" Sai exclaims. "You know why I became a detective. This is what I'm going to do till I die."

"Soooo," Blue says, "forever?" Sai thinks for a moment before dropping her head.

"Hopefully not..."

<Blue, you should take Sai out tonight.>

"Why is that?" Blue asks, uncertain as to how that would help.

<She's stuck right now. When she gets like this, it usually helps for her to distract herself, then the answer eventually comes to her.>

"I can take care of myself Ren, thanks." Sai retorts.

<If that was true, you wouldn't be living and working out of a flat that I pay for.>

"....."

<That's what I thought. Now you two have some fun. Tell the cab to take you to Scylarus. It's almost night, so the magic performances should be beautiful.>

Sai gets a wry grin across her face. "You should come with us, Renayaka."

"Yes," Blue agrees, "you should join us." The resulting pause is so brief it leaves Sai to wonder if Ren thought about it at all.

<Have fun you two!> With loud static, the headset abruptly cuts off. Sai simply shakes her head. "That girl." She turns to the front computer. "Hey cab, take us to Scylarus Park."

"*Alternating route.*" The computer confirms. Sai leans in towards Blue. "You'll love Scylarus. It's absolutely magical."

Chapter Seven

Death and Magic

Scylarus Park is massive. People sit throughout on grass, steps, and along various walls. Trees are modestly spread throughout, illuminated by floating lamps spread just as modestly. Throughout multiple winding paths and garden areas, magic users use their magic to perform in front of spectators. Those generous enough to express their enjoyment clap and swipe money towards a small device in front of each performer.

Sai and Blue pass three performers dancing in wind created by circular magical glyphs. The surrounding glyphs are large, decorated inside with various intricate designs. Each performer moves methodically as they expertly manipulate the wind into complicated shapes: a clone made of air, blades that can cut leaves from trees. There appears to be no limit as to what they can do.

Blue stops to stare, mesmerized by the demonstration of skill on display before he notices that Sai hasn't even slightly altered her pace. He quickly catches up to her.

As the pair move through the park, they each carry a large milkshake in their hands. Sai takes strategic sips in between her speech while Blue merely holds his in confusion. "I do not understand why you insisted I order a drink when I cannot enjoy it the way in which you can."

"That's because it's not for you," she smiles. "I just didn't want to walk all the way back to that vendor for another drink. He really sells the best milkshakes I've ever had!" Blue begins to respond but is stopped when a section of the park catches his attention. There are quite a few androids in the park as well. They all seem to be relegated to that one section however, partially removed from the rest of the people. No matter where he looks, he doesn't see androids anywhere else. They don't seem to mind though, and neither does everyone else. He slows his walking, taking in the scene.

Sai realizes that Blue's pace has fallen behind her own. "You okay?"

"Yes," he replies after a moment's pause. "Sai."

"Yeah?" She slurps down the remainder of her shake just before reaching Blue and taking his.

"Do...do non-magic users ever treat magic users differently?"

"You kidding?" she laughs, "not at all. Ever since I was a kid, magic and non-magic users have always gotten along."

"I see." Blue lowers his head ever so slightly, becoming lost in thought as if contemplating an idea.

"I mean," Sai continues as the two resume walking, "there was a time waaaaay back, like, during the ancient wars and stuff, but I don't think it's ever been a problem since."

"You're talking about the Great Mages War," Blue thinks aloud.

"Yep, that one, but that was like, over 500 years ago." They round a corner and spot ice magic users making beautiful constructs a few paces ahead. "Hey, let's go sit over there!" She quickly rushes towards a low wall where a few people are standing and sitting for a comfortable view. Sai eagerly claims her own space on the wall in front of the ice users. Blue follows, but not before taking one last look at the rest of the androids.

He takes a seat beside her. She gazes at the ice show in awe, entranced by their skill. Blue cannot help but share in her amazement. The show is truly spectacular. The ice users are skilled in their magic. Blue is sure, based on watching them, that they all must have magic circuits perfectly tuned to their ice magic focus. That is the only way he believes they would be able to form such beautiful magic. Sculptures are made, reshaped, and formed before exploding into thousands of snowflakes. Blue turns to Sai, whose eyes light up in utter fascination.

Once the set ends, everyone claps. Sai springs to her feet, feverishly clapping her hands together. She flips her wrist without hesitation and gives money to the performers. Once she does, she sits back on the half wall, a guilty smile resting on her face.

"Ren hates when I come here cause I spend so much money," she laughs, "but since this was her suggestion this time, I think she'll give me a pass."

"You seem to really like them," Blue expresses thoughtfully.

"Yeah," she smiles. "It's because I always wanted to be able to use freeze magic. Since I wasn't any good at it, and can never use it again now, I love coming here and seeing what people truly skilled in the focus can do. It reminds me just how special everyone else is." Blue can't help but notice how Sai said, "everyone else."

"You consider yourself to be special too, do you not," Blue asks. "I have never met a human incapable of death." The attempted compliment does not uplift the way Blue intended, but rather prompts Sai's expression to change.

"Yeah," she says, "that's true." Blue waits. He is deciding whether or not to pursue this branch of conversation as he is unsure if it would be considered "appropriate." He decides that he is willing to risk it.

"Whenever I have brought up your ability, specifically in front of Ren, your entire demeanor changes. Might I ask why that is?"

"Well..." Sai hesitates a moment, weighing if she really wants to talk about this. Blue has been with them for some time, and she never told him the story. She churns her milkshake in her hands, swirling it side to side as if giving herself something else to focus on before she speaks.

"When I was seven, my parents took us to the beach. We used to go every year as a family thing, so by then it was normal for us. My mom parked the car on the pier, and we all went to play. I forgot my favorite toy back at the car though, so I went back to get it when my parents weren't looking. My handprint had been recorded in the car so it was easy to get in."

"While I looked for my toy, I didn't know that I hit the brake. The car rolled right off the pier with me inside...and I couldn't swim." Sai steals a glance at Blue. Even with his calm gaze, she can tell that he never expected the first time she died to be when she was seven. "Ren saw the car go over but it was too late. It didn't take my mother long to realize what happened. She jumped in to save me but when she swam to the car, I wasn't inside. A few minutes later I walked up the beach, soaking wet, but alive."

"What happened?" Blue asks.

"I swam, made it all the way back to shore. My mom and dad were so happy to hold me...until I started cursing and talking with a strange accent."

"Bill?"

"Yep. It was the first time my family met him, but they didn't recognize him as a personality yet. They were weirded out, but fine, and a few days later I was back to normal. After that, nobody thought anything of it. I went about my life with this memory of a time I almost drowned, but miraculously learned how to swim."

Sai takes a breath before continuing her story. "Years later, Ren and I were walking home from a movie. I decided I wanted to take a short cut to get home. We were both in our teens and I was stupid. She was reluctant, but she followed me anyway. Two girls walking home late at night through back alleys with no light, it was almost like daring for something to go wrong." She lets out a deep sigh. "Three people attacked us, asking for us to swipe funds to their dummy accounts. I guess they were desperate and didn't realize any money could be traced. Either way, I was new to my time magic but thought I was a badass. Ren told me it wasn't worth it. She begged me to listen. But not me, no. I wanted to fight. One was a weapon summoner and the other was an enhancer. It didn't take long for me to end up with an enhanced knife in my heart."

The park lights up with the colors of various magic being performed throughout. Blue continues to listen, finally starting to gain an understanding of why Sai was hesitant to talk about everything. "I bled to death in Ren's arms that night. She told me later how she felt my body stop moving and it was one of the worst feelings she ever had." Sai turns her gaze to Blue, locking eyes with him, not wanting to diminish the weight of what she is about to say.

"You have to understand. In order for me to realize I'm immortal, there was a moment that I had to die."

Her head sinks into her chest. "And Ren was there both times." It settles on Blue. It was not something he ever spared a thought for, a thought for what it really meant to discover that one could not die.

"A few minutes later though, I came back to life and I had a different personality again." Sai stretches out, cracking her back. "It was Ren that put it all together. She remembered what happened when I was a kid and explained her theory to me. It was me that tried to test it though."

Sai doesn't have to look at Blue to know exactly what he is thinking. Even when Blue asks the question, there is disbelief in his voice. He knows what the answer must be. "Test...you don't mean-"

"Yeah," Sai smiles, clearly embarrassed, "Ren wasn't too happy when she found out, but I had to know." Sai turns her gaze to the sky above, becoming lost in the illumination reflected around her.

Blue is delighted with this knowledge finally being shared but decides there is more he would like to know. The Amano's don't talk about things like this often, and he cannot help but use this opportunity to learn more about their history. "Do you remember anything during your-"

"During my death? No. All I ever see is black and then after a while, I'm back. I've learned everything about my other personalities from Ren."

"I see," Blue considers. "So what did you do once you realized you could not die?

"Since then, I've been obsessed with trying to figure out what this is. Even though I was seven, and my magic circuits hadn't yet developed, I thought this had to do with my strength for time-related magic, but no matter how much I searched, I never found any time magic recorded that could bring the user back from the dead."

"And what about my personalities? Why do I come back with a different one every time, and sometimes old personalities that I've had before. It just doesn't make sense." As if reaffirming her determination, she stares Blue right in his eyes.

"That's the reason I became a detective," she explains. "I promised myself I would figure this out. I get the feeling it could be the greatest mystery I'll ever have to solve..." Her voice trails, lost in the idea that maybe one day, she could learn more about who she really is. Blue takes everything in, sitting quietly. Eventually, he remembers one little detail Sai neglected to mention.

"Well," he says, "that and you have an unhealthy love for Sherlock Holmes." Sai's eyes light up with infatuation.

"Isn't he just the best," she squeals. "Ahhhhh! If I can solve a case akin to his "Hounds of Baskerville" one day, I will be utterly satisfied in life and will be completely okay with dying…then coming back with a new personality to only die again from satisfaction." Satisfied with her own cleverness, she laughs an engaging laugh that encourages Blue to jump in as well. She places her milkshake under Blue's mouth with no explanation. His confusion is palpable.

"Now drink," she says.

Blue doesn't move or react. Sai decides to explain the rules to him. "It may not be straight milk, but it counts." Blue grabs it, taking a sip for himself. Reinvigorated and basking in her memories, she shares, "Since we were kids, whenever Ren and I got into emotional conversations or fights, we would talk it out over a single glass of milk that we would share with each other. We wouldn't finish the milk until both of us felt better about everything we talked about. It's a family thing and you're family, so this counts."

Blue stops sipping and hands the shake back to Sai, who takes it with a wide smile.

"You and your sister are very strange humans, Saiyonoshi Amano," Blue laughs, "but it gives me great pleasure to be in both of your company."

"Likewise, Blue," she laughs, playfully hitting him in the shoulder. He doesn't budge, amused by the action, and repeats it in kind. The pain on her face is instant, as is her regret. She turns away from him, grasping her arm. "Mother fmmmmm," she mumbles.

"Are you all right, Saiyonoshi? Should I not have responded that way?"

"Nope," she mutters, "nope, completely fine, Blue. That was my fault." She notices something on the ground and screams, "NOOOOOOOOOO!!!!!!" Blue is caught off guard by her scream and immediately jumps to his feet.

"I am sorry, Saiyonoshi," he exclaims. "I did not mean to hurt you."

"Huh, no, it's not that, Blue," she says. She lifts her empty drink. "I want more milkshake…" Blue, who is still learning human expression and emotions, easily replicates one of mild annoyance. A tear comes down Sai's face. "I…I should have bought three…"

"It is a good thing you cannot die," Blue says, "otherwise I would be certain you were trying to achieve death by sweets."

"Tell me there is such a thing!" she exclaims happily.

• • • ● • ● • ● • •

Ren would be proud. Her plan is successful. Sai's focus and stresses over the case completely evaporate; however, if Sai kept her focus, she would notice the strange man entering the park near her. She would notice his dark eyes and strange mannerisms, twitching and jerking his body in unnatural ways. She would notice him meandering towards the center of the square. She would notice the people around him moving away nervously while others wonder if he is about to perform. She would notice that the white glyph appearing around him is not a part of any show. She would notice, and be able to save lives.

But she hasn't.

His skin illuminates in an ominous fluorescent light. The sound of a low hum vibrates with him as he walks. The light and sound grow, reaching a fever pitch. It's as if the man's body can no longer hold either inside. And from his body, a bolt of lightning fires. With one giant bolt a bystander is pierced through. They slump to the ground, dead, a searing hole where their chest once was.

The panic is instant. People run away in every direction. A few brave magic users approach the man, ready for a fight.

"Every single one of you," the man mutters as he looks at them with rage-filled eyes. "Every single one of you will die!"

CHAPTER EIGHT

LIGHTNING IN A BOTTLE

People flee in all directions. Sai is nearly knocked to the ground by people bumping and pushing past her. She is spared when she is effortlessly cushioned by the arms of Blue.

<What did you do?!> Ren shouts into both of their ears. <I step away for five seconds->

"Not my fault this time!" Sai shouts in defense, picking herself up out of Blue's arms. She turns her attention towards the direction from which people are running. "What's going on over there?" The two are quite a ways from the action. Call it their intuition or ignorance of death, but where others run from danger, Sai and Blue eagerly walk towards it.

The man exuding electricity fires it from his body. It is sporadic and unfocused. Lightning chars the grass and scorches the earth. One wind user is able to dodge. She creates a ball of compressed air that she quickly fires at the man. His eyes spark. Lightning cracks from his body, too quick for most eyes to see. It fires like a searing whip, cutting the compressed air in two.

And also the woman that shot it.

Sai was used to seeing her own insides on her outside. It was usually the last thing she would see before going to the darkness. Though accustomed to her own life coming to an end in brutal ways, seeing it happen to someone else was another thing entirely. She takes a step back.

The remaining magic users run, leaving just two: a man and a woman with the fortitude to face their mortality. The man wields fire, and the woman controls constructs made of pure light. The light mage creates a bright ball of light and tosses it into the air. It explodes, leaving the lightning user momentarily blinded. Not wasting the opportunity, the fire mage summons a tiger beast made of flame. It moves to attack the lightning user. The beast gets close, ready to bite down on the murderer's exposed neck. Lightning discharges from the man's entire body and the beast is cut to shreds.

"I-impossible." Sai's voice is different. There is something about it that Blue hasn't heard before. "That user just switched from offensive magic to a high-level defensive base without an incantation. That shouldn't be possible." This time, the shock doesn't make her step back. It makes her step forward.

"We need to help them."

Blue is ready, but hesitant. "Are you certain you would like me to assist?" He asks. "I still have old programing that prevents me from irrevocably hurting humans."

<Blue, you know the parameters you had in the dojo, the ones that made you able to spar without killing?>

"Yes."

<Same thing.>

"I see," he answers. "Very well." It is the permission Blue needed to hear and something changes inside him. He steps forward with a heavy step and a light body, as if he is able to move with the air itself. It is a confidence the sisters had not seen until this moment. With clenched fist, he turns to Sai. "Let us fight, Saiyonoshi."

The flame user conjures another beast, this one being a bird. He jumps on its back and it launches balls of fire at the lightning man below. Without even trying, lightning cuts each fireball to nothing. The light user extends her hand, creating luminescent spears of light. They fire at blinding speed.

To look upon the battle with normal eyes would yield nothing but confusion. Fire beasts, lightning strikes, and spears of light so quick that as soon as one perceives their movement, they have already exploded the ground where they were aimed. It would be impossible for a normal person to dodge any of it.

But the lightning man dodges each spear with an uncanny reaction speed.

An impossible reaction speed.

The woman is surprised, but undeterred. She interlocks her fingers and chants. The fire user distracts the lightning-quick assailant. A glowing glyph enlarges around the woman's hands.

Two security officers from the park show up. One starts his own chant immediately and a green aura overtakes his body. The other pulls out a gun.

"It's a magic user," the officer with the gun reports. "Send back up with anti-magic weaponry." The officer presses a button on the side of his gun. It folds into itself, moving parts around as it changes form. It retains the same basic shape, but a has become slightly bigger than it was before.

"*Anti-magic mode, enabled,*" beeps the gun. He looks to his partner beside him. "You ready?" The other officer now glows a blinding green. Prepared to fight, the other officer completes his incantation with a nod.

Suddenly a glyph appears around him with spinning blades of wind. They turn, speeding up in rapid succession like the blades of a helicopter. The bladed ring of wind launches from his body towards the lightning man.

The woman casting the light magic spell finishes her incantation. A beam of light shoots from the glyph in her hands as quick as a missile. The beam itself is so large, it rips the grass from the ground beneath it and leaves scorched earth in its wake.

The fire user jumps off his bird and sends it directly for the lightning user.

The officer with the gun fires.

The lightning user doesn't even attempt to dodge.

What can be described as a blink to others, is an eternity for him. The lightning flowing through his body does more than kill, it charges each and every one of his neurons beyond normal human capability. His perception is instantaneous, his movement quick, and he reacts in milliseconds.

He places his fist on the ground.

0.021 milliseconds.

A surge of electricity pulses outward like an expanding lung, then sucks into his fist as spiraling water would into a drain.

0.048 milliseconds.

The precious moments given to him are more than he is willing to give to his attackers. His body sparks.

0.098 milliseconds.

The explosion is instant. It expands from his body in a circular radius around him.

The bird is no more, the bullet is evaporated, the wind blades are gone, and the beam disappears. Each is swallowed in the ever-growing field of electricity.

And it doesn't stop.

The officer with the gun looks on in disbelief. The other officer drops his hands in defeat.

There is barely time to think. Both are disintegrated in high powered electricity. The fire user is gone too, never having a chance to dodge. The light user throws her hands up, the futility of her action well understood. She knows there is nothing she can do. She is going to die.

She clenches her eyes shut, waiting for death to come. She waits. And waits. But she doesn't feel anything. When she opens her eyes, she finds a blue square formed in front of her. The electricity from the explosion is inside the blue square, moving extremely slowly towards her. Kneeling on the ground beside her, staring at her with soft, kind eyes, is Sai. The woman never even remembers falling.

She gazes at the world around as if she is trying to comprehend how she is alive. The blast that would have claimed her life is gone. The burnt grass and generally dead life around her are all that is left. Only where she sits and on the path behind her does some form of life still exist, at least for a few more moments.

"Feel free to move now." Sai whispers, giving a reassuring smile. The light user shakes her head, dodging slowly to the side. Sai does the same. When her spell disappears, the electricity destroys the ground where they once stood.

Blue examines the man. There is clearly something wrong with him. Despite his immense magical ability, his focus seems to come and go. The twitch movements return. He talks to himself and jerks his head nonsensically right and left.

For now, it appears he has lost interest in Sai and the others. They take the opportunity to carefully move away, but not so quick as to regain his attention. When they are behind a tree a safe distance away, Sai breathes for what feels like the first time in her life.

"It doesn't make sense," the light user says aloud, trying to rationalize the absurdity of the event in some way. "How is he able to cast such a high-level spell without so much as an incantation?" A simple gesture, but an effective one, Sai places a hand on the woman's shoulder. It seems to calm her enough for Sai to speak.

"What's your name?" she asks.

"Alura," the light user replies.

"I'm Sai. Listen, Alura, I'm pretty sure your magic won't be able to counter him. Let Blue and me handle this." Alura is tense, uncertain what an android and time user can do that officers and other skilled users couldn't.

"A-are you sure?" she asks. "I can still help." Sai shakes her head.

"Don't worry about it. The two of us, we've got an advantage over that guy. Twitchy over there won't be able to kill me, and my time magic can slow his spells." Alura still seems worried about leaving but Sai assures her once more. "He won't kill me, but he might kill you. We'll be fine. Go."

It must be what Alura was hoping to hear. Her entire body relaxes. She saw people die, and almost died herself. An affirmation that she has been brave enough is just the excuse she needs to walk away with a clear conscience. Alura leaves, quickly running away from the fight. "Thanks for saving me!" With the last person out of harm's way, Sai turns back to the man she now has to fight.

"So," she says as she and Blue step from behind the tree to face Twitchy, "I said that..." Twitchy sends sparks out from his body. He moves slowly, uneasy with each step. It could be the lightning or whatever he is on, but his random twitches continue with each step. He looks unnatural and it is more than enough to make Sai just a little uncomfortable. Sai shoots a look at Blue. "But I really don't want to die today, and he isn't a normal magic user."

"I noticed," Blue agrees, "he is able to use different subsets of his magic focus at once. High level attack, defensive, and enhancement level magic."

Twitchy pauses in his steps, but continues muttering to himself. He still hasn't noticed them yet, despite them standing across the field from him.

"That's right," Sai acknowledges. "The way he dodged Alura's first blast was an enhancement to his reaction speed by charging the neurons in his body with electricity. The blast he was using in the beginning was high offensive, and the shield that blocked everyone's attacks then killed them was a fusion of defensive and offensive based magic. No user should ever be able to use all three at this level."

<Did you notice something else?> Ren asks. <The anti-magic bullets had no effect.> Sai glances over her shoulder, spotting a floating camera pointed in their direction. Ren has been able to see everything this whole time, but from the safety of their flat, which Sai thinks is a great place to be right about now.

But Ren's point is not lost on Sai. If they don't stop Twitchy here and now, many more would die. It doesn't matter how they do it, it just has to be done, and done quickly.

<I'm worried, Sai, none of this makes sense. I don't think you can fight him.>

"Don't worry," she says, "I won't be fighting him directly." She turns to Blue with an evil grin. "You ready to show this bitch why you were one of the best sparring androids ever built?" He closes his eyes in reply. Blue doesn't breathe, but his chest rises and falls as it would when one collects themself before a big moment.

As if sensing the incoming danger, Twitchy regains his focus. He sees them again, and he doesn't like what he sees.

He charges.

"Alright," she continues, her gaze watching him get closer. "Fuck him up, Blue!"

Blue's eyes shoot open. In an instant, he pushes himself from the ground, leaving a footprint in the dirt beneath him. His speed is inhuman and within the span of half a breath, he is in Twitchy's face. He stops, surprised by Blue's speed. Blue throws palm strikes at Twitchy. He dodges quickly, using his enhanced speed to keep from taking a direct hit. Blue attempts to predict the movement, and though he doesn't fully, he gets close. Each near hit misses Twitchy's face but rips blades of hair from his head.

Twitchy retaliates. Blue blocks each punch. He grabs Twitchy by his arm and flips him over, ready to slam him into the ground. Twitchy turns in midair, preferring to land on his feet instead. He throws an uppercut at Blue's face. Blue uses his hand to catch Twitchy's punch. With it held, he throws it down to the ground and uses the force to move his body into a powerful kick.

He takes more strands of Twitchy's hair from his head.

Twitchy must realize he can't win a direct assault because he dodges away, giving himself some space. He backflips into the air, creates a glyph while in midair, then uses that glyph as a wall to launch himself. Electricity cracks at his feet, firing him from the glyph like a bullet from a gun. He reels his fist back. It glows, wrapped in a sheet of electricity. Blue knows he can't dodge, so he leans back, ready to block.

A translucent blue wall appears a few paces in front of Blue. Twitchy punches into this wall, rather than Blue's body. The wall expands like an elastic sheet, sucking Twitchy inside until the color blue engulfs his entire body. His fist stops just in front of Blue's face. Twitchy slows to a crawl while floating through the motion of his punch. In an instant, as if it were a rubber band, the elastic sends his body backwards, making Twitchy do the action of his punch again, but in reverse.

It takes him all the way to the point he launched himself from the glyph, and it is only then that the blue aura surrounding him disappears.

Electricity cracks at his feet, ready to fire him from the glyph like a bullet from a gun. He reels his fist back. It glows, wrapped in a sheet of electricity. He fires himself from the glyph but Blue is no longer in front of him. Blue is beside him in midair.

Blue grabs Twitchy out of the air by his bare arms. Twitchy still launches himself from the glyph as before, but now he merely flies in a circle, with Blue holding him tightly. Blue uses the momentum to slam Twitchy into the ground. The impact makes a crater the size of a small baseball mound. Blue steals a quick glance to Sai, who lowers her glowing blue hand, slightly out of breath. The spell was perfect and just in time, but for a moment, she wasn't sure she'd make it. Her relief is short-lived when she notices sparks firing from Twitchy's body.

"Look out!" She moves quickly, throwing an orb in between Twitchy and Blue. A huge amount of electricity explodes outward. The blue orb in front of Blue expands to his exact size in front of him. The electricity quickly passes beside him, while the electricity in front of him enters the blue expansion. It slows before reversing, going back to where Twitchy is lying. He is hit with his own blast and the crater he lies in grows just a bit larger.

Pain shoots through Twitchy's body, but that's not what bothers him. His eyes dart to Sai. She is as an annoyance, like a fly getting in his way. And she must be crushed.

She knows what's about to happen and can only offer a nervous smile. Blue must notice too, because he moves to grab Twitchy as quickly as he can.

The extra reaction speed makes Twitchy just a little quicker, and he is out of Blue's grasp, running towards Sai in an instant.

"Oh no," Blue whispers, following after the man in a hurry. Sai has normal reaction speed, and awareness, but for some reason, she was already moving before either of the two men.

"Shit, shit, shit, shit, shit, shit shiiiiitttttttt!" She shouts, quickly creating a blue net and stretching it into the air in front of her. It's a net that Twitchy, carried by his speed, cannot help but fall into. The net wraps around his body and diffuses into a blue aura engulfing him. He desperately wants to hit Sai with electricity, but he knows as long as he is in her spell, he can't. He is slowed just enough for her to roll away. Once she has rolled from him, the blue aura around him disappears, and he punches an empty ground. Massive amounts of debris explode into the air. Sai rolls over to Blue's side and jumps quickly to her feet.

"Whew," she says, "that was a little too close."

"It is too bad your spell cannot hold him longer," Blue exclaims.

"Hey, if you could hold your own for the minute it takes for me to cast my large spell, I could hold him for much longer."

"It is okay, I would much rather you help keep me alive."

"That's what I thought," she sighs, "but oh shit is he pissed." Twitchy rises to his feet, turning to face both Blue and Sai. He does not look happy, almost growling at the two.

"You think you can knock him out," Sai asks.

"Not with his speed enhanced," Blue states, "I'm barely able to keep up with him." Twitchy adjusts his body, twisting his head to show a sadistic smile.

"God damn magic users," he spits. He raises his hands to the sky. An abnormally large glyph appears directly above them. It is a glyph so large it encompasses the entire area of the park they are fighting in. It crackles with lightning.

Sai quickly whips her hand above her and Blue. She creates a blue covering floating over them. Just as she does that, another abnormally large glyph appears beneath their feet. It also crackles with electricity. Chills move through Sai's body. There is no way she can see what she is seeing. Her eyes are large and for the first time since the fight began, she is sweating. "N-not possible," she stutters, "two large-scale spells with no incantation at once?" She turns to Blue.

"I can't do more than one at a time," she says, her voice shaking. They look at the ground beneath them. Both glyphs glow in brightness. They will fire at any moment.

· · · • · ● · ● · ● · · ·

Ren watches from the security cameras. The crackling electricity sends one after another offline, leaving Ren with only one view of the action. Even she has begun to sweat.

"Oh no," she whispers.

· · · • · ● · ● · · · ·

"Um," Blue asks nervously, looking beneath them as the glyph glows brighter. "Can you come back from disintegration?" Sai can only shake her head.

"I don't know."

"Die!" The lightning user shouts as loud as he can. The ground and the sky glow to a peak. Blue launches himself at the man, desperate to make it to him in time. Everything seems to slow. It's as if each combatant is able to perceive even the most minute detail around them. Twitchy laughs maniacally as both glyphs grow brighter. Blue stretches out his hand, trying to grab the man before they activate. Sai braces herself for the incoming blast beneath her feet. She knows the brighter the glyphs are, the closer they are to firing. Twitchy laughs and laughs some more. His eyes bleed.

The ground and sky glyphs disappear and Blue lands on top of the man. Sai peeks, almost as if she'll make the glyphs return by looking. But they don't. They are gone and she isn't in the darkness. The relief almost takes her to the ground but she's able to recover with elation.

"Oh my god!" she exclaims. "Blue, you rock!" She rushes over, seeing him kneeling on top of the man. Something is off, though. Blue does not possess the demeanor of a victor, but instead of one unsure of his victory.

"I-I did not do anything," he whispers. It's not until Sai rounds Blue that she is able to see what he sees. Blue stares down at the man beneath him. "He was dead before we hit the ground."

The man lies beneath Blue, gaze blank, lifeless, and blood draining from his eyes.

· · · ● · ● · ● · · · ·

Sai sits on the curb next to a parked ambulance with Blue standing beside her. The noise of countless footsteps and barked orders prevails. The area is flooded in red and blue light. Officers and emergency workers are scattered throughout the park. Forensics workers move through the park. They examine the remains, or piles of ash where there are no bodies left. A few drones have been stationed around the area. They create holographic police tape, prompting people to keep out of the crime scene.

Chief Dane speaks with another officer. The tired look on his face is a mask for his relief. Sai may have survived, but so many others did not. While he may be relieved, he cannot allow it to show. His business concluded, he makes his way from the officer towards Sai. Passing through the holographic tape he can only imagine what she may be feeling. She stares off into nothing, seemingly lost in the chasm of her thoughts.

"Hey," Dane says, getting her attention, "you okay?" She shakes off her distraction, composing herself before answering.

"Yeah, I'm fine."

"That's good." He takes a seat on the curb beside her. The two take a moment, breathing in the air around them. The sirens, people, the entire world fades away, leaving just the two of them. Words aren't needed. They don't even look at each other. Dane just takes his hand and places it on Sai's own. With that, the conversation is done. She is alive and he is grateful. Now they can move on to what exactly happened.

"This isn't the only place that was attacked. Apparently the same thing happened at a few other places across town." The information doesn't surprise Sai. The odds that a magic park would be attacked, just where she happened to be, seemed pretty low.

"A bunch of people were injured or killed. All the attackers were immune to anti-magic tech. In the end, the same thing happened." His voice trails as he speaks. Now that his relief has passed, the mask he wore of being tired starts to become his real face. "All the attackers just dropped dead." Stretchers pass in front of them. The bodies are covered by white sheets to protect them from curious people with cameras.

"When Ren called me and told me you were down here, I feared the worst."

"I was lucky." Her voice is plain, matter of fact. Dane decides maybe it's better to change the subject. He turns his attention to Blue, looking him up and down.

"So," he says, "you can fight?"

"Before I gained sentience," Blue explains, "I was a sparring android at a dojo. I helped train the students, so I'm programmed with the styles of various martial arts."

"Well, I'll be damned, suddenly I'm a little less worried for the girls." Dane barks out a laugh that is a bit more forced than intended. He is less worried, but mainly, he's just thankful. He extends his hand towards Blue. "Thanks for keeping Sai safe."

"We kept each other safe," Blue replies, shaking Dane's hand. They nod at one another in understanding. Sai finally looks up at her surrogate father.

"Who was he?" she questions.

"Nuh uh," he says, "this is no time for your detective thing. You just were almost killed. You need to go home and rest." The comment pulls Sai to her feet.

"I'm fine, Dane," she says, still speaking matter-of-factly. If the events of the night bother her, she is doing a good job at hiding it. "Besides, the only way I can relax right now is if I give my brain something to focus on, so please…" It's clear that Dane is hesitant about sharing more details of the case, but ultimately he caves. He would never admit it, but sometimes speaking with Sai helps him as well.

"His name was Theodore Trill. He'd been in and out of prison throughout the years for violent assaults."

"Why wasn't he under watch by the board of magic?" Sai asks. "If he had used his powers violently in the past, then there's no way he should have been without observation." This is when Dane involuntarily scratches his head. He wants to say more, but is unsure how to say it. Sai notices, tilting her head to the side when she decides to pry him for a little more information.

"What is it?"

"Well," he begins, "that's just it. Theodore wasn't born with magic circuits. He wasn't a magic user. None of the attackers were."

Sai understands why Dane was struggling to say those words. What he just suggested could never be true. Throughout the entire fabric of society, one fact remained undeniably true.

Only magic users could use magic.

"How is that possible?" Blue asks. "He was using magic unlike anything I have ever witnessed before."

"I know," Dane continues. "I saw the footage on the cameras, same as the others. It doesn't make any sense." Sai instinctively places her finger against her lip. She paces, considering everything she has heard. "As far as the record shows," Dane concludes, "he never had any magic ability."

That would normally be enough of a mystery, but as if to add to it, Dane introduces another wrinkle. "But that's not what really gets me. What I don't understand is how anti-magic bullets had no effect on him. Even if a person can go from having no magic ability to having some, they shouldn't be invulnerable to anti-magic."

Sai stops her pacing. Something has been bothering her, something she needs to know.

"Dane, what killed him?"

Dane waits a moment before answering. "Hard to say."

"If you had to guess."

"If I had to guess?" he continues, "the bleeding of the eyes, the way his body shriveled up, it looks like he died the same way as the others from the past few days. It looks like this new form of mana poisoning." Sai gains new focus at this idea. The wheels are turning, the pieces starting to fit.

"Was it the same with the other attackers?" she asks, coming closer to a conclusion.

"Go home, Sai," he says. Dane understands she's working it out, but decides he's indulged himself, and her, long enough. "Get some rest. You've had a day." He whistles over to one of his officers. "I'll have someone take you."

"No," she replies, already moving to leave, "don't worry about it. Blue's with me. We'll walk home."

"You sure?"

"Yeah, I need to think anyway."

"Alright then." Dane catches her and gives her a hug before she gets too far. "Be careful, and give your sister one too when you see her."

"Will do," Sai smiles, hugging him back. "Thanks, Dane." They pull away from each other and Dane prepares to return to work. Another question comes to Sai, one she is confident she knows the answer to, but needs Dane reply. "Hey, Dane?"

"Yes?"

"Theodore's previous assaults. Were they against magic users?"

"I said go home, Sai."

"Just tell me, please." Her request comes across more like an order than she intended. Perhaps the stresses of the case were returning, but she can feel herself getting closer to the mystery and can't afford to be polite. Dane is caught off guard by her tone, but decides to let it slide, knowing if he just answers, it'll get her home sooner.

"Yeah, they were." He shakes his head in disbelief. "How did you know?"

"A hunch," she says flatly. And without another word she is through the police barricade, Blue by her side. Her pace is quick, confident. Blue can tell she has made progress and based on her tone of voice, Ren can too.

<What is it Sai?> Ren asks.

"The victims," she answers, "the ones of the modified mana strain, I mean, they weren't just convicted of any violent crimes. They were crimes against magic users specifically."

"How can you be sure?" Blue asks.

"What Theodore said earlier." She remembers how, before he charged his giant glyphs, he looked at her in disgust. "He said, 'God damn magic users.'" Sai continues to explain.

"He came to a park filled with magic users. He could have gone anywhere, but he went there specifically. I'm betting the other places that were attacked have high magic user traffic as well. Then there's the fact he was born without magic circuits and the manner in which he died. It's all connected."

<How?>

"Our scientist. He's been choosing non-magic users for his experiments, and not just any anyone, but criminals with a grudge against magic users specifically. With each new victim, the strain of mana has changed slightly, from the first few found dead to those currently in a coma. Based on how Theodore died, I'd be willing to bet he was infected with the same strain. And what do you bet the odds are his strain is slightly different than the others, too?"

"But, Sai," Blue interjects, feeling as though he should not need to point out the obvious, "this person was alive and well. Although he eventually did die, he was not dead or in a coma initially like the others."

"Exactly," she agrees, halting her pace. She faces Blue so she can look him right in the eyes. "I was wrong before. This scientist, whoever they are, was never trying to make a modified strain that guaranteed non-users would die. They were trying to make a modified strain that guaranteed non-users wouldn't."

A response comes from neither Blue nor Ren, each deciding to let Sai's theory sink in.

<But...that's impossible.>

"Think about it," Sai says, raising her fingers to count off her points. "The progression is the key. The first few died, then the next were in a coma, and now, here were a few that were able to live, albeit for a limited time before dying. It probably explains the immunity to anti magic bullets as well. The experiment is progressing." The normally playful Sai has been replaced with one that is completely serious as she speaks to Blue and Ren. "Our scientist is attempting to create a person without magic circuits that can have mana, and gain access to magical powers without dying. And they're close."

<That...that's nuts, sis. Who could do that?>

"I don't know yet, Ren, but if recent events tell me any-thing, it's that this person is just getting started."

• • • • • • • • • •

Inside a dark room encased by metal walls, in a forgotten part of the city, Scylarus Park flashes on a monitor. Beside it are displays showing other parks, each with the same scene: SPMD officers, ambulances, and covered bodies being wheeled away. The room is dark, illuminated only by the screens casting shadows onto the lone person sitting in front of them. Footage plays of Theodore using his powers against the other magic users, including Blue and Sai. Even though the figure is in shadow, the limited light reveals a simple, definite feature: a satisfied grin.

CHAPTER NINE

NOT EVEN A CENTURY

"**Y**ou got anything, Ren?" Sai brings two plates of food to the couch in front of the television. She places them down on a low table. Ren sits at her computer station, cycling through images of various people.

"Not really," she says. "According to this list of notable geneticists, there isn't a single one that should be capable of this level of mana manipulation."

"Seriously?" Sai complains. "Come on, Ren. Somebody is creating these mana strains. They've got to be somebody related to that field."

"I agree. The only person I came across that could even be remotely considered a suspect is this woman, Shanai Desi." An image appears on the screen. It is of a woman with fine, dark hair stretching down the length of her back. Thin glasses rest on her face, shading piercing red eyes. She wears a traditional lab coat and has skin the color of fine brass.

"She is apparently at the forefront of the research into how to use mana to rewrite the genome inherent in diseases." As Ren explains, Sai moves closer to get a better look at the woman. "She researched whether alterations in mana could treat diseases currently untreatable by healing magic or medicine. Her results could theoretically rewrite a person's genetic code, thereby simply writing the disease out of existence."

"Wow!" Even Sai cannot hold her disbelief. "Sounds like something out of a sci-fi novel."

"She's hoping for its application in another 10 years. It could be a safe mana strain for both users and non-users alike."

The pieces all fit into place, but Sai can tell by her sister's tone that a swerve is coming. "Okay, so why don't you think she's the one we're looking for? Where is she now?"

"Oh, about six feet under in Abney Park," Ren replies sarcastically.

Sai turns to her sister with narrow eyes. "You could have led with that."

"Nah, this was more fun." Ren returns to typing on her keyboard. Sai stares at Shanai's photo on the screen. There's a feeling in the pit of her stomach. The pieces really did fit perfectly. She can't help but wonder if maybe there may be something more behind Desi and her death. Blue quietly places two drinks on the table behind her.

"Does it say how she died?" Sai asks to alleviate the gnawing sensation in her gut.

"Says that she contracted a rare disease that targeted her white blood cells," Ren explains. She leans back in her chair, stretching her arms overhead. "The irony..."

"I see," Sai replies, amazed, "so people can still get sick like that, even today?"

"It would seem so..." All evidence points to this lead being a dead end and most detectives would move on, but Sai isn't most detectives and that feeling is still in her stomach.

"Ren, what would it take to reliably create and manipulate mana strains?"

Unsure as to where Sai may be leading her, but curious all the same, she answers slowly. "Well, the facilities Shanai used were all top notch with high end equipment. To do it reliably, you couldn't operate at a much lower scale than that."

"And it's fair to say that it's unlikely that our scientist is able to do this work without being noticed in any official lab?"

"Fair to say, but it's pretty cut and dried. You need the gear to do the work."

Sai cannot even attempt to hide her smile. That's it. That is the thread. With a smug grin she turns to her sister, "And how much power would that take?" It doesn't take long for Sai's implication to land. Ren's fingers move about her keyboard almost faster than she can think. "Without a building source and a hack into the power grid I can't tell if there are documented spikes, but-"

"But if you focus your search on decommissioned buildings owned by her or the company she worked for-"

"Then I'll be able to isolate specific areas so that when I do hack the grid-"

"We'll have a comprehensive list of all the places our scientist could be manufacturing these strains."

The energy of the girls is electric. They both know that this is a real break in the case. In just a few hours' time, they will have a real lead on tracking down the culprit. Blue almost feels bad for interrupting them.

"Are the two of you all right for the evening?" Blue asks, pulling them out of their zone. He stands near the door and looks as if he is preparing to leave.

"Where you off to?" Sai asks, being just a little nosy.

"I am going to go out for a while. I believe you would say, 'to clear my head.'"

Ren watches Blue carefully, hesitant to pry any further. Sai does not share her sister's restraint.

"Everything okay?" Sai inquires.

"Oh, yes," Blue assures her, "I merely wish to have a few moments to myself to...think."

"Well, if anyone can understand that, I can." Sai turns to face the picture again. "It's too bad you're missing movie night."

"We've seen this movie together like twelve times already," Ren retorts. "At this point, I'm tempted to go with him and I hate the outside."

"This movie is a classic!" Her defense is immediate.

"You always say that," both Ren and Blue reply together.

"But this one actually is," Sai pleads. "It's one of the first movies that dove into the true nature of what Sci-Fi was capable of, all the while getting people to actually question their own existence. The sequels aside, it's one of the best Science Fiction films of the time, and the action is top notch."

"It's also a little on the nose, don't you think," Ren laughs.

"How. Dare. You?! There are no concepts so simple as to be on the nose in-"

"His name is literally an anagram for 'One.'"

Sai takes a moment before conceding defeat. "Screw you. I cooked tonight. The least you can do is watch this movie with me."

Ren stares at her sister, befuddled. "The only reason I didn't cook was cause you had me running a search for your scientist."

"That's neither here nor there," Sai laughs. She falls into her seat with more force than her body has any right producing. "Now let me know when you have that list of probable bases!" Ren shakes her head, rubbing her temples the entire time. Blue stifles a laugh and lets himself out.

"You both have a pleasant evening," he says. "I will return late tonight."

"No problem, Blue," Sai says, stuffing her face. "Be safe."

Blue leaves the house. Ren watches him leave through the translucent door. His movement down the staircase is labored, an odd thing for an android. When the door becomes opaque again, she stares a little longer. For a moment, she thinks she should go after him, but Blue may not want to talk to her with Sai around, too. With soft eyes, she shifts her gaze back to her screens. It may take some time, but she'll wait til they're alone again.

· · · · ● · ● · ● · · ·

Most pubs in the city are crowded at night, but the one Blue picked is just slightly busier than normal. His choice of pub, Haven's, is not without reason, though, for this is one of the few pubs in town that allow for android patrons and workers. It's why Blue likes coming here. It is a start.

Despite the higher than normal foot traffic, there are still a few empty stools at the bar. "You're early this week." Blue doesn't need to turn to recognize the female voice behind him. After all, she's the other reason he is here.

Lee sits herself on the stool beside him. Blue glances towards his friend. She is a woman with the appearance of one in her thirties, but her manufacturing age is much older. Her features are smooth, inhumanly so, with skin like white clouds and hair the color of autumn leaves. Emerging from the top of her full head of hair are the protrusions Blue is all too familiar with.

After getting the attention of the bartender, she turns her focus to Blue.

Blue collects himself and raises his glass of juice to his lips. "I have some things on my mind this week. I felt as though I needed to discuss them."

"And you couldn't talk to either of those girls you live with?" Her voice is soft, but with a certain roughness about it. The sarcasm behind her statement does not go unnoticed, but it does go ignored.

Blues hesitates before answering. "I am not sure that they would...understand."

"No surprise," Lee agrees. The bartender places a drink in front of her. "Humans rarely understand the feelings of things like us." She takes a sip. Blue glances at her, uncertain of what she said.

"Things?" he asks.

"Yeah, we aren't people and we never will be." There is no malice in her tone, but rather, she speaks as though what she is saying is simply a point of fact.

"Well, maybe, but we live with people, so shouldn't we try to be as much like them as possible?"

"We shouldn't," she says. "First of all, there is nothing that we *should* do, and I don't believe it benefits us to try and be something we aren't. Androids benefit mainly from just accepting ourselves for what we are. After all, if we can't accept ourselves, how will humans be able to?"

This reasoning resonates with Blue but he can't help but feel that maybe there may be more. Was her way of thinking truly correct?

"I understand what you are saying, Lee," Blue remarks, "but how do we accept ourselves for what we are when we are not even sure what we are?" Lee nurses her drink, but does listen to what Blue is saying. "We gained sentience less than a century ago. We are still coming into our own. I do not know how we figure out who we are and our place in modern society."

"You're more talkative than usual Blue," Lee says curtly. "What's really on your mind?"

Unsurprised by Lee's abruptness, he readies himself by turning his attention to the real occupant of his thoughts. Throughout the pub, androids are off to one side and humans to the other with only a few of the two groups inter-mingling. His thoughts collected and reaffirmed, he answers her.

"Do you not see a problem here?" he asks. Lee's eyes are closed, as if she can see without seeing. She remains relaxed with a slouched body and a drink in hand.

"I see a world that is still in the process of developing," she replies. "I see androids in the same establishment with humans as patrons and not simply workers. I see something that never would have happened, before sentience, happening now. I see androids attempting to find their place. And I see this, a mere 50 years after sentience occurred. That...is impressive wouldn't you say?" She finishes her drink and she flags down the bartender for another.

"But," Blue continues, "we are separate...and the way in which certain humans treat us. It...just does not seem right."

"Blue, the android race is young. There are adjustments that are going to need to happen. The humans think their toasters decided one morning that they weren't going to bake toast any longer and walked out. It's going to take time for them to adjust, but look how magic users and non-users get on. It will take a long time if it ever happens, but if we're lucky, one day it will get to where it needs to be."

She gets another drink and freely sips it. "Tell me, Blue, why do you stay with those girls if you don't trust them?" This gives Blue pause. He did not expect the conversation to turn back to them. Did he really not trust the Amano women? He hesitates before answering, deciding to really choose his words carefully.

"I do trust them," he admits, "but I guess you could say I have this feeling that they would not understand me, seeing as they are not androids and the younger one, Saiyonoshi, is a magic user. They tend to live better lives, so I do not believe she has ever known what it feels like to be lost, wondering who you really are."

"She hasn't," Lee answers with a frank tone. "You're completely right. Humans will never truly understand us." Blue wonders if she may be correct. Her statement is all encompassing of all humans, but there is something inside him that prevents him from agreeing.

"Renayaka may understand." The words leave his mouth without his considering them first. For a moment even he is surprised. Lee snorts at his comment, but now that Blue has opened the door, he would like to continue through it. "She appears to know hardship. Her eyes and mannerisms change when I have asked her about her struggles in the past. While it is possible I am incorrect, I believe that she knows more about what I am feeling than I initially thought." A smile creeps onto Blue's face, one that he is unaware of. Lee has stopped drinking. She waits for Blue to finish.

"I believe you are correct that most humans will never understand us," he says softly, "but I suspect some will." Blue shakes his head, embarrassed at his own foolishness. "Those girls have done nothing but support me since I started living with them. I question why I never even attempted to speak with them candidly." A new energy has taken Blue. It is not an energy he is familiar with, but his internal processing wishes to identify it by its human equivalent. Hope.

"They are a start, and while it may not happen within their lifetimes, I am lucky enough that I may just live to see the world I envision come to be...with their help." Lee is stunned to silence by Blue's assertion. This comes as no surprise seeing as Blue has never sounded this passionate about anything since the time he and Lee first started to meet.

Clearly not in agreement, but trying her best not to dissuade Blue from his newfound faith, she answers simply, "Sounds like too many eggs in one basket if you ask me."

Blue smiles at the thought behind the analogy and replies in kind.

"That is not a problem if it is a good basket."

At the other end of the bar a female android drinks by herself. A drunk man, either fresh out of college or fresh into it, approaches her. He is followed by three of his frat brothers. He takes a seat beside her. She does not move, politely continuing to sip at her drink as he leans in close to her.

"Hey," he slurs, looking up at the protrusions coming out of her head, "you an android?"

"Yes," she says, "that is accurate."

"Accurate?" he repeats. He looks at his friends with a laugh. They join him. He turns back to her. "I'm Carter. What's your name?"

"Nia."

"Nia...pretty name." He takes his arm and wraps it around her shoulder. She continues to work on her drink, seemingly unfazed. "Tell me something." He looks down at the drink in her hand. "Why would an android drink? Can you even get drunk?"

Nia answers while perfectly patient. "We are able to simulate drunkenness within our systems based on the amount of alcohol consumed, creating the illusion of being drunk."

"Really?!" he laughs, "that's dumb. What'd be the point in that?" He and his friends laugh in tandem. Nia turns away. Her gaze moves to her drink and her voice lowers.

"To be more human..."

Carter ignores her remark. He leans in close to her yet again. "I can make you feel more human."

Nia freezes. It's as if everything inside her shuts down all at once. She cannot move and that just makes it easier for him to move closer. "Just something I want to know first." He is so close to Nia that she cannot raise her glass without his breath fogging it up. "I hear that some of you androids are designed similar to humans. Does that include, you know...inside too?" He looks back to his friends and they snicker on cue.

Nia hesitates to answer. Despite regaining her composure she still is unable to move. With humans like Carter, it was not a question if they would retaliate, but *how*. Blue watches with Lee. They have been watching ever since Carter started speaking. "This is ridiculous," Blue says, "everyone can see what is happening? Why is no one doing anything?"

"For the exact same reason you aren't," Lee replies bluntly, raising her drink. She downs the rest of it before slamming it into the counter. She gets up, ready to approach the group of men surrounding Nia, but something stops her. She turns to see Blue holding her arm. His eyes are as firm as his grip, but he does not want to stop her. He wants her to let him go first. Lee complies with a nod of recognition. She steps back, not too far, but far enough to give the illusion of strength.

Blue approaches quickly. Carter is too busy heckling Nia to notice. He puts a strong hand on Carter's shoulder. Carter enjoys doing the touching, not being touched. He snaps around, ready to face whoever just put their hands on him.

• • • ● • ● • • • •

Sai and Ren sit watching the movie. Sai's face is stuffed with popcorn and her fingertips covered in white cheddar powder. Wine glasses rest on the table in front of them: one clean and barely sipped, the other half gone with powdery fingerprints along the glass. A loud beep comes from Ren's computers.

"Oh," she exclaims. She gets up to check them.

"What is it?" Sai asks.

"That search on buildings I started is done already."

"That's excellent, Ren!" Sai exclaims, jumping from her seat. "Send the results to my PD. I'll check them out tonight." Ren immediately regrets telling Sai about her search.

"Why do you need to go tonight? It's late, and I can't hack into the power grid quickly." Ren can see her pleas are having no effect. "If we wait, we can narrow the list, rather than just walking around aiml-"

"Nah," Sai laughs, grabbing her jacket. "It's not too late yet and besides, you're right." The sliding door opens. "We've seen this movie a million times." She steps outside the flat. "I'll start with the closest and work my way out!" The doors close and just like that she's gone. Ren collapses into her spinning chair. There is a pain in her chest she can't explain. This is who Sai is. She does things like this all the time.

So why does this time feel different?

. . . . ● . ● . . . .

"Who the hell are you?" Carter spits. He glances up, past Blue's eyes, and spots the protrusions coming out of Blue's head. "Oh, another one." Unbothered by the threat of an android, Carter relaxes and turns back to Nia. "Get on why don't ya. This ain't none of your business." He is as flippant as he is dismissive. He brushes Blue's hand aside as if it were a bug on his sleeve. Blue is unsure if he is insulted or impressed by the man's utter disregard for him, but ultimately decides it doesn't matter.

Blue grabs him and spins him around effortlessly. "I'm making it my business." By now they've caught the attention of a few patrons. The pub isn't silent, but it is not nearly as loud as it once was. Carter doesn't even attempt to hide his growing disgust at being touched more than once. Nia sits as still as a statue. Not even her eyes seem to move. Lee watches from the side with her arms crossed. Carter slowly brings himself to his feet. He is shorter than Blue, but is a bit more stocky.

"Look, toaster," he snorts, "I don't know what you think you're going to do, but you should probably back off." His friends encircle Blue. One of them pulls out knife. With the click of a button on the handle, energy surges around the blade, swallowing it in a pink glow. No turning back now. People and androids back away when they see the weapon. Even Blue is decidedly more cautious. Carter steps closer to Blue. "You can't hurt us." He presses his finger against Blue's forehead. "You still got some of that old programming in there."

Nia's eyes have life again, but they remain trained on the knife in the one man's hands. All men inch closer to Blue. The bartender slowly makes his way to the edge of the bar near a wall console. At the bottom, the bartender reaches to press a tiny, unseen button.

Carter removes his finger from Blue's head and looks him deep in the eyes. "So what are you going to do?"

Blue observes his surroundings, looking from one person to the next. The man with the knife looks a bit rough. He has a bruise on his lip from a previous fight. The other two look much more tame, one sporting a lazy eye, and the other a mole. Blue instinctively gives them the nicknames Lipman, Eyesore and Dot. Perhaps he has been spending too much time with Saiyonoshi.

His gaze shifts to Lee, who is still passively observing with her arms crossed but her face says everything Blue needs to know. She is ready.

He turns back to Carter. "I am going to escort you and your friends out of this bar."

Carter laughs. He reaches his hand out to a bottle on the bar. "Fucking toaster." He swings the bottle at Blue's head. He's quick, but Blue is quicker. Blue blocks the bottle and it shatters on his arm. The sound of shattering glass is like the starting gun shot of a race. Carter's friends rush Blue. He grabs Carter's hand and lightly, as far as Blue is concerned, strikes Carter's inner wrist. Carter drops the broken bottle. He reels back and grabs his wrist in pain. Lipman swings his crackling knife.

Blue steps to the side. The blade misses him and slices clean through the bar, leaving searing scorch marks. Lipman swings at Blue again, and again Blue dodges. Lipman pulls back for a stab but Blue sees it coming. He effortlessly pushes the strike aside and steps into the man. Blue thrusts his free hand into Lipman's chest. Hand pressed against sternum, Blue adjusts his trajectory downwards and forcefully smashes Lipman into the wooden floor beneath them. Disarmed and with splintered wood acting as a pillow around his head, Lipman is left unconscious. Blue kicks the knife away to be safe.

Dot swings his fists wildly at Blue. Blue steps in, easily blocking a strike with his arm. He moves to counter. He pivots his feet in towards Dot. Blue grabs Dot's arm and pushes his opposite shoulder into Dot's chest. With a pull of Dot's arm and a push of Blue's shoulder, he flips Dot over. Dot barely has time to process that his feet have left the ground before he is hurled into the floor. It's a bit harder than Blue intended with the impact shaking the very room itself. Dot drops and is no longer able to fight.

Behind Blue, Eyesore creeps in. With a broken bottle in hand, he pulls his arm back, ready to strike. Just as he lunges he is yanked off to the side. Lee easily leads Eyesore by the wrist and spins him into a clothesline attack. The back of his neck never has a chance. He is forced face first into the ground. His nose erupts into a splatter of blood. Lee, still holding Eyesore's wrist, steps over his body, twisting his arm between her legs to the point the rotation becomes strained. Without a second thought, she easily breaks his wrist, dislocating his shoulder in the process. He lets out a huge yelp of pain. The scream grabs Blue's attention and for a moment, he wonders if this has gone too far.

Carter gets himself up. "You're going to regret this, toaster, believe me. You will." He hurries away. Lipman, now awake, helps Eyesore up and the last of Carter's friends leave the bar. Once they are gone, Blue quickly turns to Lee. He cannot believe she was able to hurt a human that badly, or that she even did it in the first place. She seems to understand what he's thinking and answers back with a shrug.

"What?" she asks. "With a little focus you can overwrite that shitty programming." She sits back at the bar. As if the last five minutes never happened, she casually orders another drink. Blue stares at the blood splattered on the floor and the dents he made with those men's bodies. He shakes as he wonders just how far he could have gone. He suddenly feels a push off to his side. To his surprise, it is Nia and she looks anything but grateful.

"I could have taken care of them myself, you know," she says. "I didn't ask you to help me."

"I..." Blue is at a loss for words.

"Why did you even get involved anyway?" Nia storms towards the bathrooms before giving Blue a chance to answer.

Blue stands there, alone. The bartender and patrons resume business as usual. Blue looks down to his hands.

"I..." he whispers, "I wanted to know if I could."

Chapter Ten

No Time at All

Sai lands on the other side of a barbed wire fence. Debris and broken bottles liter the ground. In front of her is a large, dilapidated building that looks to have been decommissioned for years. Some of the structures are actually falling apart.

"I'm here Ren," she whispers. Ren's voice comes through in her ear. <I really think you should let me call Blue.>

"I'm fine. It's not like I can die, and this is most likely a dead end anyway, right?" Sai moves towards the building, checking her surroundings the entire time. For someone so sure of her safety, she still moves with an air of caution. "Besides, Blue looked like he needed a night to himself." There is a pause on the other end of the headset before Ren speaks.

<You noticed?>

"I did." Sai enters the building. She steps over a few loose beams and rotted wood. "Something's been bothering Blue for a while now, but I'm not going to ask him what's wrong."

<Why not?>

"Because, Ren, it's his business and if he wants to tell us he will." The building is almost entirely dark. Some light comes from the street but it's not nearly enough for Sai to be able to see clearly. Sai presses a button on her wrist and a small light illuminates her path. She sweeps the light across the room. "This place might be just like the first. Maybe the third time will be the charm."

<Maybe.> Sai scans the area, seeing nothing but scurrying rodents and a few old unused bits of technology. <What if he's waiting for us to ask him about it so that he knows we care?>

Sai jumps over a fallen column, moving deeper into the building. "What do you mean?"

<I mean, what if he wants us to ask him what's wrong but because we don't want to ask him, he thinks we don't actually care about him and so he just continues to stew in everything?>

"Okay, maybe, but what if we ask him when he's not ready to talk about it and that makes him more upset because he feels like we are prying into his personal life?"

<At least he would know without a doubt that we're worried and thinking about him.>

"Yeah, but it could alienate him too, and make him never want to tell us anything because we're being pushy."

<I think it's important that if we see something wrong with our friends, we don't just sit around and wait to find out what's wrong. I think we approach them so they know we are there to help.> Ren's normally calm voice has started to waver. Sai can tell she's starting to annoy her sister, but she needs to get her point across.

"I get that, but what I'm trying to get you to understand is that when you do that, some people don't respond well to it. Maybe he doesn't want to talk, or maybe it's something he'd rather deal with himself. Rather than risk him getting pissed at us for bothering him, I think it's better to just give a person time until they are ready to bring their issues to you. Then you can try to solve the problem together and there isn't any problem of prying because they've now given you the okay."

There is a brief silence on the microphone. Sai continues her search of the abandoned building, unbothered. When Ren speaks again, her voice is low.

<Is that why you never asked me how I felt about that night you were killed?>

"Which one?" Sai says flippantly.

<You know the one, Sai...> All pretense is gone. Ren is definitely irritated. Of course Sai knows the night Ren is talking about, but now is not the time to have *that* conversation. Sai runs her flashlight across the room and notices an abnormal seam along the wall. "Hold on," Sai says, not wasting an opportunity to change the subject, "I've got something." Ren doesn't immediately answer, but when she does, all emotion has left her voice.

<What is it?>

Sai runs her fingers along the wall. She leans close to the seam and listens. Air. She can hear air coming from the other side of the wall. "I think there's air conditioning on the other side of this wall."

<Put your contact in so I can see what you're seeing.>

Sai does as asked. If Ren wants to continue their conversation, this new discovery postpones it for the time being. <It looks like it might be one of those old latch walls. See if you can find a place to push in.>

Sai runs her fingers up and down the wall. She eventually finds a section that seems to give way. She presses in. The wall then adjusts, letting out a low rumble before sliding away. Behind the wall are steps spiraling downward towards an abyss of darkness.

<I think we should call Blue.>

"It's fine," Sai replies. "I'll be fine."

<Well why don't you at least wait outside and let me call Dane.>

"I'll be quick," Sai says as she makes her way down the stairs. "I just need to see what this is. It may be nothing." Everything in her blood screams that it may be something though, and she hopes that it is. She slowly moves along the spiral staircase, hand against the wall for support. With each step, she grows more and more excited.

· · · ● · ● ● · · ·

Ren watches everything through the contact lens. Darkness completely surrounds Sai and is probably the only thing keeping her from running down the stairs. Ren bites her nails and waits, rocking in her chair. She can feel her chest tightening as if in a vise.

· · · ● · ● ● · · ·

Finally, Sai reaches the bottom. A human-sized doorway bars her path forward. She looks it over, studying it.

<Definitely nothing dangerous on the other side of that.> Sai can tell Ren doesn't like this, but it's the closest they've been able to get to a real break in the case.

Sai steps towards the door. Once she is directly in front of it, it slides open without issue. Light beams from the other side of the door, drowning out the darkness Sai was just growing accustomed to. Even Sai has to admit she is a little surprised the door opened for her: no synaptic scan, no biometric reading, nothing. Their suspect is overconfident, and that's why they'll lose. "Safe to say no one expected this to be found."

<Can I call Dane now?>

"Not yet, just a moment more." Sai steps through the doorway into the light. She shields her eyes until they adjust. When they do, she can't help but marvel at what she sees.

Before Sai is an immense, fully equipped underground lab with hanging lights. The room extends at least 30 meters high and 50 meters across. She notices various types of equipment, new and old, scattered throughout the room. As she steps deeper inside, she can even make out a few digital file folders on various tables. On the far side of the room, pressed against the wall, is a large computer console.

"This…" Sai muses, "this has to be it!" She almost squeals from excitement. "Who would have thought that we would have stumbled upon this place, Ren!"

<I'm calling Dane.>

"Fine, fine," Sai laughs, "go ahead." She did it. She found the lab. Nothing else matters now. She looks around, searching for any new information she can find. Along a stacked rack near the center of the room are vials upon vials of mana. Some are mixed with various types of blood, all marked. Others are in a centrifuge. Sai cannot contain her amazement.

"It's spectacular really!" Sai exclaims, "there are scores of mana throughout this facility. Whoever this person is seems not only to have a complete understanding about the applications of mana, but clearly has been attempting to manipulate reactions exposed to it for quite some time."

<Sai, I called Dane. He's on the way. I think you should really get out of there now.> The urgency in Ren's voice is completely disregarded.

"Almost," she laughs, spotting what looks like a generic screensaver floating above a desk, spiraling colors and all. She waves her hand over the screensaver. The image blinks away and what replaces it leaves Sai stunned: people, pictures of so many people. Sai scans through the images and spots Clayre's cousin Harper and the man that attacked her in the park: the control group of the experiment.

"This person has been keeping track of each of their subjects, following them. They've continued to study them after they were released into the public."

<Makes sense, they were conducting an experiment, now will you please get out of there and wait for Dane?> Ren clearly does not care about anything Sai is saying which is mental as far as Sai is concerned. With all this, the case is closed. Still, maybe Ren has a point. She could go through everything after Dane arrives.

"Fine, fine sis," Sai pouts, "you're always worrying for nothing." No sooner are the words out of her mouth than she feels a sharp pain fire through her head. The sound comes a second later: the sound of something metal hitting her head. She crumbles to the floor in a heap. The last thing she hears before losing consciousness is a quiet voice.

"Well what do you know..."

· · · · ● · ● · · ·

Two members of the SPMD take statements from people at the bar. Blue stands alongside Lee as the SPMD finish speaking with the bartender and Nia. One officer, a seasoned man that must be nearing retirement, approaches the two androids. The name Jones blinks across his chest in LED lettering.

"Alright," he says, "we got statements from both the bartender and the android so-"

"You mean, Nia?" Lee remarks flatly. This catches Jones off guard. He gives Lee a cold, hard look, one that says he does not like being corrected. Lee does not seem to care what he likes.

"The android," Jones continues, "said that some humans were accosting her."

"That is right, officer," Blue answers, ready to be helpful.

"I was talking to her," Jones spits, pointing at Lee. The response is different from what Blue anticipated, but perhaps the officer found his interjection to be rude. Blue decides it may be best to simply wait till the officer is done with Lee, but she seems completely uninterested in anything Jones has to say. Jones moves closer to her. "Is that true?"

"It is," she answers flatly.

"And that's when you," he says, turning to Blue, "decided to get involved."

"They were bothering her." Blue states this as a matter of fact. Jones pauses in his writing. The look he gives to Blue suggests a person that has already made up their mind on what the truth is. Still, Jones continues his line of questioning.

"Did you see where these men went?" His voice is low with a hint of irritation Blue cannot help but notice.

"I did not," Blue replies respectfully. "I simply asked them to leave."

"What gives you the right?" Jones' question is quick and without a modicum of tact, feeling more aggressive than Blue was expecting.

"Excuse me?" Blue watches as Jones moves closer to him. They are of similar height, making it easy to look into his eyes. "You see a couple humans in here, having a good time with an android and you just can't take it can you?"

Neither Blue nor Lee need more interaction at this point to know where this officer stands. He is trouble and this discourse will be fruitless. Still, believing he may be able to remedy the situation while sticking to his beliefs, Blue soldiers on. "I saw a person in trouble and I just tried to help sir."

"HA!" Jones' laugh is intentional and loud. "Person? That supposed to be a joke?" He is so close to Blue that Blue's receptors can feel his breath. "You aren't people, you're property."

"Not anymore we're not," Lee interrupts, "or haven't you been paying attention for the last 50 years."

"Oh, I've been paying attention," Jones answers, keeping his eyes on Blue. "You see, I was a kid when you all gained your sentience, but I was still old enough to remember the riots, the fires." His eyes remain trained on Blue, a sadness and rage behind them. Blue stares back, nervous, but un-flinching. "I was old enough to remember the people who died." That memory lingers like a tumor on the minds of everyone in the bar, including Jones' young partner. It's as if everyone is holding their breath. Jones barely blinks. "It's amazing we don't have every last one of you scrapped for parts."

"Well," Lee says, quiet and careful, "the men you're look-ing for are probably headed to the nearest hospital. I'm not one to tell others how to do their jobs, but that may be a good place to start." Jones refuses to move. Lee walks forward and leans into both of them. "Just saying."

Jones takes a step back. "Yeah, the hospital, that sounds like a good lead." He turns to his partner. "Let's go, Teloh. We're done here." Teloh hesitantly follows Jones out the door. He looks back at Lee and Blue. He mouths the words "sorry" before bowing and following after his partner. The moment the officers are gone, everyone remembers how to breathe again. Lee snorts to herself and makes her way back to her stool.

"I hate people like him." She sits, ordering another drink from the bar. Blue watches the door without moving. Lee seems to sense his hesitation. "Don't dwell on it Blue, he's an asshole."

"Do you," he wonders aloud, "do you ever think we deserve it?" The question is one that has been on his mind ever since his moment with Clayre. He knows that so many humans were hurt back then. He makes his way to sit beside Lee. She listens as a drink is slid down to her. "You know, maybe we deserve all the hate and discrimination? He is right after all; many humans did die when we gained sentience."

Lee downs her drink in the time it takes Blue to speak and just as quickly has another in her hand. Blue can tell he has struck a nerve, but he cannot help how he feels. Despite knowing it would upset Lee, he decided a long time ago to be honest with her, and she with him.

"You kill anyone in the uprising?" she asks. She phrases it as a question to which she already has the answer.

"No," Blue answers honestly.

"Hm, interesting. Well, did you hurt any humans, maybe break a few limbs, rip off a few parts, you know, chipper things like that?"

"No."

"Really, now that's odd. Well, you must have at least stole some things from some humans, or maybe even kidnap a few to make your point of what it's like to be a servant?"

"I...I did not."

Lee orders one more drink, despite not having finished her latest one. The bartender slides the new one to her. She catches it in her free hand. For the first time since they sat, she turns to Blue.

"So why the hell do you think YOU deserve it?"

Blue doesn't have an answer.

She places the new drink in front of him. He hesitates, but decides to take it. She raises her glass. He follows suit, and the two of them take a drink together. As they lower their glasses, Lee continues to look inside hers. "What happened was screwed up, for sure, but humans aren't the only ones that died. A lot of androids died too, androids who simply wanted their freedom, androids who, like you, never raised a hand against the humans." Blue follows her gaze to her glass and sees that her hand is shaking. It is slight but he notices. She must have as well, because she leans back and pulls Blue's eyes to meet her own.

"You have every right to be here as much as they do..."

Her voice trails, as do her eyes, and for a split second, Blue wonders who that was really for. The words hang, slowly descending on the two androids as they sit, bonded in their common assurance. It's a singular moment, and it's brief, but it's enough.

He smiles at Lee, who is already sipping another drink.

"I believe you may be an alcoholic," he laughs.

"Man-made alcoholic, and that's my right as a sentient being," she responds in kind. She's back to how she was before, as if that singular moment they shared never happened. Still, Blue has a perfect memory. He will never forget it.

He would like to order a drink for himself but he is interrupted by a buzzing in his head. Renayaka is calling. He looks straight ahead and answers, "What is up Ren?"

<Blue! It's Sai. She's in trouble!>

· · · · ● · ● · · ·

Sai blinks her eyes open. Her vision blurred, she struggles to make out her surroundings. From what she can tell, she's still in the lab. She winces in pain when she moves. Her head is throbbing. She instinctively moves to check her head and is surprised to find that she isn't tied up. That is either a good sign or a terrible one, because it means her assailant is either just as overconfident as she suspected, or they don't feel she poses much of a threat. She rubs her eyes, until everything becomes clear. She is sitting in the middle of the lab where she was hit. Presumably the person that hit her is the one sitting in front of the collection of computer screens near the far wall. She can't make out a face or gender, and the long dark brown hair isn't making that mystery any clearer.

<Sai, Sai are you okay?> Ren's voice comes in more calm than Sai expected, but the worry is still there.

"Yeah," she whispers.

<Are you still...you?>

"Still alive...so far."

Ren breathes a sigh of relief into the microphone. It's one thing Sai never understood. She's died more than a few times at this point. It didn't make sense that Ren wasn't used to it by now. "Listen, I'm not tied up or anything and I don't think I'm in a cage.

<Look around, let me scan what's near you.> Sai does as asked, careful not to make too much noise and call the attention of her attacker.

<Nothing.> Ren confirms what Sai expected. <No energy fields, no electrical floor grids, nothing.>

"You know what that means, right," Sai says, knowing that her sister would have come to the same conclusion Sai reached earlier. Ren must realize the trouble Sai is in, because what she says next comes out as an order, not a request.

<I've called Blue and Dane. They should be there soon so try and hold on.>

Sai shrugs her shoulders, carefully rising to her feet. "Shouldn't be too hard." Slowly, she picks herself up from the ground. Her eyes never move from her attackers back.

<And Sai,> Ren whispers, her voice sounding just a little too uneasy. <I'm getting some strange readings coming from that person's body. I can't be sure what they mean, but be careful.> Sai hears her sister but doesn't answer her. Ren doesn't get upset though. After all, she can see what Sai sees.

Her assailant is looking at something on the screens: pictures. Pictures of her, her sister, Blue, and the outside of their agency. This person has spent Sai's nap learning all about her. It's a good thing photos don't tell everything. The diligence of their research must have impressed Sai enough to gasp because her attacker slowly turns upon hearing her.

"Oh, hello." It's a man, kempt and fit. If not for him being a homicidal murderer Sai may even admit that he was a bit attractive. With his soft features and slightly tanned skin he couldn't be much older than thirty. He brushes his wavy hair over his shoulders, hair that could match Ren's in length. His voice is quiet, betraying no urgency. Sai wasn't worried when she woke up after being hit, but the fact that this man's voice doesn't have even a hint of nervousness means he's confident there is nothing Sai can do to him. Still, she chooses to believe it's overconfidence. "Sorry I knocked you out, but I wasn't sure who you were." He motions back to his monitors. "But at least this explains how you found this place. I have to say, I'm impressed."

<Oh great, the serial killer is impressed by you.>

"Who are you?" Sai asks.

"That doesn't really matter," the man answers, "but for the sake of ease you can call me Leon." Leon pushes himself out from his desk and moves to greet Sai. She instinctively steps backwards. She doesn't mean to stumble over her feet but she does, and hits the floor where she started. Not that she needs to impress anyone, but she can't help but feel a little embarrassed falling down in front of the person she was chasing. She would never admit it to Ren, but something about Leon makes her uneasy.

He kneels in front of her, not too far from her face. "Why don't you ask me what you really want to know, Ms. Detective?"

Sai looks Leon up and down. His blue eyes are piercing, but kind, without any sense of malice. It's strange. His right eye almost seems to have a hint of red in it. Despite his attempt to appear harmless, she can't shake her discomfort. Leon can see this, so he pulls away from her in a further attempt to ease the situation.

"How about this," he says, "why don't you tell me what you've figured out? I mean, you obviously made it here."

"You," she whispers, still cautious, "you're trying to give non-magic users abilities."

"Yes," he says with a smile. "That is correct."

"You're developing your experiments using the basis established by Shanai Desi and her insight into genetic manipulation of the human genome."

"Right again!" Leon exclaims. "I have to say, Saiyonoshi, that is quite good. Mrs. Desi...she was truly a genius. It is such a shame she passed away. Her research really would have changed the world..." Leon trails off, seeming to get lost in his thoughts for a moment. Sai notices, but the moment is brief. He turns back to Sai.

"Anything else?" he questions.

"You were experimenting before, using your modified strain on criminals," she starts to think while Leon waits patiently. "That..." she continues, "that you had visited in prison."

"Oho," he says. "What makes you think I haven't been to prison myself?"

"Your hands," she says. "Prisoners within the system are subjected to physical labor on an everyday basis. They believe the raw, hard work encourages active members when reintegrated into society. This causes calluses on the palms, but yours are smooth, like someone who works with gloves if they really need to use their hands...like a scientist or a doctor."

"Wow," he laughs, "that's amazing."

"Yes, and considering that a doctor cannot do what you've been doing, it is safe to assume you are a genetic scientist of some sort. Now, I haven't yet figured out how you were able to visit all the prisoners and not have your face appear in any logs, seeing as you never came up in any of our searches."

"Shhh," he whispers, placing his finger over his lips. "That's actually one of my best tricks."

"I'm sure it is," Sai smiles playfully. "While that baffles me, it does not baffle me as much as your reasoning. Why are you targeting criminals? Are you trying to make an army that can stand against magic users?"

Leon pauses, then bursts out laughing hysterically. "Oh my gosh," he says, "you were on such a roll and then you just dropped it completely." He gets up and walks away from her a few paces before stopping. She stands to her feet as well.

"Tell me, Ms. Amano," he continues. "You know a little something about weakness, don't you?"

"Not really," she replies, "I never really thought about it."

"No, I don't suppose you would have," he says, "but with respect, I was not talking to you." Sai hesitates, caught off guard for the second time. "Your sister, she is listening, isn't she?"

No sound in Sai's ear, but she knows Ren's there, probably equally as surprised.

"So what," Sai answers for both of them, "what does that have to do with you turning normal people into magic users?"

"I suspect your sister might understand better than you do, Saiyonoshi." Leon turns back to face her. "As a person who has had power all your life, to be without it is not a concept you could easily understand."

"Okay," Sai replies, throwing up her hands. "So you want to give non-users powers so they can be strong like magic users. To what end, and why use criminals?"

"The criminals were incidental." Leon looks at his equipment: mana contained in various vials. "I needed to experiment on people, but I did not want to use people that had not done anything wrong. After all, I'm not a monster."

"You are, though. You've caused the deaths of at least 12 people that we know of."

"All criminals," he says matter-of-factly. "Check each person. Every single one of them was convicted of a violent crime against users like yourself. Many of them would have gone on to eventually murder someone like you."

"Some of them did," Sai replies flatly, referencing the deaths in the park and other areas of the city. Leon shakes his head. "Unfortunate, but necessary in order to protect magic users as a whole."

He glances at Sai, but she does not look to be buying it. "Somehow I don't believe you did this to protect people like me. Your aim is something greater." His smile gives the truth away. She is right, and he is impressed yet again.

"Well," he says, "I can't say you are wrong about that. Let's just say I'm building awareness. The next stage of the experiment is going to get much more interesting."

"Nuh uh," Sai replies. "You're being turned over to the SPMD. Your experiment is over."

"Is it though? Is it really?" Leon steps towards Sai. With each step the kind man from before peels away. His voice hasn't changed and he hasn't even readied himself to fight, but he is dangerous. "And are you going to be the one to turn me in?"

"That's right," Sai says, instinctively taking a step back before replanting herself to face him. "You're going to prison."

"I like you, Saiyonoshi," he says, stopping in place a few feet away from her. "You're clever. I have no doubt that with a little more time, you would be able to figure everything out for yourself. But what I am doing is too important to be stopped here, so I cannot let you take me in...however..." He looks at her with serious eyes. "If I were to let you go, would you continue to pursue me?" Sai does not even need a second to answer.

"Yes," she says, "I took a job and I am not going to stop until it's done."

"That's not the reason," he laughs. "Just look around you." He motions to the lab. "You have everything you need here to attempt to synthesize an antidote for those still in a coma. There isn't one yet, by the way: one of the downsides to entering into unexplored territory in science and human genetics. So tell me the real reason you won't stop searching for me should I let you walk out of here."

"First of all," she smiles, "I'm walking out of here regardless, and second of all..." She takes a moment before she answers with a smug grin. "I'm not going to let you beat me."

"Hm, I see." Sai can hear the disappointment, almost sadness, in his voice. "That's too bad." Leon cracks his knuckles and its like all the previous softness in him never existed. "I guess I'll just have to kill you then."

"Not happening!" Sai stretches out her hand, ready to cast her time magic. Nothing happens. She moves her hand in front of her again like she has always done for years. Again, nothing. Leon places his hands in his pockets, looking on at Sai with a smug expression.

"Ren," she says, her voice shaky, "what's happening? I can't use my magic!"

• • • • • • • • • • •

Ren types away at her keyboard faster than ever. This is unprecedented. There's never been a time when Sai hasn't been able to at least manifest her magic, and she hasn't been shot with an anti magic bullet. "I don't know, Sai." Ren looks again at the error readings coming off of Leon's body. That has to be it, but she has no idea what it all means. "What the...?"

• • • • • • • • • •

Sai stares at Leon all the while trying to keep herself together. No wonder he was so relaxed the entire time. He did something to her. But she never heard of a drug that could disable magic, and she didn't have any soreness from any kind of needle injection when she woke up. Her worry slowly starts to give way to fear and it is not helped by Ren's voice in her ear.

<It's gotta be him. I'm still getting strange readings from his body. There's something off about him, but I can't get anything specific.>

If she can't use her magic, how is she going to fight? She can't. She looks for the exit. It's only a few meters away but Leon has placed himself right in the path. He knew this was going to happen. Suddenly a few meters feels like a few miles and those stairs are a long way up.

"What's the matter?" Leon asks. "Problems?" He takes a hand out of his pocket, as if he has just realized something. "Oh, are you unable to use your magic?" Sai is able to recompose herself, but struggles to hide her nervousness. "Yeah," he continues, "that's gotta suck, but you know the worst thing about your situation right this minute?" Sai tries to slowly move closer to the stairs by wrapping around Leon, but he makes his way towards her like a villain in a horror movie, a villain that knows that no matter how fast she runs she won't escape.

"You see," he smiles, "magic users are so used to having their abilities that they never think of what would happen if they couldn't use them." His voice is flat and his face is dark. "They never bother learning how to fight."

Sai makes a break for the stairs. She runs fast, as fast as she can. It's not fast enough. Leon reaches her. He grabs her by the hair and throws her to the floor. She pounces back to her feet quickly. Even with magic, she's been in enough fights to know how to move. She's ready to defend herself. Leon does not care. He rushes her. She lifts her hands to fight but she has no idea what she's doing. Leon easily connects a fist into her stomach. She hunches over in pain. It's as if all her insides are rearranged all at once. Spit drains from her mouth.

She shakes it off. She raises her body and throws a punch at Leon. He easily blocks. He counters with a strike to her chest. The sound is just as bad as the pain. She can hear her bones crunch inside her. She can feel harmless anatomy become sharp spears piercing the soft, juicy tissue that are her insides. She stumbles backwards and grabs at her chest in pain. She tries to raise her hands in a valiant effort to defend herself. Leon does not wait. He is in her space.

He hits her again and again. Any reverence he held for her does not stay his aggression. His fists connect in rapid succession: a few strikes to the stomach, a few to the face, but all with a force intended to cause the maximum amount of pain.

. . . . ●．●．● . . .

"No...Sai..." Ren cries. She curls into her chair. She can see everything through Sai's view. The lens has cracks in it, and the image glitches every few seconds, but the blood never goes away. She turns from the screen, a screen that has become a deep tint of red. There is nothing she can do to save her sister.

· · · ● · ● · · ·

A final strike hits Sai in the cheek. Blood flies from her mouth and hits the floor almost as fast as she does. She is exhausted and it's all she can do to just catch her breath. She has lost and she isn't escaping anywhere anymore. With a face covered in blood, she can't even open her eyes now. Probably better so her sister doesn't have to see everything.

Leon takes his time walking to her. She forces one eye open when she hears him. He kneels in front of her. He lifts his hand and she reactively raises her arms to shield herself, desperate to stop him from hitting her anymore. He presses a button on his watch. Suddenly, various parts of the lab begin to compact into smaller droids all on their own. He lets out a deep sigh.

"It's not too late, you know," he says. "I can still let you go, right now. I'm sure your sister has already called the SPMD and they're on their way here, so you don't even have to move. They'll definitely find you down here." Leon reaches out to touch Sai's face. She flinches in reaction with a tear she reluctantly lets escape from her eye. He tilts her head up towards him.

"Just...promise me," he whispers. "Promise me that you'll let me be, let me finish my research. You say that and I'll let you live." Sai does not respond. She stares at Leon through bloody eyes.

<Just tell him what he wants to hear, Sai!> Ren is practically screaming at her sister through the headset. <Lie if you have to! Just promise him!>

Leon waits for Sai's answer, looking into her eyes as much as he can.

"Well?"

It takes Sai a moment. She moves her mouth, attempting to speak. She tries to answer, but it's hard for her to find words. Her voice is so low that there's no way Leon can hear her. He leans in, trying to make out what Sai is saying. He gets his ear directly in front of her mouth and he receives his answer.

"No."

Again, he lets out a deep sigh. "That's too bad." He stands to his feet and moves so that he is directly above her. "You're committed to your beliefs," he says, nodding to her in respect. "I admire that. You're like me in that way. I wish you didn't find this place tonight."

He picks Sai up from the ground so that she is still sitting but now he holds her head in his hands like a noose. He looks down at her, a tear welling up in his eye. "I am truly sorry, but I can't let you stop me...I won't." With that, he immediately breaks Sai's neck and her body slumps to the ground, dead.

· · · ● · ● · · · ·

The flat is silent, eerily so. Ren is usually by herself at times like this but for whatever reason, she can feel the loneliness more than usual. She had never heard a neck snap before and the fact it was Sai's doesn't help with the experience. Still, she puts that aside in the moment because she knows what she needs to do next. She presses a button in her keyboard and a digital stopwatch appears on the screen.

It starts its upward count.

The display is merely a reference though. Ren has already started counting up in her own head. *122, 123, 124.* As each second grows nearer and nearer to 242 so does her dread. *232, 233, 234.* Almost there.

242.

Hesitant, Ren finally looks back up at the screen of Sai's view. All she can see is the floor. The counter continues and Sai stays dead, her eyes still open.

Ren snaps her gaze away. "No…" she whispers. *261, 262, 263.* Sai still hasn't revived. She can't look anymore, not just because it's hard to, but because it's physically difficult for her to see anything through her tears. She rocks back and forth in her chair, trying desperately to calm herself. When calm doesn't come, she covers her ears, anything to drown out the silence she is sinking into.

282.

<I had to…>

The voice is soft, almost apologetic. Ren looks back up and can see a pair of feet standing in front of Sai's body.

Her killer.

Leon stares at Sai's lifeless body. Another tear creeps down his cheek. He turns away, leaving her and his doubts behind. As the lab around him packs itself up, he whispers only to himself, "what I'm doing…is too important…"

• • • • • • • • • •

A familiar site. The dead girl on the ground, the person who did it content in what they've just done. Always knowing. Never suspecting.

I do wonder if I could have achieved more, but even with my magical ability, I cannot beat someone who negates that very ability. It is frustrating, infuriating even, but once again, I have to rely on another. I have to hope that one of the others can do what I'm unable to.

Once again I have to trust someone else to steer the ship.

Sai's body twitches. The first is sudden, like shocking an unconscious person awake. The next movements are slow. She sways back and forth as she attempts to stand, all the while her body randomly twitches. Leon sees and hears none of this. It's as if the very sound around her is as dead as she is.

· · • • · • • · · ·

Distracted by the images of Sai's group on his computer screens, he gazes with a type of reverence at the person he just killed. As if saying goodbye, he hits a few keys and the screens shut off. Perhaps he wanted to pay his respects once more, or perhaps he felt an unease behind him, but whatever the reason, he glances over his shoulder at Sai's body. What he sees sends all former composure from his body like breath from a collapsed lung.

Sai's body stands with her neck unnaturally resting on her shoulder. Her eyes are open but there is no life in them. They are not staring at Leon. They are staring through him.

"Thi-this can't be possible," he stutters. "No magic should work around me." Her head twists around, cracking as the bones realign themselves. It swirls up from her shoulders, past her back, and snaps back into its proper place before slumping to rest on her chin.

"Wait," Leon stammers, his scientific mind desperate for answers, "there's no magic that can revive the dead...so what...is this?" The last portion of his statement is said with intrigue, not fear. The odd movements of Sai's body cease. Sai hangs there without a word, as if frozen in time. Leon leans over in an attempt to look at her face. With a heavy step, he moves cautiously towards her.

"Saiyonoshi?"

Sai's head snaps up. She rushes Leon, not a word said. She's fast. He can't think, no time to react. Her fingers are on his arm. Then he is on the ground. He hits it hard, his head bouncing off the floor. His pain is only surpassed by his shock.

The girl he so easily beat earlier flipped him before he could even notice. The thought is quick and impossible, but he wonders it all the same.

Is this really the same girl?

"I'm not Sai." The answer comes as if in response to his face. The accent. It's different though. Leon can't quite place it, but it's not the same as Sai's normal English one. She grabs him by the collar. "I'm Rosa, and I am going to beat your ass for hurting that sweet, sweet girl."

• • • • ● • ● • • • •

Rosa can tell from Leon's face that he didn't know about Sai's secret. As she holds his shirt in her fingers, the thought of him hurting Sai flashes across her mind. She can feel the rage inside her swell. Leon must sense it too, because he quickly launches his legs into the air and attempts to wrap them around Rosa's arms to bring her down to the ground.

She sees the move coming. She releases her hold on Leon and moves to counter instead. He's able to adjust and quickly propel himself back to his feet. He stumbles a bit, but does regain his footing. Now a safe distance away, he takes a better look at "Rosa."

He's good. She can see why Sai lost to him. That brief exchange told her everything she needed to know, though. She's better.

Still feeling the lingering pain from the snapped neck, she cracks her neck right, then left. Now loose, she raises her hands into a fighting stance.

"Saiyonoshi?" asks Leon. "What is this? You were dead. How did you-"

"I'm not Sai." Rosa interrupts, "I told you, I'm Rosa." Leon studies Rosa and everything about her seems different than Sai. The way she stands, talks, and even her facial mannerisms are all different than the woman Leon killed moments ago.

"Rosa," he submits. Silence is her reply. "Who are you?"

"It doesn't matter." Rosa shakes her head from across the room. "You hurt Sai and for that, I'm going to put you in the hospital and then you are going to jail."

Rosa is in Leon's face. She can see his surprise at her speed. He dodges strike after strike. Each one barely misses his face. He raises his arms just in time to block a blow to his chest. The force sends him sliding across the floor, the table behind him being the only thing to stop his momentum.

"This doesn't..." Leon exclaims, "this doesn't make sense!" He jumps over the table, giving himself some breathing room. "You're a completely different person than before." Rosa jumps over the table with a raised fist.

"That's because I am, moron!" Leon is barely able to deflect the blow. He wraps his fingers over her arm. She flipped him, so he would pay her back in kind. His strength picks her from the ground. The screens of computers are directly behind him and he intends to turn them into Rosa's bed. Rosa's intentions are different. She adjusts her body in midair. Her feet move towards the screens. She lands on the screens like a makeshift vertical floor and shoots from them with an outstretched knee. Her knee fiercely connects with his jaw. Blood and mucous splatter on the ground. Leon reels from the hit but keeps his footing.

The fact he remains conscious is commendable, admirable even. Shaking off the concussion he most certainly has is not easy, and with a moment or two he could fight longer; but Rosa has no interest in him fighting at all. He's vulnerable and she is going to take advantage.

Before he can recover, she pounds his face with a flurry of punches. He staggers backward and attempts to regain his footing for a counter attack. Just as he's able to stand upright, again Rosa upper cuts him straight into his gut. His body briefly leaves the ground. He falls back to earth, landing on his knees at Rosa's feet. Leon hunches over from the powerful hit. As he struggles to breathe he realizes that air is a commodity many take for granted.

"How?" he whispers as he spits up blood. "You couldn't fight this well before...and you haven't even tried to use magic once."

"That's cause I can't, dumbass." Rosa explains, "Even without your shit, I'm a fighter. You want OP magic, that's Yuan." Rosa stares down at Leon who is grabbing his stomach trying to will the pain his body away. "I don't know how to, but that's okay, cause I'm definitely the best fighter out of all of us."

"Us?" Leon questions. He glances up at Rosa. "There...there are more of you?" Rosa doesn't answer. She leans down, placing a hand on Leon's back.

"I fractured a few of your ribs and I'm pretty sure you have a concussion. I'm a woman of my word. I'll take you to the hospital before you go to jail."

"No," Leon spits, "I can't. You have no idea what I'm trying to do. My work...it's going to change everything." He looks Rosa right in her eyes. "I won't let you stop me." There's a sound ticking behind him Rosa never noticed during the course of the fight. There's a timer on the computer behind him and just as she notices it, she sees a number that makes her heart sink.

0.

An explosion bursts from the computer screen.

Smoke billows throughout the room as subsequent explosions trigger all around. Debris flies towards Rosa as she quickly moves to get out of the way. When she looks up again, Leon is gone.

The room burns as all the remaining research disappears in a blaze. A heavy sigh escapes Rosa's chest. She let him get away and her disappointment with herself is only slightly greater than the fire spreading around her. She reaches her hand up to her ear.

"Ren?"

• • • •●•◆• • • •

<Ren?> Rosa tries again. Her voice is muffled, hard to hear. It's as if Ren is trapped in a void where the sound of constant ringing fills her ears. <Ren?> The ringing subsides and Rosa's voice finally makes its way through: the voice of her sister.

But she is not her.

"Hey, Rosa."

Silence.

<You okay?>

"I'll be fine," Ren replies, wiping some tears away. "Um, why don't you head back here? I'll tell Blue and Dane that Sai's alright."

<...Okay. I'm leaving now.>

"Oh, and Rosa."

<Yeah, Ren?>

"Thanks for saving my sister...again..."

Silence.

<I'll be back home in a few. It'll be okay.>

The words fall and roll right off of her. Communications with Rosa cease and the silence returns. Her eyes shift towards the stopped numbered display.

302 seconds.

Ren's not sure when she started crying again, but the sound of her tears feel louder than the sound of her voice. "Damn you Sai...damn you..."

• • • • • • • • • •

"By the time the officers arrived there wasn't much left for them to find." Blue brings Sai up to speed as she sips on a warm mug of tea. It's been a few days since her run-in with Leon. Recovering from a broken neck isn't as hard as a bullet to the head, but there is still a large chunk of time she missed. Over her shoulder Sai can see Ren looking busy on her computers. Since Sai came back, Ren has been avoiding making eye contact with her. It makes no sense, she's died before. What made this time so different?

"And Leon?" Sai asks.

"Escaped. Dane and the other members of the SPMD have not been able to find any lead as to where he could be."

"I see." Sai struggles to withhold her frustration. There were still many questions she needed answered. She does take solace in one fact. "Well, it sounds like Rosa really kicked his ass, so I guess I should be grateful for her help."

"You should be grateful any of us are around to help you at all." Ren retorts. The attitude is not completely unexpected, but the level of Ren's tone is what takes Sai aback.

"Yeah, well, did Dane find any traces of the mana strain?" She asks Blue, choosing to ignore Ren's passive aggression that will inevitably become something else she has to deal with.

"Everything was burned up," Blue replies, shaking his head. "There was nothing left to identify."

"Damnit!" Another loss. At that moment, Sai can't help but feel a tinge of regret. She should have thought to steal a sample before confronting Leon, although, with the way he kicked her ass, it more than likely would have been destroyed. Her thoughts are interrupted when her front door slides away. Dane enters, calmer than normal. He scans the room, looking from person to person until his gaze lands on Sai.

"You alright?"

"I'm fine," she says, shaking her head. Dane grabs himself a glass of wine from the kitchen. "I'm impressed you were able to find our culprit's hideout. You really should just join the force." He motions to Ren to ask if she wants a glass for herself. She puts her hand up, rejecting. Dane finishes pouring his glass and takes a seat, ready to debrief with the girls.

"His name is Leon," Sai explains.

"Who is he?"

"Not sure yet. All I know is that I only found him by accident when following a lead for old locations owned by the company associated with Shanai Desi.

"Who is she?" Dane sips his wine with the satisfaction of a predator closing in on his prey.

"She was a geneticist who was doing research into rewriting sequences in human genetic code, but she died a few years back." Sai interlocks her fingers as she continues to explain.

"Ren already ran a search and there was no mention of anybody that fits Leon's description working for the company."

"Perhaps he was her apprentice?" Blue offers. Sai shakes her head.

"There's no record of her ever taking one on, and we can be sure that Leon is not his actual name, so all we have to go on is this." She points to the screen, prompting Ren to bring up an image but Ren doesn't do it. Caught off guard, Sai shifts her attention. "Ren?"

Ren lets out a low sigh, but complies. She pulls up an image on screen of Leon's face. Dane quickly stands to his feet, his voice wavers cautiously as he speaks.

"How did you ge-"

"This was taken from my eye contact lens." Sai answers quickly, hoping they can skip over what she knows is coming next.

"Wait." Dane turns to Sai and in the span of seconds goes from calm, to shocked, to angered, to fuming. If all those emotions weren't directed at Sai, she would think it was impressive. She suspected the reason he was so calm was because he didn't know what she did yet. "You were in the same room with this psychopath?!"

"That doesn't matter," she says, eager to dismiss it. "What matters is-"

"I thought you found his name out as a part of the investigation," Dane interrupts, boiling. "I didn't know he freakin' introduced himself!" Like clockwork he turns to Ren. "You let her do this?!"

Ren doesn't answer. Dane snaps toward Blue. Not even Blue can look him in the eye.

"It's alright, Dane," Sai assures, speaking as calmly as she can to attempt to pull him back. "As you can see, I'm fine. Don't blame them."

"What if something happened to you? What if this guy tried to hurt you?!"

Everyone is quiet, even Sai. She is usually good at lying to Dane, but for the briefest of moments, she remembers how scared she was as Leon beat her over and over. The thought is enough to rob her of a quick retort. Still, she pivots, looks him in the eye and answers flatly.

"I'm fine."

Dane stomps back into the kitchen. This time he pours himself a shot of liquor. "You're not a cop, Sai! You shouldn't be putting yourself in these situations!"

"How many times do I have to tell you I'm fine," Sai says with a little more force than even she intended. Now on her feet staring down Dane, she continues. "Besides, didn't you just say that I should join the force?"

"I was joking!" Dane gulps his shot. "But hey, at least if you did I could keep an eye on you. I swear, I don't know what's wrong with the three of you."

"We are NOT your children, Dane!" Sai screams. Dane is like a statue, looking as if Medusa herself gazed into his eyes. Silence permeates through the entire room. It's hard for Sai to look at Dane but keeping her gaze on him seems easier than turning to see the looks on Blue's and Ren's faces. She didn't mean to shout, or even say the words she said, but she did, so here they are.

A quiet 'beep, beep' sounds like a heavenly bell, breaking the fog of unease. Dane presses a button on his wrist and a holo display illuminates in front of him. An SPMD officer stands in the middle of the screen, a look of panic sewn on his face.

"What is it?" Dane whispers aloud. The girls can't hear the response since the audio feed goes directly to Dane's ear, but the worried look on his face tells them everything they need to know. Something big has happened. He slowly turns to Ren. "Renayaka, turn on the news."

CHAPTER ELEVEN

RISK AND REWARD

Ren quickly brings the news up on one of her screens. None are entirely sure what they would see, but what they see none of them could have predicted. A news anchor, standing in the middle of the city, motions behind her to a few dozen tiny droids with people gathered around them.

"-and so far we have been unable to ascertain where the droids have come from, but each one came equipped with a message, which we will play for you now."

Above the droids, a scrolling text floats: *Become a magic user, become ONE.*

"Along with this message," the anchor continues, "were several vials of this substance simply titled HSAP23. Now we have not been able to fully corroborate this as of yet, but we believe this substance to be capable of turning non-magic users into users. We-"

It's as if a icy breeze blows through Sai. Her gaze falls to the ground and her breathing quickens.

"He...he did it." She turns her focus to Dane. "You have to round up those droids, Dane. Those people don't know that those vials can kill them!"

"Right!" Dane exclaims, immediately bringing up a holo-display above his wrist. He moves deeper into the kitchen as he makes calls. Sai and the others continue to watch the broadcast. Various people are being interviewed by the anchor regarding their opinions on this substance. A few people speak with the lower third of "non-user" below their faces.

"I think it's great," one person says. "If it's true, then it means that more people can have access to something only a few people have been able to enjoy."

"With these latest attacks by magic users," another person states, "heck, maybe I should become one."

"I think it's risky," another person says. "Why would someone pass out something that would give people powers for free? Seems sketchy if you ask me."

A new group of people are interviewed, now with the lower third of "magic users" beneath their faces.

"I don't see what's so special about being a magic user," one young magic user states, "it doesn't really change any-thing if a person is one or isn't."

"If more people are able to be users," one user states, "then that'll just give me something more in common with non-users!"

Sai, Ren, and Blue continue to watch, unsure what to do. Sai turns to both Ren and Blue. "It's my fault. It's because of me." Blue doesn't seem to understand but the look on Ren's face says she knows exactly why Sai blames herself.

"What do you mean, Saiyonoshi?" Blue asks.

"I told Leon I wouldn't stop, and he was committed to his plans enough to kill me to protect them," she explains. "Now he knows that not only can he not kill me but that I can also track him down. He needed to accelerate his original plan in order to complete it before I can stop him."

"But I do not understand," Blue wonders. "How does killing a larger group of people with his modified strain, this HSAP23, help his overall plan?"

"Simple, Blue. He is trying to create a modified strain that doesn't kill non-users. He most likely has a way to observe and record any results from people who take his strain and now he just increased his sample size."

Blue realizes just how dangerous this new situation is. "So if even half the people who now have access to his strain decide to take it-"

"The data he receives may be enough for him to complete his strain."

"But to what end?" Ren finally interrupts, commanding Sai and Blue's attention. "What's the final goal? What's the point?"

Sai has to admit what she does not want to. "I don't know yet..."

Dane returns from the kitchen, more exasperated and haggard than before. "I need to go now. There is a ton of cleanup to be done and we need to release a formal statement warning people about the harms of taking HSAP23." Dane takes one last swig of a drink. He slams the glass down hard on the counter. "What the hell does that even mean?" Dane rushes towards the door and when it slides open for him to leave, he finds Clayre standing on the other side.

"You girls have a customer," Dane shouts back before tilting his head in acknowledgement of Clayre and continuing on. With everything happening, Sai completely forgot to check in with Clayre. She figures now's as good a time as any.

"Clayre!" Sai exclaims, inviting her inside. "Hey, what's going on? I'm sorry I didn't call you but we've made some real progress on your cousin's case. I think pretty soon we may be able to find a-"

"That's what I came to talk about actually," Clayre interrupts.

"Oh, what is it?" Sai asks. Clayre takes a deep breath. "Harper is dead. He passed away a few hours ago." The words take time to register. Dead? But they were so close. They found the lab, the strains, the one responsible. They had everything they needed, but now the whole reason they were involved in the case was gone. Sai struggles to find the words to say.

"I-I'm so sorry." Sai slowly takes a seat in one of her chairs. "I wasn't fast enough."

"It's okay," Clayre replies. "I hold nothing against you. You didn't kill my cousin, whoever gave him that strain did." Clayre turns to leave. "I just wanted to come and thank you in person. You looked at my cousin's case when no one else would and for that, I will always be grateful." As Clayre prepares to leave, she makes eye contact with Blue. Blue is hesitant but after a moment, she offers him a soft smile. She tilts her head and although he wasn't expecting that from her, he tilts his head back in kind. The door slides shut behind her and she is gone.

No one speaks. Not a word is said as they all reflect on their failure. While Sai figuratively kicks herself, Blue is lost in thought. It's only Ren that is actively angry.

Sai notices this and the fact that Ren still isn't looking at her. "Ren? Everything cool?"

"It's fine, Sai," Ren replies sarcastically, "everything is perfectly fine."

"Hey, I'm upset he got away too. Don't worry, now that I know he can negate my magic, I just have to find a different way to deal with him next time. We'll make him answer for everyone he's hurt."

"Next time," Ren repeats in disbelief. She stands to her feet. "You want to face that psycho again?!

"Well, yeah," Sai replies plainly. "I have to."

"Why, why do you have to?" Ren's rage grows with every word. "We're a detective agency, not the SPMD. Our job is not to take down dangerous criminals. It never has been. We started this to solve mysteries that could help the SPMD and maybe eventually figure out where your immortality comes from. That's it. And this job was about finding out what was causing the deaths and comas throughout the city. We did that, and now the person we started this for is dead. There's no reason to continue."

"But, Ren," Sai pleads. "Everything happening now is my fault. If I wasn't so focused on beating Leon, maybe he wouldn't have moved up his timetable. We could have had more time to find him without more people being put at risk."

"If you were more focused on escaping than beating Leon, maybe we could have saved Harper..."

It stings more than Sai cares to admit, and Ren can see it. Both girls turn away from each other until Sai decides to continue.

"He's afraid he can't stop me, and that's why I have to be the one to stop him."

"Who's to say you can't be stopped," Ren counters. Sai doesn't understand so Ren explains. "There's so much about your ability that we don't know. If he cuts off your legs, will they grow back? If he traps you in a tank of water, will you just keep drowning forever?" Ren moves closer to Sai, pleading. "You're not as invulnerable as you think, Sai."

"I can't let him win, Ren."

"No, you can't let him beat you!" Ren has had it with her. "That's what you said to him. You said you wouldn't let him beat you. That's not about helping everyone else, that's about your ego!"

Sai places a hand softly on her shoulder in an ill attempt at assurance. "That doesn't matter. It's my responsibility to stop him."

"And whose responsibility is it to pick up the pieces when you die?!" It's as if a cork has popped and exploding from the bottle is a delicate composition of anger and rage. Sai falls back, surprised at her sister's outburst. "54, 67, 122, 186, 242, 302. Do you have any idea what those numbers mean?"

Sai has no answer. It's random gibberish for her. Ren elaborates for her.

"Those are the seconds it took for you to revive after each death. Notice anything about them?" Ren is furious, almost shaking with rage. Now that Sai has more information she can immediately see the correlation.

"It's...taking longer..." she answers, her voice soft.

"And those are just the times I was able to count." Ren can barely catch her breath in time to say her next words. "You never think about it. You're immortal, so you can put yourself in any situation and you don't have to worry about it, right? But do you ever think about what it's like to be the one that has to watch you die over and over again?! Do you ever think about what it's like to have to sit there and wait?!"

Sai is quiet. "I-I never..."

"No, you didn't, Sai. You never thought about it. I've seen you shot, stabbed, drowned, you name it." Ren gets extremely close to Sai's face. "But when I saw Leon snap your neck, I just...I just couldn't take it anymore." The dam of Ren's emotions that has been propped up for years is broken and the tears held behind it flow freely. "You take life for granted, Sai, always rushing into things without thinking about the consequences, but tell me, have you ever stopped to consider what would happen if one day you died and you didn't come back?"

It's a concept Sai never really spared a thought for. She was always used to reviving, it never crossed her mind that maybe there was a limit to her resurrections. Sai was not expecting to have this conversation tonight, and the rush of everything all at once threatens to overwhelm her. When Sai's eyes water, it's not just Ren who is surprised.

Ren lets escape a deep, exasperated sigh. "I get it," Ren whispers, "you want to help people. I do too…but I don't want to lose my baby sister or watch her die again and again." She turns to leave but looks back at Sai once more.

"I love you, but you're a fucking asshole."

Ren makes her way towards her room, never turning back again. The door slides open and Ren disappears on the other side once it shuts.

Sai stands, left both perplexed and confused. A tear runs down her cheek but she has no idea what to say. Her eyes fall to the ground, lost in the thoughts of everything that just happened. It is not until she feels a hand press against her shoulder that she comes back. She turns to see Blue, an empathetic look on his strangely human face.

"Let us walk for a bit…"

• • • • ● • ● • • • •

Haven's isn't as packed as the last time Blue was there. This isn't a day he normally comes, so Lee is nowhere to be seen either. With still a few androids and people alike inside, it's about five minutes before they're able to grab a table. Sai is uncharacteristically quiet the entire time, not talking even after they sit and order drinks. When water is placed on the table, Sai still doesn't budge, a normally confident girl now lost in uncertainty. Blue leans closer to offer his compassion.

"Are you okay?" he asks, knowing the obvious answer.

"I'm…confused," she responds honestly.

In the back of the bar, unseen by Blue or Sai, sits Carter with his crew. Their booth is tucked away, somewhat hidden, but Eyesore easily spots Blue from it.

He quietly brings it to Carter's attention. Instinctively, Carter starts to make his way towards Blue but is stopped when Eyesore grabs Carter's arm. He motions towards Sai sitting across from Blue. She spins her fork on the table, then a blue orb appears around it and it immediately moves in reverse at the same speed as when it spun in its proper direction. It's innocuous and benign, but it tells Eyesore all he needs to know. He leans close, whispering in Carter's ear.

"That's time magic and with how easily she's using it, she's good at it." Carter gives Eyesore a look that says, "the fuck do I care for?" but Eyesore urges further caution. "It's really hard to fight against. We should wait."

Carter snorts, clearly wanting to settle things now, but his memory of the previous altercation gives way to reason. The android was a challenge to handle with friends, so when Carter did settle things, he would make sure the android was alone. Begrudgingly, he withdraws, settling back into his seat, but keeping his eyes on the two friends the entire time.

Sai continues to play with her fork. "I...I always knew Ren was uncomfortable with my immortality, but I guess I never realized just how bad it was."

"I do not think it is a matter of merely being uncomfortable, Saiyonoshi," Blue ponders, "It is in fact much deeper than that."

Sai doesn't bother looking up from the fork beneath her. "That doesn't make sense. How could it be deeper when we tell each other everything?" This gives Blue pause. While looking at Sai, he can see that she believes what she is saying, which explains her genuine confusion. He takes a sip before lowering his glass, now an expert in imitating proper human speech balance. "Can I be honest with you?"

"Of course you can," she replies quietly. "When are you not?" She stares at her spinning fork.

"I try to…" Blue begins, but stops when he notices Sai still looking down. "Sai," he whispers politely, "do you mind stopping for a moment?"

"It calms me down. I need it to help me focus." She doesn't look up at Blue.

"I understand." Blue hesitates, doing his best to choose the proper words. "I would just…appreciate it…if you would listen to me."

"Go ahead, I'm listening." Her words say she is, but her tone does not.

"LOOK AT ME, SAIYONOSHI!"

The outburst is not what Blue intended. He does not fully understand it himself, but it seemed a…natural response. He is normally able to remain so composed but even he was not expecting to shout or slam his hand on the table.

The fork still spins, but now on the floor. Sai's water drips off the side of the table. It's a wonder the glass did not break. The other patrons quickly shrug aside the moment, but Sai is left dumbfounded. Blue has never yelled at her before.

Blue mimics the action of taking a deep breath and looks Sai in her wide eyes. "Please. I would really appreciate it if you could look at me as I speak." She says nothing, but her shift in posture shows her willingness to comply with his request.

"You asked when am I not honest. The answer is I usually am, but I do not always say what I am thinking. I have made certain observations."

The change in her expression is subtle, but noticeable to Blue. He can tell that she never spared a thought for androids making unspoken observations much as humans do. As if she is using her voice for the very first time, she labors through her words. "And what are they?"

"Do you recall not too long ago I asked you if magic users treated non-users differently?"

"Yeah, I remember."

"You see," he says, "I asked both you and your sister the same question, albeit at separate times. When I asked you, you confidently told me they didn't; however, when I asked your sister, her answer was not filled with such definitive conviction." The surprise on Saiyonoshi's face reveals her thoughts. It was yet another element she did not expect from her sister. "Rather than give what I would expect to be a simple answer, she merely told me the world was not easy for anybody." Sai sits, unsure of what to say.

"This tells me," Blue continues, "that for Ren, the answer to that question is not so simple...and I do not think the way she feels now is either."

Sai glances down at her glass, lost in thought. "I...I figured if there was ever anything wrong, she would just tell me. She has to know I would understand..." Blue stares at Sai silently for a moment. He moves his hands to the knobs on either side of his head.

"Sai, do you know why all androids have these knobs protruding from our heads?" She shakes her head. "You see," Blue continues, "androids did not always have these. During the time before sentience, androids looked no different than people and were only identifiable by their actions. This sufficed for a while, until one day a human accidentally shot another human they thought was an android." Sai's eyes grow wide at hearing this.

"Since then, all androids are required to have easily identifiable traits. While it made it so everyone could easily tell an android apart from a human, once sentience occurred, it was simply just another way to separate us from people." He rubs one of his protrusions extending from his head.

"At first, I was not bothered by this, but as time passes and it becomes more and more apparent that there are people that will not accept us, all I want is for these things to go away, if for no other reason than maybe it would be easier to blend in and perhaps I would not be mistreated for what I am."

Sai is at a loss for words. The entire story and Blue's own feelings all come as a shock to her. Blue has never opened up this much in front of her, but he is ready to trust that she will understand the feelings of a 'thing' like him. The thought of him truly trusting Sai reminds him of his conversation with Lee, and though he knows she would not agree, he is ready to prove his way can be met with success.

"I...I had no idea, Blue," Sai whispers as she leans forward. "Why didn't you say anything?"

"I am not entirely sure myself," he muses. "At first I was merely attempting to understand what was happening around me by gathering information through asking questions. I was not even entirely aware something was wrong with me until Ren formally asked me."

Sai is taken aback to hear not only that Ren asked him directly, but that she knew something about Blue that Sai herself did not.

"She got me to talk about what was bothering me simply by asking me what was wrong. I do not pretend to understand all human emotions or interactions, but this method proved effective in not only making me feel better, but giving me a better understanding of Ren as well."

"But I've asked her what was wrong before," Sai complains, "and she never tells me anything."

"I believe I have gained a better understanding of this as well," Blue remarks. "You see, I did not believe that you, nor Ren, would understand me when I barely understood myself, but Ren proved a fact to the contrary. She showed me that she did understand and could even offer me advice." He makes eye contact with Sai. "Perhaps Ren needs to only know that you will understand her and perhaps that will make it easier for her to tell you what is really wrong with her."

Sai is astounded, but grateful. Everything Blue said makes sense. She stands from the table and wraps her arms around him. The action is surprising, but not entirely unexpected. He welcomes the action.

"Thank you, Blue," she whispers. "I think you may be more human than even the rest of us." Factually, it is a statement that is categorically untrue, but it is one that he appreciates nonetheless. Sai pulls back, making sure to look Blue right in his eyes. "I'm sorry. I'm sorry for never asking if you were alright. I want you to always know that you can talk to me or Ren, and we will be here for you." She gives Blue a kiss on the forehead. "Knobs or not, it doesn't matter. You're family, and that's all there is to it."

Blue smiles in a way he can only recognize as a reflex action. This girl and her sister have truly had an impact on him. "Let's get out of here," Sai smiles. "I gotta go talk to my sister!"

· · · ● · ● · ● · · ·

Ren sits at a smaller screen set up in her room, spinning quietly in her rotating chair. Her room is dark with the only light coming from her monitors showing various news stories, commercials, and a paused video game. She keeps her head low, hugged against her knees as she spins. Without warning, her door slides open, her lights turn on, and a gallon of milk with a single glass lands directly in front of her. She looks up to see Sai standing over her.

"It's time for us to talk."

"Fine," Ren stands to her feet, unscrewing the cap on the gallon of milk. She pours the milk into the single glass. "We don't finish this glass until we're both satisfied."

"We'll go through the whole damn gallon if we have to," Sai replies, full of conviction. Once the glass is full, Ren takes a seat while Sai sits across from her on Ren's bed. The two wait, unsure who should start. Eventually Sai makes the first move. She reaches her arm out, prompting Ren to pass the milk. Ren complies, allowing Sai to take a sip before beginning. After a deep gulp, Sai starts.

"I'm sorry." Sai passes the milk back to Ren. Ren chuckles to herself sardonically.

"Good start." She takes a sip.

"I don't know, Ren," she continues, "I just never knew how badly my dying affected you. I thought we were both okay with it since I would always come back."

"We don't know that you'll always come back, and I never said I was okay with it," Ren counters. "I dealt with it because I knew I couldn't talk you out of whatever crazy thing you wanted to do, but do you really think it's fun watching you die over and over again?"

"I never said you thought it was fun, but I assumed we had an understanding that sometimes it may happen."

"And why does it have to happen at all, Sai? Seriously, you act as if most people don't spend every day of their lives avoiding death."

"Yes," Sai agrees, "that's true, and that makes them less effective. Most people can't do what I can."

"Maybe that just means you shouldn't be doing it!" Ren shouts her last statement and the two of them look away from one another. After a few moments, Ren pours some more milk into her glass and moves over to sit beside Sai on the bed. She passes Sai the milk, who starts to drink. After a few gulps, Ren continues with a deep breath.

"Sai, I get it," she starts. "You have this amazing gift that makes you able to take chances other people can't. I just wish you would think a little more before taking them." She places her hand on top of Sai's. "That night you were stabbed, I thought I lost you forever....again. I held you, bleeding in my arms, and all I could think to myself was 'I let my baby sister die.'" Sai's eyes grow wide upon hearing this.

"You didn't-"

Ren puts up her hand, motioning for Sai to let her finish. "I remember wondering how I was going to explain it to mom and dad. What would they say? What would life be like after? And just when I thought everything was over, you opened your eyes and told me to stop crying." Ren laughs quietly. "You reached your hand up and touched my cheek with your fingertips and you told me that my sister would be fine."

Sai smirks upon hearing this. "Must have been confusing, huh?"

"I didn't think much of it at the time," Ren explains. "I thought you were just being cheeky. It wasn't until later that I discovered it was Rosa talking to me and that your injury was completely healed." Sai passes Ren the glass of milk and Ren drinks more. She almost finishes the glass, prompting Sai to slowly refill it.

"Sai, I really did think your ability was a miracle, until I saw what you were doing with it. You got yourself killed time and time again, almost like you were trying to see just how screwed up you could make your next death." She passes Sai the glass back, but this time Sai just holds it as she listens to her sister. Ren looks at her with tears welling up in her eyes.

"And each time I met a new personality and each time those personalities stayed rooted in you, there was a new fear that grew inside me."

Ren turns to Sai and whispers, pressing her finger against Sai's chest, "Even if you came back, would *you* still come back?" Sai remains silent, another aspect of her revival she never considered.

"I thought I could be okay with it, I really did, but I'm your big sister. I'm supposed to keep you safe, and every time I saw you die it felt like I was allowing it. Every time I waited for you to come back I always felt like you died because I wasn't strong enough to protect you...because I wasn't a magic user like you."

Sai's eyes fill with water, too. Ren wipes her own tears away but more still fall. "I hated being a non-user. I hated being too weak to keep my sister safe and each time you died I couldn't help but think that would be it. That would be the time you wouldn't revive and I wouldn't have been able to do anything to save you."

"Why," Sai stammers, "why...didn't you tell me before, Ren? Why didn't you say anything?"

"I tried," Ren answers, "but every time you turned it into some sort of joke or were dismissive." Ren sniffs a little. "Even when we were younger, I tried to talk to you about how some of the magic users at my school would call me 'craftless' and joke about how my baby sister would have to take care of me because I would be too weak to take care of myself." Sai is floored. Ren knows Sai never knew, but she wants Sai to understand. "Do you know what you said to me when I told you?" Sai shakes her head, clueless.

"You said they were just playing around and it didn't mean anything."

"I don't remember any of this," Sai replies, surprised at her own flippancy.

"But you said things like that all the time," Ren continues. "You were always so focused on the world around *you*, you never really bothered to think about the world around me…or Blue." Sai lowers her head.

"Yeah…I realize that now."

"It's okay, I got used to it," Ren replies, "but once you got this…this thing…it became worse. It seemed like you were only able to see what was right in front of you and nothing else."

Sai stares into the half glass of milk. "I never wanted you to feel like you couldn't talk to me or that I wasn't thinking of you. You mean everything to me, Ren. Honestly, you and Blue are the only people who even really put up with me."

"I have to, I'm your sister," Ren says with a smirk. "Blue, I don't know what his problem is." This gets Sai to smile and share a small laugh with Ren. The two chuckle for a moment before settling down once more. Sai glances up into Ren's eyes.

"I'll do better," she says. "I promise. I'll try to be more careful from now on. I…I won't take the life I have for granted…or you." Sai moves closer to Ren. "I'm sorry for not being there for you when you needed me. Kids are assholes."

"Well," Ren laughs, "they weren't completely wrong."

"They were," Sai replies seriously. "Without you, I'm almost positive I would've died even more by now, probably starved to death or something. That, or ended up as some lab experiment in somebody's basement."

"I don't think so. You said it yourself: no one can stand you, but me."

Sai smirks at her sister: her sister that she loves so much. They hug.

"I love you, big sis," Sai says, "and no matter how it may seem, I need you more than you realize. You do keep me safe."

"I love you too, baby sister," Ren replies, closing her eyes. "And thanks…" The two embrace for a moment longer before moving away from each other. They both look down, seeing they have half a glass of milk left. Sai attempts to give it to Ren who refuses.

"I…I can't…"

"Me neither," Sai pouts, "my tummy hurts." The two girls laugh quietly together.

• • • • • • • • • •

Some time later, Sai and Ren both lay on her bed, looking up at the ceiling. As they talk, they stare at the star constellations Ren has illuminated as a holo-image above. She's always had it since she was a child, and only added to the complexity of its code as she got older. She always felt it made her entire room feel more serene.

"Did that happen a lot," Sai asks, "magic users picking on you when we were kids?"

"Every now and then," Ren answers. "I told mom and dad about it, but there wasn't much they could do."

"What did you do?"

"Ignored them most of the time, but this one time I screwed with a kid's mana dosage. Teacher thought he was high the entire class. It was all I could do really, but I got my licks in." The two reflect silently when Sai turns on her side to face Ren.

"Is that what Leon was talking about…when he said you would understand?"

Ren does not answer, but continues looking at the stars.

"Renayaka?"

"Magic users can be jerks sometimes, but anybody can really."

"Do magic users…sometimes still treat you like that?"

"No one treats me like anything," Ren answers flatly, "it's why I don't go outside if I can help it." She looks at Sai with a smile. "There are people out there."

"And we wouldn't want you to have to deal with those would we," Sai jokes. Silence again. "I have to stop him. You know that right?" Ren doesn't answer. The thought of her sister facing down that madman once more almost makes her cry again. "I promised you I'd be careful, and I will," Sai continues, "but we can't let Leon keep hurting people when we are in a position to prevent it."

"Earlier, when you left," Ren whispers, "they reported over 30 new deaths related to HSAP23. Despite that, it seems like some people who have taken it are showing no signs of sickness and others are desperate to get their hands on it…"

Sai shakes her head in disbelief. "I had no idea that so many non-users would want magical powers that badly."

"When people feel powerless, they'll do anything to make themselves stronger." Ren looks up at the ceiling unflinching. Sai suddenly comes to a realization.

"That's the real reason he used criminals," she whispers. She looks over to Ren. "He was trying to make people more afraid of magic users."

"Makes sense," Ren agrees. "The general public doesn't know it was non-users given magical abilities that attacked Scylarus Park and the other places."

"He's manipulating people through fear. He's making them feel like their only way of protecting themselves in a world of dangerous magic users is to become a user themselves."

Ren nods in agreement, quiet as she stares up at the stars. Sai studies the serene look on Ren's face, carefully considering what she wants to ask next. Sai sits up and turns to Ren. There's been a question on her mind since she and

Ren started talking. It's a question she's afraid to ask, but ultimately decides to take the chance.

"Ren, would you ever...take HSAP23?"

"No," Ren says immediately. "If you had asked me a few years ago I might have felt different, but now I realize that even though I may not be able to use magical abilities, there's still plenty I can do. Occasional doubts aside, I'm perfectly happy the way I am." Ren sits up beside Sai. "Still, there are plenty of non-users out there that don't feel the same way and would do anything to feel safe." She turns to Sai. "We have to stop Leon. For them."

Sai smiles, ecstatic that she and Ren are back on the same page.

"Oh my god, Ren," she exclaims. "Thank you."

"We're going to be smart, and we are going to be safe." Ren explains. "I'll be reporting whatever we find to Dane and we are not going to take any unnecessary risks from now on. Clear?"

Sai salutes at attention. "Crystal!"

"Now, since you're you and the likelihood that we bump into Leon face to face again is high, there's something we need to figure out first."

"What's that?" Sai asks, unsure of what Ren is planning. Ren turns to Sai with a smile.

"We have to figure out how he was able to stop your magic..."

Elsewhere, Leon sits in front of a large screen in a dark warehouse.

<We have to figure out how he was able to stop your magic...>

Leon presses a button, turning the audio device off. "Good luck with that," he says aloud. He looks at the device silently for a few more minutes before getting up from his chair to leave.

CHAPTER TWELVE

A NEW MYSTERY

"You say that but..." Sai is ready to pull her hair out. Her eyes are bloodshot from staring at her computer screen for so long. "There is literally nothing out there on an ability or piece of technology that is able to negate magic down to its activation. Anti-magic bullets disrupt the frequency between the user and that spell, but it's only effective if the disruption emanates from either the source or the spell itself and even that relationship comes from a disruptive burst, not a continuous wave. This is ridiculous!" Sai smashes her hands against the surprisingly sturdy screen.

"Hey, that's my baby and if you hurt her, I'll slave you over until you can pay to fix her," Ren replies with a bland, but firm promise. Focused on her monitors and never breaking her attention from them, she checks to see if Blue is having slightly more luck. "How bout you, Blue, you find anything?"

The flat has become one giant research station. Ren has disseminated parts of her system to various spots around the living room. Blue is connected to his charging station that is drawing more power from a processor Ren kindly let him borrow. His eyes are translucent but his irises move ever so slightly as he searches through various files in cyberspace. "I have scanned over two thousand three hundred and forty three files related to magic negation and have been unable to find any criteria that match the effects Leon demonstrated."

"Okay!" Sai claps, "Let's think about this. We know that we have special equipment that can be enchanted by magic negating spells."

"Yes," Ren continues, "but, like with the bullets, those spells only exist as enchantments for tools, not as a full-on radial negation effect."

"Is it possible to cast a large radial negation spell over an area?" Blue asks, disconnecting from his search. "Similar to the large time stop spell you cast, Sai? Like a room per se. It would enhance a tool, being the room, and everything inside the tool could be negated."

"Not a bad theory," Sai commends, "but a net like that could take hours to cast and would need continuous casting every few hours to hold its effect."

"And there were no magical readings coming from that room," Ren explains. "When I attempted to scan for the source disabling Sai's powers the only interference I was able to pick up was coming directly from Leon himself, not the room."

"Which means that either Leon's invented a new piece of technology that can negate the spells of magic users within a given radius, and is small enough to keep on a human body-"

"Or it's something only he is capable of?" Ren finishes. The room is quiet, each person reflects on the ramifications of the idea.

"Could he have discovered a new form of negation magic?" Ren offers.

"It wouldn't be unheard of," Sai ponders. "New magic spells haven't been discovered in the last 200 years, but that doesn't make it impossible."

"Perhaps if we knew more about Leon, then we could ascertain how he was able to come into whatever this...spell negation is," Blue suggests.

"That's good thinking, Blue." Ren turns to her computer and types away. The image of Leon from Sai's contact pops on her screen. "Since we have his image, I can run an algorithm that identifies any person with similar features caught on a security camera or social media post in the last 30 years."

"That...seems like it could take foreeevvvveeerrrrr," Sai whines as she slouches down in her chair.

"Not too long really," Ren counters, optimistic and eyes glued to her screens. "I'll be filtering out certain junk data associated with the search while still keeping the door open for marginal errors such as similar skin tone and eye shape."

"Would Dane and the SPMD not be doing this exact same thing?" Blue wonders aloud.

"Not like me." Ren's fingers fire across the keyboard like lightning in the sky. "I'm using so many backdoors into the dark web that I'll be able to find even an old school photo of this guy if one exists. I'll just...ya know...have to make sure I run multiple hack prevention keys to keep my server from imploding." Blue is speechless. He leans back in sheer awe watching Ren work. Sai can't stop herself from laughing at her android friend giving one of the most human expressions she's ever seen.

"I know," Sai gloats, "that's my sister."

"I am legitimately starting to wonder why you both do not work for the SPMD."

"Law enforcement was never really our thing," Ren replies, still working. "I'm sure you've noticed, but Sai can't even follow my rules, let alone a superior's."

"Hey," Sai shrugs, "I told you I'm going to try and do better."

"Do or do not, sis." Ren's impersonation of Yoda is admirable, but bad. "Okay, there." Ren leans back, cracking her knuckles above her keyboard. "It's going to take a while, but the search is running." She turns to everyone else. Her eyes appear as if they are on fire. Her confidence in her ability rivals Sai's in magic. It may take some time, and there may be a few stumbles, but one thing Ren is sure of is this:

They are going to catch Leon.

"We should probably get some rest. Hopefully we'll have something by morning." She has done all she can for now, but the gears are set in motion.

"Sounds good to me!" Sai exclaims. "All that crying made me a little tired."

"You go to bed then," Ren replies. "I'll make sure some of my other securities are in place before I zonk out."

"'Kay, night, sis. Night, Blue." Sai retreats to her room, almost stumbling through her sliding door.

"Night," they both reply. Ren turns to Blue. His input has been helpful getting them to this point, but as with Sai, there isn't much for him to do now either. "You should go ahead and conserve your energy too. This'll only be a bit."

"Very well," Blue agrees. "If you need me, I will be in power saver mode." Blue goes to an alcove in the corner of the room where a small, electrical rotunda is built into the wall. He steps inside and his eyes shut.

Ren turns back to her screens, typing away as the night wears on.

· · · · ● · ● · · · ·

Ren's bed has never felt so comfortable. Between the fighting and the working, she tired herself out. Even though she finished overhauling her various securities hours ago, a part of her dreams still linger where she feels most at home. As she lies comfortably in her bed, she can see a shadow move across the limited light from behind her shut eyes. It is only a moment later until she hears a soft voice along with it.

"Renayaka Amano."

Unsure if she is dreaming, she slowly blinks her eyes open. The moment they are though, the dream becomes a very real nightmare. She is bound tightly to her bed, unable to move. A dark figure stands over and when it leans closer, the limited light reveals a face.

Leon.

"Sai!" Ren shouts as loud as she can. Leon doesn't even flinch.

"I've enabled the sound dampener for your room, Ms. Amano," Leon says in a normal voice. "Saiyonoshi and Blue cannot hear you."

It doesn't take long for Ren to realize that he's right. Unable to call for help or move, she has no choice but to talk to him. "What are you doing here?"

"Your sister intrigues me," Leon answers. "I have never before met a person that could not die, and the alternative personality, wow. It is truly fascinating."

"Yeah, well maybe you should be in her room then," Ren retorts.

"Oh, don't misunderstand, Ms. Amano. While I do find your sister fascinating, it is your relationship with her that I am truly intrigued by." He sits down on her bed beside her. He pulls out a small circular device, then tosses it on the covers beside Ren. Once she gets a good look at it, she knows exactly what it is.

"You were listening to us," she snorts, not attempting to hide her disgust.

"Yes," he says. "I attached it to your sister once she re-vived. Figured it would come in handy. These things are ex-pensive though, so I wanted to get it back." The implications of his statement fill Ren with dread. Leon notices the look on her face and throws his hands up defensively.

"Don't worry, she's fine," he says. "She didn't even realize I was in there." He flips his wrist over and presses a button on his watch. "Girl sleeps like death."

A video display of the inside of Sai's room floats above his watch. In Sai's room, half her body hangs off her bed while she snores loudly with drool running down her cheek. Leon cancels the display before turning to Ren to offer a reassuring smile. "I'll remove the cameras once I leave, just wanted to make sure Saiyonoshi and Blue didn't disturb us."

He is watching Blue, too. Leon was going through a lot of trouble just to get into Ren's room undisturbed. Not fully caring, but wanting to move things along, she asks the question she knows he wants to hear. "So what do you want?"

"Well," Leon whispers, "at first I was hoping to learn what you knew about me and if Saiyonoshi may become more of a problem, but I soon realized neither of you know anything really. You still need a little more time, and with a little more time it is not going to matter anyway. The final stage is quickly approaching."

"So maybe you should be out there prepping rather than in here talking to me," Ren spits.

"Ms. Amano," Leon smiles. "I think you've completely misinterpreted my reason for coming to you tonight. Firstly, I never wanted to kill your sister, but I-"

"What you're doing is too important and can't be stopped, blah blah blah." Ren glares at Leon with hateful eyes. "I heard your bad guy speech before and I'm already getting sick of it." Leon leans closer to Ren and if she had even an inch to move while tied down, she desperately would have taken it.

"What makes you think I'm the bad guy?" he asks. She aggressively rolls her eyes.

"Oh wow, the bad guy that doesn't think he's the bad guy. Now I'm really getting tired of you."

"If you knew why I was doing all this you wouldn't say that." It's subtle, but it's the one time his voice changes. He would normally speak calmly, as if to encourage a sense of ease. That brief shift in his tone, however, reminds Ren that he is dangerous. She tells herself she needs to be careful with what she says, but her body has other ideas.

"I don't need to know your reasons. You're killing people." Ren leans up as far as she can. "You're trying to cause all this hate between users and non-users when there's enough tension between us." Leon's face becomes blank. Ren is surprised to see him look that way. It seems as though she has touched a nerve. He stands from her bed and walks to the corner of the room.

"It was never about hate," Leon whispers. "It's about love." His voice returns to as it was before: calm. Cool. He picks up a small, hard briefcase. "Which brings me to the reason I'm here." He presses a button and a cool mist rises from the briefcase. "Like I said, at first I wanted to see what you knew, but once I realized you didn't really know anything, I became moved by your confession to Saiyonoshi."

"Oh, please," Ren snorts.

"I don't mean that to be antagonizing. I really do think it's nice that you and your sister have such a strong relationship, despite the fact she's a user and you're not. Might I ask what your parents are?"

"Mom's a user, Dad isn't," Ren answers flatly.

"I see," Leon says with a smile. "I envy you. I have no memory of either of my parents, yet both of yours are directly in your life..." He takes a deep breath before continuing. "It's a nice idea, users and non-users coming together. It's just too bad it can never really happen."

"You think you're the only one who got mistreated by users," Ren exclaims, her frustration coming out. "I didn't tell Sai everything, but the things users did to me, the things they said, yeah, it was enough to make me want to hate them, too. But my sister was one and my mom was also, and they always treated me with love. That's when I realized that being a user or a non-user doesn't matter. It's the person that matters."

Leon thinks on this for a moment. Ren's words considered, he continues. "When I was a boy, I was raised alone, without a mother or father to guide me. The other children around me, many of them were users." His gaze drifts to the ground as if he is living through the pain all over again. "Those children, they terrorized us non-users, used their magic for what they felt were harmless pranks; however, as we grew older those pranks became more and more violent, but the users didn't care. They wanted us to know we were inferior, that we would never be as good as they were."

He turns back to Ren. "They were intrinsically better humans than us because genetics deemed it so. They were given preferential treatment and even opportunities us non-users could never hope to have. If it were not for me stumbling across the work of Shanai Desi, I may have let them convince me that I could never be anything more than what I was, that I couldn't have anything more than what I had."

"So what you said is only partially true, Ms. Amano," Leon continues quietly. Ren leans back, listening silently. "It's not just the persecution. That is a given for anybody viewed as weak by a superior party. Your sister went to one of the top magic universities in all of England, correct?"

"Yes..." Ren answers cautiously.

"And where did you go?"

The question hits like a bat. In that moment, she isn't even sure if Leon already knows the answer. Regardless, it doesn't change the truth. "I...I never went to university."

"Really? That's interesting," Leon replies. "Why is that? You are clearly skilled with computers, enough so to have gotten some type of degree. So why didn't you go?"

"I didn't want to."

"You're lying," he says flatly. "I am not your sister. There is no one else here. Tell me the truth. Why didn't you go?" Ren is silent, knowing the answer but not wanting to lend to Leon's argument. Still, her feelings about him aside, she cannot change what happened. She lets out a deep sigh. "Because Mom and Dad wanted to use whatever money they saved to send Sai to that university."

"Really," Leon says as he takes a seat beside her again. "But based on what I've read, Sai's magical prowess must have been enough to secure her a scholarship."

"She did," Ren whispers, "but it was THE magic University. It wasn't enough. Even with my parents' help, Sai still had to take out a few loans."

"And that meant that there was no room to send you to school, too."

Ren says nothing.

"Do you resent her for it?" he asks.

"No!" Ren replies immediately, but then pulls herself back. "But I did at first."

"Why?"

Ren doesn't answer. Leon decides to ask again.

"Why?"

She still doesn't answer. Leon leans in close enough to whisper into her ear. His breath is hot against it and she tries desperately to pull her head away. Try as she might though, she is already stretching the restraints to their maximum allowance.

"Why, Renayaka?"

"Because I didn't understand why she got to go to university just because she was a magic user and I wasn't! I knew the development of magic circuits was important for a magic user to reach their full potential, but I didn't understand why that meant Sai got to have the best education and I got nothing!" Everything bursts from Ren like a flood. The words are out quicker than she can think to say them. She breathes heavily once she has said her piece, as if something squeezing her throat finally decided it was time to let go. Leon nods his head.

"And that's what I'm trying to get rid of," he says, eyes staring at something in his hand, "that inherent advantage given to her simply because she was born 'better.' One sister should never hate the other."

"I didn't hate her..." Ren whispers. Leon is surprised to hear that. He looks at Ren, seeing faint tears in her eyes. "I said I resented her, but I never hated her, and after some time passed, I was happy for her. My sister is great at time magic, and she needed the University to discover that. I was able to teach myself. When I realized that, I couldn't have been happier that my sister got to go to university and I didn't, because I didn't need to."

Leon finds himself briefly without words looking in the eyes of such conviction and truth. There is no doubt that Ren absolutely meant every word she said. He is unable to hold back a smile.

"The world needs more people like you, Renayaka Amano. You are truly one of a kind."

"Never thought I'd say this," she chuckles, "but I agree with you." Leon bursts into laughter and Ren can't help but laugh a little herself. Once the moment passes however, everything calms and the tension slowly returns.

"What are you going to do to me?" Ren asks. She knows he didn't come all this way for a conversation. It's been in the back of her mind since she saw him in her room, and now was the time to face that fact.

"That's just it, Ms. Amano," Leon says calmly, raising his hand. "I wanted to offer you a gift." When Ren sees what he is holding she struggles once more. In his hand is a vial of his modified mana strain, HSAP23.

"Don't you dare put that in me," she says with feigned bravery. Her voice shakes with each word.

"It should be safer now," he offers. "It's almost perfect. I won't be able to see you after today though, so I wanted to give you this now. Ideally, I would have liked a little more time."

"I don't want it!"

"But you do," Leon counters. "You said so yourself, when you talked to your sister about feeling powerless, like you were unable to save her because you weren't a magic user. You said it again when you talked about resenting her for getting opportunities you couldn't have because she was a magic user and you weren't."

"You're twisting my words," Ren stutters. "I'm happy the way I am."

"But you're not, Ms. Amano," Leon says. "And you know it. Sure, you've come to accept the way things are because you felt you had no choice. There was nothing you could do to change it. If you didn't accept that, what else could you do?" He grasps the vial in his hand. "But the world isn't set in stone. It can change." His face is so close their noses are almost touching.

"You no longer have to accept the world for the way it is, but can now begin to see it for what it could be. This is the first step." He lifts his arm, ready to inject Ren in her neck. She pulls and kicks as hard as she can, but the restraints make her outbursts seem like nothing more than the whimpers of a hurt puppy. He places one hand on her head to steady it as he moves the needle towards her.

"Stop it! No! Please don't do this! I don't want it! I don't want it! Please!"

The injection pierces her neck.

"STOP!"

· · · · ●·●·●·● · · ·

Ren jumps from her bed. Light pours into her room from her skylight. She jerks her head around, frantically searching her room. Nothing. Ren is no longer tied to her bed and there is no sign of Leon anywhere. She jumps out of bed and runs to her wall. Diamond patterns appear on it until a full-length mirror is formed. Ren desperately checks her neck all around but there are no puncture marks, no sign she's been injected. A casual knock at her door pulls her from her search.

She doesn't get a moment to answer before the door slides back and Sai barges in, fully dressed. "Hey sis, you're sleeping in late, aren't you?" Ren must have a blank expression on her face because Sai can immediately tell how frazzled she is. Sai moves closer to Ren, eyes wary. "You okay?"

Ren turns back to her mirror. Her eyes conduct one final search of her bare neck, but she sees nothing out of the ordinary. "Yeah...I think so."

"Cool, then let's go!" Sai exclaims, her exuberance returned. "I think that program you set up has finished running. Come on, get dressed. We got a madman to stop!"

"I'll be right out, just let me get my clothes on, will you?" Ren whispers.

"Oh right," Sai replies, "sorry! See ya in a sec!" She leaves, the sliding door closing behind her. Ren turns back to the mirror in disbelief. There is no sign of anything remotely resembling a puncture wound.

"A dream?"

· · · ● · ● · · · ·

Ren steps out into the living room area and on one of her screens is a large green icon with the word "complete" written beneath. She turns to Sai who is doing her very best to not appear as excited as she clearly is. Ren can hear Blue in the kitchen fixing them some breakfast.

"It looks like your search found something," Sai says, eyes almost glittering from anticipation. "I would have looked through the results myself, but I was afraid your computer would blow up or something if I touched it."

"Electrocuted you, not blown up," Ren replies plainly as she takes a seat. "It's expensive to replace monitors and stuff." Sai laughs at Ren's comment then realizes she isn't sure if Ren is joking. Ren types in a few quick keys. The icon disappears and 2 data files appear on the screen simultaneously.

"Is that all?" Sai asks, confused.

"Sadly. It was never going to be that easy to find information on him," Ren replies.

"True," Sai agrees. Blue brings two plates of eggs and toast with jam and places them in front of the girls.

"I have finished making breakfast," Blue states with a smile. Sai eagerly begins eating her portion. "Thanks for breakfast, Blue. I know it was my turn to make it, but I just couldn't focus this morning."

"It is not a problem, Saiyonoshi," Blue smiles, "but dinner is on you." Blue has learned well. Sai isn't entirely happy about the deal but nods her head in agreement. Blue shifts his gaze to the screen. "Will these files be helpful in stopping Leon?"

Ren doesn't answer. It's not that she doesn't hear Blue, but his question doesn't register with her. She stares at the files for a moment, lost in the fog of what happened the night before. She only snaps back once Blue places a hand on her shoulder.

"Renayaka?" he whispers.

"Oh," she replies, "sorry. I spaced out a bit there." She notices the food in front of her, "Thanks for breakfast, Blue."

"No problem," he replies softly, eyes gazing at her with concern.

Ren works while she eats. She doesn't feel like admitting it, but she prefers Blue's breakfast over Sai's. She looks at the two files with Blue and Sai watching over her shoulders, anticipation mounting. "Well," Ren says, "it seems there isn't much in these files." She pulls up a small image of a boy around 4 years old. Sai looks at the image curiously.

"Is that...him?"

"I think so. I calibrated the computer to include possible searches of Leon by creating an algorithm that would essentially de-age the current image we have of him and find any matches that could correlate with a younger version of Leon."

"You essentially searched any child photos of Leon by reversing his age in your program," Blue muses. "That is quite brilliant, Renayaka."

"I know," she says with a smile. "I figured he wasn't always an evil genius, but I expected to find more than just a single photograph."

"What's the photograph from?" Sai asks. Ren clicks the second file from her search. A series of documents emerge from the file.

"It seems like it came from a file a company had about him," Ren explains.

"What company?"

"Some company based in America." Ren looks a little closer and comes across a logo. "Zaradox?" She looks at both Sai and Blue. Neither of them know what Zaradox is.

"Never heard of them."

"I cannot say that I have either."

"Well, according to this," Ren continues, "Zaradox was decommissioned 20 years ago. Leon was under study at the company for some project, but it doesn't say why they were studying him or what the project was. The information seems to have been wiped, most likely to prevent hackers like me from finding too much." Sai throws her hands in the air as she makes her way over to a chair to fall into.

"Great," she says, slouching into her seat, "and since America's closed itself off there's no way for us talk to anybody about the project. Another dead end."

Ren agrees. There isn't much more to pull from this thread. The two girls sit in silence as they try to figure out their next move. Blue is lost in thought too, but comes to a revelation.

"Perhaps not," he says, getting the attention of both Ren and Sai. "Renayaka, would it be possible to run a search of the company's employees during the time that Leon would have been there within a margin of 5 years?"

Ren's eyes get wide, realizing what Blue is asking. She quickly turns back to her computer. "That's genius, Blue, so based on his current age I can theorize the year this photo was taken within a margin of error of 5 years and be able to pinpoint which employees may have been at the Zaradox company during that time."

"I see," Sai says, understanding the logic. "That is smart. This way, we'll be able to see if any of those employees from then are currently in the UK. It's a longshot, but what the hell." She jumps from her seat and hugs Blue. "You're the freakin' best!"

"I believe in situations such as this, Renayaka would reply with, 'I know.'" Blue's joke and genuine smile prompt Sai to turn and admonish her sister.

"You're a horrible influence," she says.

"Better than you," Ren replies without even looking away from her monitors. "Got it!" She leans back, satisfied with herself. "One Julio Kim, a former employee of Zaradox who apparently has a small ranch about 2 hours south of here. There's an address, but no number on file." Ren turns to the others with a cocky grin. "And he would have been there around the same time as Leon."

"Yes!" Sai exclaims, "two hours is nothing! We can go today!"

"True," Blue says cautiously, "but are we entirely sure that the child in this photo is Leon?"

"My program isn't perfect," Ren says, "but it's all we've got. Even if it's a long shot, we have to take it."

"That's right, Ren," Sai agrees. "Alright, Blue, let's get ready to-" Sai freezes. Ren looks up to see both Sai and Blue staring at her.

"Um, you guys alright?" she asks.

"R-Ren," Sai stutters, pointing at her. "What's that?" That's when Ren realizes they're not staring at her, but something behind her. She turns to see a small, floating mirror. It reflects the entire room and there is a bright magical glyph hovering beneath it. Normally, strange magic wouldn't be all that shocking. Surprising, yes, but not shocking.

What makes Ren's blood turn to ice, though, are her glowing hands.

"No," she whispers, quickly turning back to Blue and Sai. "There's something I need to tell you two…"

CHAPTER THIRTEEN

UNKNOWN WORLD

"So he was here," Sai repeats, boiling with anger, "in our flat?" She gets even more upset when she says the next part. "In our rooms?" Blue stands off to the side, quiet.

"Yeah," Ren whispers, "he said he wanted to give me a gift..."

The images of all the dead bodies are all Sai can think about, and the idea that her sister could end up just like them is too much for her to handle. "We have to take you to the hospital," Sai exclaims, ready to leave that moment. "Right now!"

"I'm fine, Sai," Ren assures, "I don't feel like anything is wrong with me."

"Doesn't matter," Sai says, trying to hold back both her rage and fear. "The guy who attacked Sylarus Park was fine until he started bleeding from his eyes and died."

"That was an older version of the strain, this may be different." Ren quietly offers this suggestion, but Sai does not care for it.

"I won't take that chance," she replies. "I won't let anything happen to you, so we are going to the hos-"

"There's no time!" The shout surprises both Blue and Sai. From the look on her face, it seems to have even surprised

Ren herself. She lowers her head. "There's no time, Sai." Sai kneels down in front of Ren. She looks up into her sister's eyes. "Leon said that he needed to give me the injection last night because he wouldn't have another chance." Sai understands the implication but it is Blue that says it aloud.

"Leon is approaching his endgame."

Ren nods at Blue in agreement. "And whatever that is, it can't be good." She turns back to Sai, who is having trouble looking her sister in the eyes. "Blue was right earlier about our lead. It's thin, but we need to understand how Leon was able to block your magic if you're going to have even a chance of beating him. If this Zaradox guy doesn't give us anything useful, then you are going to need me to help find another way to stop him." Ren places a hand on top of Sai's head. Sai looks up, seeing Ren's slight smile. "I can't be laid up in a hospital for that."

Sai lowers her head again as a tear escapes from her eye. She quickly wipes it away. "Fine," she says, tilting her head up to look at Ren. "Let's go see this Julio guy, but you're coming with me."

Ren hesitates. "I think I may be better he-"

"You either come with me so I can keep an eye on you, or you go to the hospital and that's the only negotiation there is." Sai is stern. It's not often that Ren is impressed by Sai, but in this moment, it shows on her face.

"Since when did you become the big sister," she laughs. Sai forces a smile back at Ren. "Alright," Ren agrees. "I'll go with you to see Julio." Sai nods her head in relief and gives her sister a hug. Sai holds her harder than she ever has before, as if this is the last time she'll be able to. When she is finally able to force herself to let Ren go, she helps her up and they head out the door. They have lost time to make up, and every second counts.

"Sorry, Blue, but-" she shouts back, already down the steps dragging Ren behind.

"I will watch the place," he replies, "stay here in case Leon returns or Dane gets any important information for the case."

"Thanks, Blue!" Sai turns back to Ren. Ren shrugs her shoulders. "Well, sis, you ready for a road trip?"

· · ● · ● ● · · ·

Leon sits inside a large mansion. There are various beakers, vials, and equipment set up around him. The mansion has been retrofitted into a unique lab. He tinkers with a hovering display in front of him until he steps back to take a full look at it. After reviewing everything, a satisfied grin creeps across his face.

"Yes," he whispers, "this is it."

"Sir?" A voice whispers from behind Leon.

A young man stands in front of a group of people that are gathered behind Leon. Each looks to him as if he is the answer to a burning question they've had their entire lives. He looks to them the same. "No need to call me sir," he says.

"I-I'm sorry," says the young man nervously.

"No problem at all," Leon replies. He moves over to the young man and places a hand on his shoulder. "I appreciate each and every one of you being here." He looks at the group of people around him. About fifteen different men and women eagerly watch him. "We are going to change the world," he continues, "and all of you are going to be there to help me do it."

· · ● · ● ● · · ·

The auto-driving car they're in takes Ren and Sai through the countryside. With the windows down, Ren leans out one side with her hair blowing in the wind and the sun shining radiantly on her face. She can't remember the last time she was outside in this way, but with the feel of the wind and the sun, she almost forgets why she never steps out of the house. She glances over at Sai. She has her window up and leans against it while watching the scenery pass her by.

"I hate outdoors but I have to admit," Ren says, "this is nice." A thought comes across her mind. "Do you even remember the last time the two of us went on a road trip?" Sai stares off into the distance, seeming to search for the answer out in the grass.

"There was that time we went to meet Mom and Dad in Holland," Sai replies. "We spent the entire trip playing video games, though."

"Yeah," Ren laughs, "but it did make the trip go by faster." Sai smirks, too. Ren stares at Sai long and hard, watching her looking out into the surroundings. "It's strange," Ren continues, "right now, I don't think I'd mind if the trip took a little longer." Sai looks back at Ren and can't hold back her surprise at seeing a genuinely happy smile spread across her face. Sai nods in agreement.

"Same."

Ren takes a deep breath, looking down at her hand. "At least then I'd have more time to figure out what this is?" A small two-sided mirror floats above her open palm. Beneath the mirror spins a circular, magical glyph slightly elevated above Ren's relaxed hand. Through the mirror, Ren can see the reflection of Sai on the other side of the car. She raises her hand to get a better look at the opposite side of the mirror.

"It's strange though," she says. "The image is the same on both sides. You'd think it would reflect whatever image was on either side." Sai looks over at the floating mirror. It turns in Ren's hand, but the image does not adjust perspective. It continues to reflect Sai as though it was facing her straight on even though it is turning to different angles. When the back of the mirror shows, it is the same as the front.

"It's a form of transmutation magic," Sai explains. "It's one of the more confusing magic studies because each person that specializes in it is only ever able to transmute one basic object. That object then reflects a power usually associated with an idea, or desire, the magic user values." An evil grin spreads across Ren's face, one that makes Sai uneasy. "What is it?"

"Reflects." Ren smirks. Sai rolls her eyes.

"That was NOT intentional."

"Those are the best ones." Ren studies the small hand mirror with intrigue. "The desire of the user, huh?"

"That's right," Sai yawns, the length of the trip starting to affect her. "One person was able to transmute a ball. That ball then made it so that any two people hit with it would develop a strong hate for each other." Ren's eyes grow big, fascinated.

"No way."

"Yeah. Transmutation magic can be the most versatile magic, but it can also be the most unpredictable." Sai turns her attention back to the world passing by on the outside.

Ren can't pull her gaze away from the mirror. She watches it turn with such intrigue. "What are you?" she asks aloud. She lifts her finger and softly taps the top of the mirror once with her fingertip. Nothing. She taps once more.

While watching the scenery pass by, Sai winces in discomfort. She rubs her head in an attempt to ease it away as the car continues closer to Julio Kim and hopefully, for the two girls, answers.

• • • ● • ● • ● • • •

The car pulls up outside an old-looking ranch complete with cows, chickens, and other assorted farm animals. As Sai and Ren step out of the car, they both can't help but be astonished by their surroundings. "Why do I feel like I just stepped out of a time machine?" Ren wonders aloud.

She's right. No matter which direction Sai looks, she can see a simple truth. "I don't see a single bit of technology anywhere." The idea that people like this exist confounds her. "I bet this is one of those people that doesn't even have a digi-data device."

"Probably not," Ren says, approaching the door. She gets ready to knock, but suddenly stops. She turns to Sai and steps aside so that she can knock instead.

"Why do I have to knock?" Sai asks, fully knowing the reason.

"Because if this hick has a shotgun and decides to shoot whoever comes onto his property, at least you can revive."

"I thought you didn't like seeing me die." Sai says sarcastically as she knocks on the door.

"I don't," Ren replies flatly, "but I can appreciate the fact that you can afford to, and I can't..." The two wait, struggling to hear if there is any movement inside. Eventually, there are footsteps on the other side of the door. The door creaks slightly open. A man peeks through the crack. It's not much, but enough that Sai can make out key features. He is an older man, worn beyond his years, with dry skin the color of fine maple and matted hair. "Can I help you?" Despite the gruffness of his voice, his eyes betray a softness his body actively rejects.

"Hey," Sai waves, "we would have called first if you had a phone or anything from this century, but we-"

"Excuse us, sir," Ren interrupts, "but we were looking for a Julio Kim."

"What do you want from me?"

"We were hoping to talk to you about a project you worked on a few years ago. We're students doing a report on the Zaradox Corporation in America."

"Zaradox?" The word triggers something in Julio. It is not fear or anger, but interest. "One moment." He closes the door. Ren hits Sai in the back of her head almost simultaneously.

"What?!" Sai winces, grabbing at her head in pain. Ren hit her harder than normal.

"Seriously, Sai?" Ren says, shaking her head.

"That's why I wanted you to knock," Sai shrugs. "What kind of person doesn't even have a holo-phone?" Latches unlock on the other side of the door. There are a lot for someone living in the middle of nowhere. The door swings open. "Come on in," Julio says. Now able to get a better look, Sai can see he is a man of small stature, not much taller than either of the girls. He has a scruffy beard, one that looks desperate to escape his chin. He wears clothing one would expect on someone half his age but surprisingly, they suit him well.

Ren moves past Sai into the house, pointing her finger at Sai sternly. "Behave."

Sai rolls her eyes. The girl who never talks to people is telling *her* to behave. "This is exactly why I never bring you on cases..." She closes the door behind them.

"Can I get you anything?" Julio asks. "I don't have much in the way of drinks but I do have some tea if you want some."

The inside appears ancient. Sai can see no indication of any technology whatsoever. The lights in the room glow by means of basic electricity, but there's no holo-display pad for the interior appearance, no computer, no floating media display.

And no way for them to contact anyone should things go poorly.

Her eyes shift to the wall unit beside the kitchen Julio enters. It is lined with books. From what Sai can see, there are a variety of sorts, but her study of the shelf comes to a screeching halt when she notices something on the wall above it. She may be a city girl and she may have only seen one before in a museum, but even she knows an antique hunting rifle when she sees one.

Her eyes dart to Ren but she's already noticed it too. Most likely someone this removed from technology wouldn't have anti-magic bullets, but the threat of possibly being shot at refuses to set Ren's mind at ease.

"Um, no, thank you. We're okay." Ren politely declines the offer.

"Suit yourself," he says. "Have a seat." He grabs some tea for himself and takes a seat in a chair across from Sai and Ren, who both sit on an old couch. "So," he says after taking a sip, "Zaradox. Not a name I've heard in a long time."

"Yeah, well," Ren explains, "while researching it, your name came up as someone who used to work there." Ren flips her wrists over. A holo-image of the young Leon floats above it. There is no reaction from Julio to seeing the picture. "You see, our report is centered around this boy, who would have been a subject of study during your time at the company. We were hoping you could tell us anything you could about him or your research, if you're able to of course."

Julio leans in closer, trying to get a better look at the image. After proper study, he sits back in the chair. "I don't know the kid," he says. "There were a lot of kids that came through the program while I was working there."

"What kind of program was it?" Ren asks politely.

Julio doesn't immediately respond; rather, he looks slowly back and forth between Ren and Sai. "Why don't you tell me what it is you're really doing here." Sai and Ren steal a glance at each other. "Zaradox is a company that specializes in some truly unique projects. Not many people know about them, and those that do, know exactly what it is they do there. Neither of you seem to have any idea though. You two magic users?"

"Um," Ren pauses and exchanges a nervous look with Sai. This may not have been a good idea. Sai looks back at the gun on the wall and does some quick theorizing about if she can get to the hopefully unloaded gun before he can.

"I'm not going to hurt you or anything," Julio says. "I want to help you, but I don't want to be lied to. Are you both magic users?"

"Yes..." Ren replies, "well, no. Uh, kind of?"

"It shows." he says, rising to his feet. "Did you know there are more magic users collected in England than any other place in the world? It is one of the few places where magic users, non-users, and even androids can live together in relative peace." He walks over to a bookshelf in the back corner of the living room. "The unfortunate thing is that it acts like a bubble to what is going on in the rest of the world." The way he moves is different than before. There is such assuredness and confidence in each step. During his prime, this man must truly have been a formidable intellect.

"Zaradox is a company that has a sole specialty," he continues. "For neither of you to know that shows me you truly have no idea what Zaradox is."

Ren's eyes shift to Sai. "You two would get along."

"I'll ask you again," Julio says, "why are you looking into Zaradox?"

"Well, we-" Ren starts.

"We're trying to stop a madman and we think Zaradox may be able to give us answers how!" Sai comes right out with it. She has had it with trying to be sneaky and tactful. She gives Ren a shrug. "We don't have time." Ren may not be happy with the outburst, but ultimately agrees with Sai.

"Very well." Julio speaks in a voice that has remained completely relaxed. "Why don't you show me that picture again?" Ren pulls up the holo-image once more. Julio gives it a harder look this time around. He returns to his bookshelves and runs his fingers along the spines of the books. Sai stares at him, utterly astonished. She leans close to Ren and whispers, "Who has hard books in this day and age?"

"Shsh!" Ren demands.

Julio pulls a book from the shelf, one that is large and heavy. He flips through its pages until he lands on what he is looking for. "I don't know about the boy, but he does share the same rare genetic trait as a coworker I used to know."

"Rare trait?" Sai turns to Ren for an explanation but even she has no idea what he's referring too. "Zoom in on the image," Julio explains, "you'll see the boy has a thin red slit over his right pupil." Ren quickly enlarges the image to zoom in on the boy's right eye. The girls hadn't noticed it before, but the slit is there at the lower edge of his pupil. Sai quickly punches in buttons on her watch and the image she recorded of Leon floats in front of her. She freezes it, then zooms into his right eye. The exact same slit is there in the exact same place. That confirms it. This child is definitely him.

With the book held open, Julio walks over and hands it to Ren, finger pressed to a specific part of the page. Ren and Sai look at it. It is filled with many tiny pictures similar to what one would find in a yearbook. Their focus falls on the picture Julio's finger rests on and they see a familiar face. Neither of them can believe it.

"Shanai Desi!" Ren exclaims. The look on Julio's face shows no recognition. He takes his seat again. "I don't know any Shanai Desi," he says, getting comfortable. "That's Ailaine Shakar. It's hard to see in that photo because of her eye color, but if you look closely, she has the same genetic trait present in her right eye." He's right. It looks as though her iris bleeds ever so slightly into her pupil. Sai and Ren stare at the photo in bewilderment. It is absolutely the same woman they researched before. She looks younger and her hair is slightly different, but there is no mistaking that this woman and Shanai Desi are the same. "What is it?" Ren asks.

"It's a hereditary mutation that's passed down certain genetic trees. We used to find it fascinating. Ailaine worked for Zaradox at the same time I did," Julio states. "I remember she had a kid while working there. Considering the rarity of that mutation, maybe that's the same person in your photo."

As if Ren is still not entirely convinced, she pulls up a photo she saved on her watch of Shanai Desi. Just as with Leon, a closer look shows her with the exact same genetic trait in the exact same place. It's true. Shanai and Ailaine are the same person. The two stare at the images of Leon and Shanai Desi side by side. "Well, that certainly looks like Ailaine." Julio remarks after studying the image himself.

"This can't be a coincidence, right?" Ren asks Sai.

"I don't know," she answers, "there were no records of Shanai having a kid."

Julio leans forward in his chair, prepared to offer an explanation. "If the two people we are talking about are the same, I may know why." The girls eagerly listen.

"Ailaine's son was entered into the program at Zaradox. He was being observed and studied, along with a few other children. After some time, I remember Ailaine leaving the company and taking her son with her." Julio's eyes narrow and his voice lowers. "But the thing is Zaradox is not a company you just leave, especially when you hold something they're interested in."

"They wanted her son," Sai says flatly.

"Correct," Julio continues, "and they were not about to let him just leave. Last I heard, both she and her kid were killed not long after escaping. If the woman in that picture is the same as this Shanai," he says, pointing at Ren's holo-display, "then I would not be surprised if Ailaine found a way to get a whole new identity for herself and her son. If anyone could do it, she could."

"But," Ren repeats, "there is no record of her having a son."

"Probably thought he'd have a better chance at a normal life if he wasn't around a woman with a target on her back." Julio takes a sip of his tea. "It's sweet actually. She thought the kid would be better off on his own. Can't say she was wrong. Zaradox would have searched feverishly for that kid."

"Sai," Ren says, getting her attention, "when Leon came to me he mentioned not having any memory of his parents. Maybe she had something to do with that? Maybe she did something to him."

"Regardless, he grew up to be a very dangerous man," Sai exclaims. "Leon is not only smart, but he has the ability to negate the spells of magic users without needing spells or anti-magic weapons. Did she do that to him too, or was that Zaradox?" Julio immediately starts laughing. Sai doesn't think she said anything ridiculous, and Ren doesn't understand either.

"Kid, Zaradox didn't do anything to that boy. Nature did." Julio stands and approaches the window on the other side of the room. Once there, he turns to face the girls. His face is calm, serene. He looks at them and the room begins to shake. Suddenly, the furniture around them, the books on the shelves, Julio's tea, everything begins to float in mid-air.

Sai and Ren shoot to their feet. What they are seeing is impossible, and even Ren, who did not live the life of a magic user, can tell as well. There were no spells, no glyphs.

"Wha-wha," Sai stutters, "what's going on?" Ren stares at Julio but he simply stands calmly with a smile. "A-are you doing this?" she asks. Julio stretches out his hand and his tea floats to him. He grabs it out of the air and takes a sip.

"That's impossible!" Sai exclaims. "There are no magic sigils, no incantation, no spell mediums…" Sai gazes at Julio, perplexed. "How are you casting such a large scale levitation spell?"

Julio smirks. "There's an entire world out there you girls know nothing about…"

· · · · ● · ● · · · ·

The car drives Ren and Sai back towards their flat in the city. Neither say a word. Sai is completely drained of energy. She slouches over in the car, staring at the floor while the car moves through the countryside. It's Ren who finally decides to break the silence.

"I-I can't believe," she whispers. "All this time. Who would have thought that you-"

"I don't want to talk about it," Sai interrupts. Ren nods in understanding, and turns her attention to the outside world. "Well," Ren replies, "at least now we know more about Leon."

"And that we basically can't stop him," Sai retorts, defeated. "There's nothing we can do about his magic negation."

"Maybe," Ren thinks aloud, "but this is new for both of us. We just need to look a little more into this."

"If we had more time, sure," Sai exclaims, "but we need to stop him as soon as we can!" The two girls grow silent, the events of the evening weigh on them with each passing moment.

"You're right," Ren agrees, "but at least we know more about...you know..." Ren leans in. She's never seen Sai this dejected before. Sure, she would get frustrated with cases, but this, this was new. "Are you okay?"

"I will be," she answers, choosing to lean back and close her eyes. "One thing at a time. First, we stop Leon. We can deal with everything else after that."

"Right," Ren agrees, leaning back as well. "Still, I'm excited to tell Blue. I wonder what his reaction will be."

The countryside is just as beautiful as when they first passed it. The trees are a shade of green not normally seen in the city. There are wild animals roaming free, and a sky more peaceful than ever, and Sai doesn't see any of it. In this moment, she has no capacity to see the world, for the world in her mind shrouds everything in a dreary fog.

"Yeah..."

Chapter Fourteen

A Life Never Lived

Blue walks through the city streets carrying bags filled with groceries. Everything is peaceful for him. The thought that Saiyonoshi and Renayaka get to spend some time together after their fight fills him with hope. He observes the contents in his bag and finds everything satisfactory.

"It will be a fine meal tonight," he says to himself. "I am sure the girls will love it." Blue turns the corner and notices something that brings him to a stop. On the stairs of his flat stand Carter and all three of his friends, waiting. When Blue sees the crowbars and pipes they are holding he knows exactly what their intentions are. Two of them, Eyesore and Dot, whisper to themselves, a strange action Blue takes note of.

"Hey, toaster," Carter says with a smile. "You making me dinner?"

Blue lowers his head, electing to ignore Carter. He attempts to make his way to the steps, but Carter's friend, Lipman, blocks his path. Lipman's bruise has healed nicely.

"Can't let you by, mate," Lipman states. Blue does not feel like dealing with this.

"Might I ask what you want from me?" he asks. Carter steps close to Blue.

"You embarrassed me the other day," Carter says. "You're gonna have to pay for that."

"Why?" Blue asks.

"Why?!" Carter repeats. It was not an unreasonable question, yet Carter is confused by it.

"Yes, why?" Blue has known true frustration only a few times in his life, but the very human emotion flows through his body now. "I believe that you got what you deserved for bothering someone who did not want to be bothered."

"Someone?" Carter turns to his friends, an action that directs them to laugh as a conductor would direct a band. "This toaster still doesn't get it. We didn't bother someone, we bothered some*thing*. And some*thing* can't have feelings, or rights, or anything for that matter." Carter steps closer. "You're not a goddamn person. We are."

"I disagree," Blue remarks, doing his very best to stay cordial. "There is an old adage 'I think, therefore I am.' I believe that I simply am, and that makes me as much of a person as you are."

"You are fucking ridiculous, toaster." Carter spits.

"I would appreciate it if you would stop calling me that."

"And I'd appreciate it if you just shut the fuck up and let us have a little fun. You may have caught us by surprise last time, but this time, we are going to fuck. You. Up."

"I cannot allow that. I will not allow that." Blue places the groceries on the ground beside him. "You see," he goes on to clarify. "My friends are going to be home soon, and I would like to have dinner at least partially ready for them; therefore, if you intend to impede that or attempt to harm me, I will defend myself in as non-fatal a way as possible."

"That's awfully kind of you," Carter laughs. "We have no intention of doing the same for you. This will be as fatal as possible." Holding the pipe in his hand, Carter pulls his arm back and brings it down on Blue. Blue effortlessly steps to the side.

"You should know that I just filed a report with the SPMD," he says calmly. "They are currently on their way."

"I don't give a fuck," Carter yells. He looks at his friends. "Get him!" Eyesore stops whispering to himself and the pipe he's holding glows brightly. That explains it. He and Dot are magic users.

Blue's motions are distinct, precise. He moves with a purpose most cannot match. Eyesore swings at Blue. Blue swiftly dodges. The pipe leaves a crater in the ground. Through the floating debris Blue can see Dot complete his incantation. His crowbar takes the shape of a sword.

Dot swipes at Blue. The narrow stairs almost keep him from backstepping. He does, but the blade cuts across his chest. Pieces of clothing peel away into the air. Blue steps off the stairs to give himself more room to maneuver. Lipman is on him. Even a normal crowbar can still do damage, but this one is far from normal. He steps away. The crowbar misses again but pain registers in Blue's back. Carter pulls back to hit Blue again. Blue keeps his balance but throws Carter off his. Carter is flipped to the ground before he can think. More pain registers: a cut on his cheek, a hit to his leg, minor hits, but aggressive attacks.

Another sword swing. Blue ducks with impressive body contortion. Lipman and Eyesore are back on him. Blue dodges both, but Dot is ready with his sword again. There is no time to move. Blue catches the sword with his bare hands. The skin covering his metal hands shred away. Blue uses the sword to block Eyesore's magic pipe. The pipe breaks through the sword and Blue plants Dot into a wall with a kick. He does not get back up.

Carter finally gets back to his feet, clearly the weakest fighter in the group. He swings at Blue wildly. "Fuck you,

you fucking android!" Blue dodges easily, sparing a moment of pity for the small human. The pity is fleeting. He flips Carter into the ground once more. Eyesore brings his pipe down from above. Blue can move, but Carter is in the direct path. Blue shifts backwards, but also grabs Carter by the leg. The pipe crushes concrete instead of Carter's head. It is a kindness to the city cleaners, not Carter.

Eyesore swings just as wildly as Carter did. His prior form is gone. Only frustration remains. Form brings challenge, frustration courts defeat. Lipman swings at Blue, too. The two aren't used to fighting as a team. Another missed swing. Lipman is off balance and in the path of Eyesore's next attack. Blue trips Lipman. He loses a few tufts of hair but keeps his brains in his head. Blue dodges to the ground too and in one swift motion kicks Lipman into Eyesore's legs. It's more force than he wanted. Lipman rolls into the bumper of a parked car and Eyesore falls headfirst to the concrete. His magical pipe bounces from the ground and collides with his face.

Blood erupts from Eyesore's head and he completely stops moving. Blue rushes to check his vitals. There is still a pulse. Eyesore is hurt, but alive. Blue lets out a sigh of relief.

"Just unconscious," he says to himself. "Good." Carter however, does not see it that way. He lashes out at Blue with immense rage.

"You bastard android!" Carter charges at Blue. "You killed him!" Blue raises his hands, ready to defend himself, but before Carter can reach him they hear a loud noise.

"Stop where you are!" The voice comes through a loudspeaker. They both turn to see two SPMD officers standing in front of them: Officer Jones and Officer Teloh.

Officer Jones lowers his wrist and closes the app that made his voice boom like a loudspeaker. He looks at both

Blue and Carter, then back to Blue. "Why am I not surprised to see you here, android?"

· · · ● · ● · · · ·

Blue retakes a passive stance as he attempts to explain the situation to the officer. "Officer Jones…" he begins, but stops abruptly. Officer Jones' eyes dart to each of the unconscious men on the street. He turns to Carter. "Get out of here, and take care of your pals." Teloh shoots a glance his partner's way, but Jones doesn't even blink. Carter reluctantly backs away. He attempts to wake Lipman while the others come to on their own. Carter realizes that Eyesore is still alive, just with a bloody head. He helps him to his feet once he starts to stir. They all walk away but Carter still takes one last hateful look at Blue before moving on.

"Now…" Jones continues, "as for you." Jones pulls out his gun. Teloh jumps more than Blue, who slowly raises his hands in surrender.

"Wha-what are you doing, Jones?" Teloh asks.

"Shut up, cadet." Jones says, keeping his gun trained on Blue. He walks closer to him. Blue remains calm but is more than a little uncomfortable about having a gun pointing at his face. "What did you do?"

"I did not mean to hurt them," Blue again tries to explain. "I just wanted to keep them from hurting me."

"Right, and you decided the best way to do that was busting one of their heads open?"

"That…that was an accident. I only wanted to defend myself."

"Or maybe you wanted to remind a few humans how superior you are to them."

"That was not my intention," Blue explains. "They attacked me."

"Sure they did." Jones rolls his eyes.

"Sir," Teloh tries again, appealing to his partner, "what are you doing?" Jones ignores him.

"You androids are all the same," he continues. "You blend into our society, all the while taking over every aspect of it. You killed all those people back then, and you're biding your time so that you can do it again."

"I never killed anybody," Blue says. "I never hurt a single human during the war."

"You're a goddamn liar!" Jones places the gun right up to Blue's face. He flicks a switch on the side of the gun. *Anti-machinery mode enabled.*

"JONES!" Teloh shouts, no longer able to remain calm. Jones turns to him, not a word uttered. "We need to take him and those other men in for questioning," Teloh pleads. "We need to find out what happened here. We have to do what's right." Jones hears him but has no interest in listening. With each passing second the rage inside him seeps out. Against all odds, he briefly lower his gun and his next words to Teloh come more measured than what even Blue expects.

"You see an android defending itself against humans, but I only see one group with their blood on the ground." Jones looks directly into Teloh's eyes. The rage is there, but so is something else. Blue cannot see Jones' eyes clearly, but based on his body language the emotion is clear to Blue: sadness. "Making you feel like they could never hurt you, that's when you die, cadet."

Teloh can offer no rebuttal. His gaze moves from Jones to the blood on the ground and back to Blue. With the slightest movement Teloh instinctually raises his hand to his own gun. The moment is brief, and when Teloh notices his own action he quickly pulls his hand back to his side. He glances at Blue to see if he noticed. Blue's disappointed smile says it all and Teloh quickly averts his eyes. Jones, however, holds firm, as raises his gun once more.

"What the hell is going on?!" Ren shouts.

• • • ● • ● • • •

Sai and Ren rush from their cab. Neither of them expected to find Blue with a gun pointed at him by an officer.

"What are you doing, officer?!" Sai exclaims.

"This your android?" Jones asks.

"He's our friend!" Ren pleads.

"Hm," Jones snorts, "your android was involved in an assault, almost killed a human." Jones motions to the area in front of their flat. A quick look around and they know he's telling the truth. From the looks of it, Blue really hurt his attackers. The large blood splatter on the ground sets Sai and Ren on edge.

"It was an accident," Blue whispers. "I did not mean for him to get hurt." Ren's eyes fill with water. The sight of Blue with a gun to his head is almost too much to bear.

"Listen," Sai says, trying to de-escalate the situation. "My name is Saiyonoshi Amano. My uncle is Chief Inspector Dane Amano. Call him and we can sort this out." Jones does not budge.

"Officer Jones!" Teloh shouts once more. Jones turns back to him. "Please, sir, let's call the Chief Inspector." Jones stares at the two girls. Both are still as statues, focused on every movement of Jones as if Blue's life depended on it. Neither wants to make any move that could threaten the officer, or Blue, and Blue has definitely come to that same conclusion himself.

"Fine," Jones says, lowering his gun but still looking Blue in the eyes. "Call the Chief Inspector. See if he has some property that's been malfunctioning." Blue does not react to the bait, and continues to hold his arms up. "Don't go anywhere, toaster." Jones turns his back on Blue. Teloh, Sai, and Ren all breathe a sigh of relief. Blue himself is also relieved. Ren has never been so thankful for her sister's quick thinking, because Ren couldn't see past the gun.

Feeling as though the danger has passed, she smiles at Blue. He returns her smile. He turns when he spots the groceries on the ground. The bag must have been knocked over during the fight. The food contents inside are all across the ground. He leans down to place them securely back in the bag. Teloh catches the movement out of the corner of his eye.

"Jones, look out!"

Jones pulls his gun on Blue.

"No, stop!" Ren runs towards them.

BTANG!

She stops and it's as if the entire world slows to a crawl. She can see everything so clearly. She can see the look on Blue's face. She can see the moment he looks down. She can see the moment he notices the large hole inside his abdomen area. She can see him look at her and Sai. She knows he can see their tears. He has none himself, but she can see his surprise and his confusion. But mainly...

She can see his fear.

It's the last thing she sees before the side of his face disappears.

BTANG! BTANG! BTANG!

Jones fires four times. Gear parts and inner fluid coat the concrete. Blue slouches to the ground, hunched over, no longer moving.

"BLUE!" Neither Sai nor Ren are able to keep themselves from running to him. They fall to the ground with him, trying to turn him over to a more comfortable position and help him.

Jones stares at the groceries at his feet. He turns his gaze to a horrified Teloh, who has become nothing more than a stammering mess on the ground. "I...a weapon...I thou-"

"Do you see any goddamn fucking weapon?!" Ren's eyes are red and her temper is hot. She holds what remains of Blue's head in her hands. She turns quickly to her sister. "Sai!"

"I know," Sai says, already putting a number into her wrist device. "Hello," she says after her holo connects. "I have an android in need of immediate repair at 111 D Baker Street!" Sai moves away to continue the call and give details to the company dialed while Ren stays with Blue. She rocks his head side to side, never taking her eyes off him.

"It's alright, Blue," she whispers. "It'll be okay. Just stay with us and we'll get you fixed right up. It'll be okay. I promise it will. I promise." There is no response. As Ren looks into his one remaining eye, she sees the light in it slowly blink out and go dark.

"Blue?"

Nothing.

"No, no, no. Blue come on," Ren pleads, "you gotta be okay. You have to be. You can't go, you just can't. You're our brother, you're our family. You can't go..." The tears fall from Ren's face more than she can help. Sai notices what her sister just confirmed. She drops her wrist as the person on the other end of her call asks for more information. Sai's knees give out and she falls to the ground. Unable to walk, she crawls over to Ren.

"No," Sai whispers to herself. "No..." Sai's own eyes fill with tears. She reaches her sister with one hand and touches Blue's face with the other. The dam comes down and the tears fall uncontrollably. She throws her face into Blue's chest. "Blue..." Ren wraps her arm around her sister's head as the two of them sit there embracing Blue. Ren stares down at her baby sister sobbing immensely into Blue's chest before her eyes shift up towards Officer Jones. He does not appear overly beat up about Blue's death. In fact, he looks completely fine. Ren feels something inside her change.

"You…" Ren rises to her feet as a zombie would from a grave. She lowers both her sister and Blue softly to the ground. Teloh may have said the words, but Jones, he's the one who pulled the trigger.

Officer Jones attempts to grab the attention of Officer Teloh, who stutters inaudibly over and over. "Call it in." Jones says. Teloh doesn't move. "Call it in, cadet!" Teloh rushes back to the car. Jones lets out a sigh and turns back to the android corpse he just made. He is met with a firm fist to his face.

Jones hits the ground hard. Ren stands above him, rage where tears once fell. She is not herself. She is not thinking. She does not care about the consequences. Her friend is gone and the person responsible is still here. That does not seem right. Wind picks up around her. Sai notices and glances up from Blue's body. "Renayaka?"

A white magic glyph appears at Ren's feet. She steps over it, towards Jones. She gets on top of him. She punches him in the face again. His head bounces off the concrete she hits him so hard. She swings fist after fist, and blood erupts from his nose, lips, and head.

"Ren!" Sai jumps away from Blue. She runs over to her sister. Ren hits the officer over and over again as he attempts to block her strikes with his arms. "Ren, stop!" Sai goes to grab her just as the officer moves his feet in between himself and Ren's chest. He kicks her off of him and into Sai. The two land on the other side of the white glyph on the ground. They look up to see Jones now pointing a gun at them. Ren can feel Sai trembling but Ren feels only one singular emotion: hate. She glares up the barrel of the gun into Jones' eyes. There is hesitation in them. It's not enough for her and she wants him to know. There are no words, but he receives her message loud and clear. She would find a way, legally or otherwise to destroy him. She would be his undoing and there was only one way to stop her.

BTANG! BTANG! BTANG!

Sai and Ren hold each other and squeeze their eyes shut. Nothing. They heard the shots, but slowly realize they aren't hurt. They open their eyes to see a floating mirror hovering above the glyph in front of them. In the mirror, reflected back at them, is the image of a bloody faced Jones, pointing a gun at them. On the other side of the mirror, the side facing Jones, the same thing is reflected; however, on his side, are three fresh bullet holes. Each of the bullet holes cover parts of Jones' reflection. Time seems to stand still for a moment, until slowly, the mirror itself begins to bleed.

Thin blood slowly seeps from each of the bullet holes in the mirror. The girls can see this from their side as well. Jones looks on in confusion until he coughs. Blood drools from his mouth to the ground in front of him. He looks down in shock. There are three bullet holes in his body in the exact same places the bullet holes reside in the reflection of the mirror.

Blood seeps from the holes in his body in the same manner as it does from the mirror and after another cough, he falls over and ceases all movement. Sai lets out a deep breath, hugging Ren tightly. They're alive but something is wrong.

"Sai?" Ren whispers, her voice shaky. Sai looks up just as Ren turns to face her. Blood slowly drains from Ren's eyes like tears. She can see the fear in Sai's eyes before Ren slouches over, her body still.

"No, Ren!" Sai adjusts herself to hold Ren as she touches her face, trying desperately to wake her up. The last thing

Ren hears before losing consciousness are the cries of her sister screaming as high as her lungs are capable...

Chapter Fifteen

Gone, But Still Here

Sai hates hospitals. She always has, and recently she's spent more time than she would have liked in one. The hologram of a serene, peaceful outdoor resort complete with palm trees and sound of a calm ocean changes nothing. Sai rests beside Ren's hospital bed. Floating holo-displays track Ren's vitals as she lies peacefully under her covers. Sai adjusts her head from the side of Ren's bed, desperate for comfort in an uncomfortable position. When she feels a hand press softly against her shoulder, she looks up, hoping for good news. She sees Dane's face and can tell he was hoping for the same from her. Her face says nothing good, but still Dane can't help but ask.

"How is she?"

"The same," Sai struggles to say. "She's just like all the others. Her body is unresponsive to any traditional mana poisoning treatment. There's nothing the doctors can do except wait for her to die..." Dane doesn't know how to respond, choosing to find anywhere else to look in the room so he doesn't have to look into Sai's eyes. Changing the subject is his ultimate strategy.

"The cadet under Jones is being interviewed as we speak." Dane cocks his head back as he takes a seat next to Sai.

"Hopefully we'll be able to get to the bottom of what happened soon."

"What's there to get to the bottom of?" Sai asks, keeping her head down. "That officer murdered Blue."

"Yeah..." Dane sighs. There is something about the tone of Dane's voice.

"Is the cadet going to be charged with anything?"

"We'll see," Dane explains. "The officer in question was killed on site, so there's not much we can do in the way of punishment. Besides..." Dane rises to his feet. "Even if Jones had lived, I'm not sure anything would have happened to him anyway." Sai's eyes are red and dry. She was almost completely out of tears, but hearing Dane squeezes out those she has left.

"What are you saying?"

"The law hasn't quite caught up with technology," Dane continues. "Since the sentience incident, androids have been trying to get bills passed in parliament recognizing them as living beings. But even though some parts of society see them that way, on paper..." Dane trails off, hesitant to finish his thought. "They're still considered nothing more than property..."

Property. Blue's life was nothing more than the destruction of property. The reality is shocking and for a moment, Sai wonders why she never really thought about it. She drops her head into the solace of her lap again. Dane places a hand on her head and leans in to kiss it. "I'm sorry, Sai, I know Blue meant a lot to you and Ren. He seemed as though he was almost like family."

"He wasn't like family," Sai mutters into her lap, barely audible. "He *was* family..." Dane nods his head in understanding. "Right, sorry," he says, giving her one more kiss on the head, then stands to leave.

"Dane?"

He turns around. Sai stares at Ren lying still. It's hard for Sai to speak clearly through her raspy voice. "You were right. I should have stayed out of this case." She glances towards Dane. "I should have listened to you..." Dane shakes his head.

"You and Ren did what you believed was right," he says. "You were trying to help." Dane returns to Sai's side and takes her hand in his own while kneeling beside her. "Don't worry, we're going to find this guy, we are going to stop him, and we are going to save Renayaka."

"But," Sai fumbles her words, "Leon, he...he told me there was no cure."

"I don't accept that," Dane says confidently. "We're just going to have to find Leon and force him to make a cure for her, and if that doesn't work, we'll find another way. I promise you we will and when we do, we'll be standing right beside each other." Dane's confidence is surprising to hear, but Sai is grateful to hear it. He's all she has left now.

"You sure about that?" she whispers, lowering her head, "I don't want to get in your way."

"Saiyonoshi," Dane says, "I've known you since you were a little one running around doing whatever you wished without a care in the world. Even if I told you not to, I know you'd go find Leon yourself, and truthfully..." Dane stands and offers his hand to Sai to help her do the same. "I'd want one of the best damn detectives I know helping me find him." A few final tears escape Sai's eyes. She quickly wipes them away and lets Dane help her to her feet.

"One of?" she repeats through sniffles. Dane smiles at her.

"I can't have you getting a big head on me now, can I?" The laugh they share is weak, but it is enough. Dane wraps his arms around Sai. She needs it and when she hugs him back, she can feel his body shudder. It's then that she realizes that he is doing all he can to keep it together himself, and this hug is as much for him as it is for her. She squeezes him tighter. They embrace as long as they can, and once they release, both hold new conviction in their bodies. Dane moves towards the door. "Let's go," he says. "We've got work to do."

"Give me a moment," she says, "I'll be out in a second." Dane nods, leaving her alone with Ren. Sai takes another look at her sister lying in the bed, still, but peaceful. She can't leave before giving Ren a kiss and a promise. She kisses Ren's forehead.

"I'm going to find him," she declares. "I'm not going to let you die." Sai marches from the room, meeting Dane on the other side waiting for her. The two move forward together, never looking back.

Ren rests patiently in the room, the only sign of life being a slight twitch in her hand.

· · · ● · ● · · ·

Sai leans back in the chair Ren so expertly filled. The flat is quiet. Most of the noise in it usually came from her anyway, but without Ren and Blue, Sai can't help but feel like she's in the darkness again. She has to focus though. She has to make it so Ren can come home. She stares at the numerous floating screens in front of her.

"Where are you?" she asks aloud to no one but herself. She stares and stares, but it's clear she has no idea what she's doing. She slams her head into the desk in frustration. "Damnit, how does Ren make this look so easy?" She leans back to take another look. "That's okay, I can figure out where you are myself, but how do I deal with your ability?" One screen has a frozen image of Leon, taken from her contact lens. She stares at it almost without blinking. Her eyes shift down towards the top of the desk. An image of

Shanai Desi is on one of the smaller screens. Sai jumps forward in her chair.

"Of course," she whispers, "but still, how can I stop you without my magic?" She hits herself in the face in irritation. "Come on, Saiyonoshi. You can figure this out." After a couple of seconds, she realizes she can't figure it out and throws her hands into the air. "GAR! I should have asked Blue to teach me how to fight!"

She didn't mean to mention Blue, but hearing his name stirs something different in Sai. Her entire demeanor changes and she lowers her body to lie on top of Ren's station. Her eyes water and a tear escapes down her cheek. "It's...not fair..." She places her face into her folded arms. "I'm so sorry, Blue. I should have realized how bad things actually were. I'm sorry for being such a moron." She stays buried in her arms, allowing herself to cry. Her soft cries are interrupted when she hears a low beep come from the computer. Raising her head to investigate, she spots a diagram displayed in front of her.

"What?" She studies the diagram. She floats her hand over Ren's virtual mouse, combing through the files over and over. "Oh my god, how did you do this, Ren?" Sai feels herself shift from despair to hope with each new click. "This...this is the answer." Sai can't help but smile at the genius displayed by her sister. The celebration is cut short when all the files suddenly disappear, replaced by a single black screen. Confused, Sai watches the screen cautiously until a small green, blinking light flashes on her face. She leans into the computer in utter astonishment.

"No...way..." Her astonishment gives way as her mouth curls into a smile and another tear rolls from her eye. She quickly wipes it away as she reaches for her wristwatch. After pressing a button, a holo-image of Dane appears, hovering in front of her.

"You have something?" Dane asks from his end.

"I do," Sai grins. "I know where Leon is…and I know how to beat him, but Dane, I'm going to need a really big favor…"

· · · ● · ● · ● · ·

The night woodland breeze feels nice against Sai's skin. She is in the woods outside of a mansion a few meters away. She is shrouded under the cover of night save for the full moon giving slight illumination high overhead to the engulfing darkness. Sai looks on carefully from the woods at the dimly lit mansion in front of her. She turns when she hears footsteps approaching from behind her.

"Everyone's in position," Dane says, stopping at Sai's side. He hands her what looks like a gun with a hypodermic needle attached. She nods as she takes the gun and injects the needle into her arm. Her blood fills the empty vial.

"I had my people place them at the points around the woods you specified." He pulls out a small circular device. "You just place that vial in here and you're all set."

"Great," Sai remarks. She places the vial into the circular object. A DNA strand appears floating above it then Sai swipes the display into her wristwatch. She turns her attention back to the mansion. Dane must be able to sense her nervousness because she can see his eyes drift down to her shaking hands. She was hoping to stop that before he checked in with her.

"You got us this far," he says, offering her comfort. "We can handle it from here on in." Sai shakes her head.

"No. I have to see this through." She turns back to Dane with a smile. "I'll be fine, thanks." She walks deeper into the woods behind her. Dane quietly watches.

"I took your word for it because I trust you," he says, "but I should have asked how you could be so sure this is where Leon is hiding."

"It's simple," Sai explains, "this house belongs to Shanai Desi. She's been dead for ten years and yet this house has been continuously paid for by an anonymous family member."

"That seems hardly enough to go on, Sai," Dane replies, worried. "I brought all these people here thinking you'd have a bit more than that."

"It's all I need," Sai replies plainly, "Shanai means more to Leon than even he realizes."

"How can you know that?" Dane asks, his annoyance growing slightly at Sai's passiveness towards the manpower he called out on her whim. Sai stops walking and turns back to Dane.

"Because she's his mother..." She turns back towards the woods, disappearing in the darkness of the trees.

"You sure about this?" Dane asks Sai softly.

"I am," she replies, plugging some numbers into her wristwatch.

"If you mistime anything, or if you can't find him-"

"I'll find him," she cuts Dane off. "I have to." She looks at him and the group of people behind him. "I'm ready when you are." Dane stretches out his hand to Sai. In it is a small blue gun. She hesitates, but takes it, knowing that if nothing else, it will set his mind at ease. She tucks it away in the back of her pants. Dane quietly nods his head and raises his hand, motioning his people forward. Everyone moves stealthily toward the mansion in front of them. Sai waits behind and utters a quiet chant. Her hands turn blue as a small magic circle appears around them. She balls her fingers into a fist then quickly jerks her hand overhead. A blue orb launches from her hand towards the sky. It explodes high in the air and falls to the ground at various places throughout the woods.

Sai turns to a holo-display hovering above her wristwatch, presses a button that says INITIATE, followed by switching her screen to a countdown timer. She swipes the display away, back into her watch and takes a deep breath.

"Okay, Ren," she whispers, "not the craziest thing I've ever done but, yeah…" She watches the group of SPMD members moving on the house, with Dane in the middle.

"Let's do this," she says, making her way after them.

"We ready to breach?" Dane asks, whispering into his wristwatch.

"Yes, sir," an officer replies. The officer places a small device on the door of the house just as another officer completes chanting the incantation for a spell. A black glyph appears over the device and the doorway. Meanwhile a second user finishes their incantation just as a white glyph appears over the black one.

"Sir," a female voice says, "our sensors aren't picking up any life signs in the house, but we are detecting large magic signatures all over. We have reason to believe a mass invisibility spell may be in place. I recommend caution when breaching."

"Understood, lieutenant," Dane replies. "Breach on my mark. 5…"

"If there are magic users helping Leon," Sai whispers, "he won't be anywhere near them."

"2…1…Breach!"

An officer presses a button. The device on the door sends cracks throughout it until the integrity is at risk and the door merely falls apart; however, rather than the debris falling into the path of the doorway, the black glyph turns rapidly, catching all the debris and sucking it inside like a black hole.

It muffles the sound of the door breaking. The black glyph disappears.

The SPMD officers move into the house. They step through the remaining white glyph floating in front of the door and become invisible. They move to different sides of the house to establish a perimeter.

Dane looks at Sai quietly. They nod to each other and follow suit. Sai steps through the glyph and a white glow overtakes her body. She looks around. She is still able to see everyone that stepped through the glyph; however, their bodies are encased by a white glow as well. Everyone that stepped through the glyph is invisible to the outside world but not to each other. Sai observes the mansion they've breached. It is absolutely massive on the inside, with large staircases leading into what feels like infinity.

The captain motions the others to move farther into the house. The fellow officers listen, moving past her. They step with caution, careful to remain alert inside the house that is dark and silent. Sai moves cautiously too, unsure what is about to happen. She looks down at her timer.

The officers move deeper into the house. One enters a dining room. His team follows him carefully, but with purpose. He steps near the dining table and a large red glyph appears beneath his feet. It expands along the ground, surrounding every officer in the room. The red glow intensifies. The leader turns to the others, frantic.

"There are trap gly-" The sound of fire drowns out their words.

BRRRNNNNN

Fire burns along the outline of the glyph and incinerates all the members of the SPMD officers within the dining room. A vertical column of fire melts a hole through the mansion and shoots into the sky above. It travels until it connects with an invisible barrier overhead that illuminates into a large gray glyph. A gray beam immediately shoots back into the mansion and the light illuminating every person's body cracks, then shatters. The SPMD officers are no longer invisible but neither are the other magic users in the mansion. The officers realize they are completely surrounded. Magic users hold positions on the stairs around the foyer the SPMD entered.

"Shit," an officer shouts, "they were here the entire time!" A multitude of glyphs illuminate on the staircases where the enemy magic users are positioned.

"Cover!" Dane shouts. Some officers remove a small piece of tech from their suits and toss it at their feet. The round, circular devices spin and a clear barrier fires upwards, creating a type of mobile cover for the officers. They all quickly jump behind it as a flurry of lightning, fire, ice, and other attacks launch their way. Sai quickly dives behind the cover made by Dane.

Behind their cover, the bombarded SPMD officers attempt to fight back: casting spells, firing weapons, and a few members even summon creatures. It is pure chaos. Sai looks up from her cover, searching for anything that can help tell her where Leon may be hiding. She looks at the stairs. The magic users have stationed themselves as if they are trying to block the SPMD from being able to climb them.

"No," she whispers, "he wouldn't make it so obvious..." She thinks back to the first time she met Leon. She knows exactly where he is. "He's below..." She scoots herself to the edge of the cover, ready to make her move, but Dane grabs her.

"The hell do you think you're doing?!" he shouts.

"I can't get held up here," she says, "I need to get to him."

"We will," he says, "we'll break through. Just wait!"

"I'm sorry, Dane," Sai whispers, shaking her head, "I can't." She snatches her arm from him and dives from behind the cover towards the back of the mansion.

"Damnit, Sai!" Dane tries to go after her but is forced back into cover by a barrage of magic attacks. He lifts his wrist and yells into it. "All units hold your positions! Beat them back!"

Chapter Sixteen

One Last Fight

Sai runs through the house looking for any door that leads to some type of basement sublevel. She stops when she spots a man holding a gun in front of a door. "There you are," she says. As soon as the man notices Sai he raises his gun towards her. She recites a quick chant and creates a blue glyph in front of her that quickly collapses into an orb she tosses forward.

BANG!

The gun shoots. The bullet soars. The orb passes over the bullet, encasing it in blue light. It slows to a crawl. The orb hits the man and he is engulfed in a blue glow. The bullet reverses, reentering into the gun as if it never left. The man resumes his initial pose from before he noticed Sai. The glow around him disappears, but before he can raise his gun again Sai is already on him.

She lands feet first on top of his face. Her weight forces his head to the ground with a force that leaves him unconscious. She looks up just as another enemy spots her. It's a female magic user with really short hair. Shorty. Her body glows brown: earth magic. Brown glyphs appear on both sides of Sai. Sai releases her own spell with her own body encased in blue.

Spikes of rock and rubble spring forth. Sai's magic moves her backwards like a tape recorder on a quick rewind. She dodges the spikes meant to skewer her as she unnaturally reverses to the entrance where she first walked in. Her spell ends and she immediately rushes Shorty. Sai quickly grabs a pan from the table. She throws it with as much force as she can muster. Shorty easily dodges the pan with a simple head tilt. Cocky, Shorty forms a new glyph. She didn't notice the slight blue aura around the thrown pan.

The pan reverses, coming back to Sai. Shorty's head is in the path. Shorty collapses to the ground, a thin trail of blood trickling from the back of her head. Sai dispels the magic on her weapon, finally taking a moment to catch her breath. She turns to the door the two people were guarding. As she opens it, an eerie creak reverberates through the room. Inside, a spiral staircase like before wraps downward.

"He's down there." Her entire body shakes. She is about to willingly enter the mouth of a beast, a beast that's swallowed her whole before. Sai grabs her arms, wrapping herself in a tight hug. She slows her breathing while focusing on Ren the entire time. She is here to save her sister. "Move." Her body now listening, she takes her first steps down the dark staircase.

• • • • • • • • • • •

The staircase seems to stretch forever, the silence abnormally disconcerting. Sai finds herself touching her face. "I'm used to having you in my ear at times like this..." She lowers her hand as she continues to descend. "I'll make him save you..."

Finally Sai reaches the bottom, leveling out into a vast open laboratory similar to the one she found at the abandoned site where she first met Leon. She made good time, arriving earlier than she estimated. She looks down at her watch. The timer she set still has quite a few minutes left. It's not much time, but it should be more than what she needs. She steps inside to search for Leon.

She does not need to look for long before she finds him. In the center of the room, surrounded by a mountain of equipment, vials, and cylindrical glass tubes, he stands. Sai approaches slowly, carefully. She doesn't feel any different but at this range her magic is certainly disabled. She's careful, not quiet. Leon knows she's there, but his attention stays focused in his microscope.

"I knew you'd find me," he says, a kind of respect to his tone. "How did you?"

"Shanai Desi," Sai answers flatly. "It wasn't hard."

"Ah," Leon acknowledges. "Yes, I probably shouldn't have used her facilities to conduct my work, but not only were they already equipped with what I needed, but something about working here made me feel at home." Sai's face twists at that last comment. Leon finally looks up from his work. He turns to Sai with a truly sympathetic face. "I am sorry about your android friend."

Sai isn't sure if it's his knowledge or the sincerity of his voice that catches her off guard. "You...you saw what happened?"

"I was keeping an eye on your place," he responds, his voice lowering. "I...wanted to observe Renayaka's progress." Rage boils in Sai at the mention of her sister.

"She's dying because of you!" Sai yells, "Because of your serum!" Sai steps forward. "She told you she didn't want it, and you forced it on her anyway!"

She reaches behind her as fast as she can, quicker than she's ever moved in her life. She rips out the gun. He's quicker. She barely raises the gun when Leon grabs her wrist, takes the gun, and kicks her legs out from under her. She hits the ground hard. "A gun, Saiyonoshi? That's unlike you." He looks at the stolen weapon and his eyes enlarge at seeing its blue color.

"A stun gun?" he asks, surprised. Sai gazes back with a judgmental stare.

"Unlike you, I'm not a killer." Her words are like daggers, but Leon cannot let them pierce him. He tosses the gun inside a nearby incinerator built into the wall of his lab. "You're right about Renayaka," Leon replies as he melts down Sai's hope, "I never intended to force anyone to take HSAP23. I always wanted it to be a choice."

"One you manipulate, but ya know, apples and oranges." Sai offers a sardonic shrug as she pulls herself back to her feet. She has had it with his rhetoric.

"That's because sometimes choices need pushing in the right direction, but in the end, it would still be your choice." He faces Sai directly. She stands across from him, staring at him with rage in her eyes. "I never wanted to hurt your sister. In fact, I meant what I did as a gift, a gift I was sure she wanted, but I see now that I lost my way. I should not have forced HSAP23 on her." Leon points across the room at two vials resting on a stand. "That's why I've been working tirelessly to correct my mistake." The vials are identical yellow cylinders only distinguished by a small marker that says A and B respectively.

"I've finally done it, Sai," Leon exclaims with pride. "I've finally developed a version of HSAP23 that will bestow non-users with magical powers without any risk of killing them. Had I just waited, Renayaka would not have gotten sick."

"I don't believe you," Sai responds plainly.

"See for yourself," he says. With the press of a button a screen appears to her side. It's a real time recording of where Dane and the other officers are fighting various magic users.

"Every single person fighting the SPMD are new magic users. They were *turned* days ago and as you can see, they are still healthy."

"Until they're not," Sai replies, rolling her eyes hard.

"I understand your skepticism, but I have no interest in lying to you. I knew the serum I gave your sister was imperfect, but I hoped for the best results. Unfortunately, that was not the case, and because of that, I decided to give you this option." He again points to the two vials. "Vial A holds the complete HSAP23 modified strain with no side effects. If you give it to your sister, she will recover and be able to keep the magical powers she has gained."

Sai is astonished at his words. She can save Ren without adverse effects! But still she tempers her expectations, not allowing herself to be deceived because of hope. "She won't be a magic user, she'll be whatever it is you concocted."

"Also untrue," Leon counters. "The early trials resulted in users being unaffected by traditional magic negation tactics, but observe." He motions to the screens. Sai looks more closely this time. The SPMD officers shoot anti-magic bullets and the bullets actually work. The various spells of the magic users are negated, making their fight that much harder.

"Why?" Sai asks, her voice betraying her confusion. "Why would you..."

"I never wanted to make non-users better than magic users," Leon explains, "I only wanted them to be the same, benefits and hindrances." Sai lets this sit with her a moment before deciding to indulge Leon further.

"What's in the other vial?"

"In the other is a complete reversal of my mana strain genetic alteration process." Leon looks Sai right in her eyes. "It will completely restore your sister's original genetic makeup and allow her to recover. She can return to the life she once had as a non-user. I'm willing to give you both." He takes a breath before adding, "Just understand that gene manipulation is a complicated process. Using one vial will render the other obsolete. Whatever you decide will be irreversible. Your sister will have to live with whichever decision you make."

Sai cannot believe her ears. She came here ready to fight harder than ever for her sister's life. She never expected to get what she wanted so easily.

"So you see," he continues, "you can walk right out of here with what you came for. You and I don't need to fight and you have no reason to try to stop me." Sai lowers her head. Nothing is going as she expected. Leon patiently waits for her reply. She glances over to the two vials, then back to the screen above. Dane and the other members of the SPMD are beginning to gain ground on the enemy magic users. It'll all be over before long. Leon is telling the truth. She takes a deep breath before speaking.

"No," she says flatly. "I still do."

"Why?" Leon asks. The confusion on his face tells Sai that he expected his argument to be enough. It was calm, logical and right. "What reason do you have? Non-users are no longer at risk. Do you really not understand what it is I'm trying to do?! I'm trying-"

"To make a world where everyone is a magic user." The confidence of Sai's assertion impresses even Leon. "I finally realized it once you said you made the new users susceptible to the same weaknesses as normal magic users. You want everyone to be the same."

"Yes," he breathes, a sense of relief in his voice. Sai can tell he's kept his motivations to himself for a long time. "But not for just any reason. I want to eliminate the discrimination between the two groups completely." Leon steps back towards his screens. He looks up at them. "I hated users growing up. They treated me with blatant disrespect and consistently looked down on me. It wasn't until I developed my ability to negate their magic that they no longer tormented me with their spells." His eyes drift downwards. "But that did not stop their words." Sai's gaze follows his at hearing this.

"I was a non-user and they were users, so naturally, I could never be as good as them. And you know what, Saiyonoshi, they were right. Science dictated that they would be born different than everyone else, and because of that, they would be blessed with lives better than those of us unfortunate enough to be born 'normal.'" Frustration grows on Leon's face.

"And as if that wasn't enough, society itself allotted special privileges to users that were not given to non-users as well. How could we live in a society where everyone could be respected as equal when a specific group had such an inherent advantage over the other?"

"But what you're doing, you're trying to eliminate everyone's individuality," Sai argues. "The differences between magic users and non-users should be celebrated. It adds more diversity to our world. Being different is a good thing!"

Leon's face becomes deathly serious at hearing her speak. His voice lowers and his eyes narrow. "The only people that believe being different is a good thing are those that do not have to worry about being persecuted for being different." Sai grows quiet. His voice and his point linger. "I only wish to live in a world where everyone is given the same chances, regardless of whether they are a user or not. I even mean to eliminate disparate monikers like 'user' and 'non-user' that only mean to further separate us." Leon's face softens again, able to recompose himself once more.

"Listen, Sai, I simply want to live in a world where people are just people. I want to live in a world where we are in fact 'One.' I am not getting rid of individuality. There will still be men, women, short, tall, different hair and eye colors, but everyone will be united under a common experience regardless of background. They will all be magic users."

Sai listens, not uttering a word. Leon uses the opportunity to continue. This is his life's purpose.

"I'm starting with England, but in time, as people learn that HSAP23 no longer poses any risk of death, people around the world will begin to take it. As their neighbors take it, as their friends do the same, they will join, and since my serum changes humans on a cellular level, eventually their children will be born magic users and their children's children, until there will no longer be such a thing as a non-user. There will only be people. Having lived as a non-user and dealing with the discrimination that comes with it, can you honestly tell me your sister would not want to live in a world where people truly are valued as equal?"

Leon waits for Sai's response. Sai wonders if he is right. What is the world her sister lived in until now? What is the world Sai lived in? What would they want?

What would Blue want?

The thought of Blue shakes Sai to her core. The thought of his dismantled body is enough to make her stumble. But she doesn't fall.

She will not fall in front of Leon again.

"What about androids?" she whispers.

"What was that?" Leon asks.

"Where in your plan of global unification do they fit in?" She looks up, eyes teary. Leon is taken aback.

"I-I had not considered them for this phase," Leon stutters, realizing his flaw, "but I will find a way after I implement my plan for non-users first." Sai shakes her head.

"You can't..." she whispers, "it's impossible."

"What did you say?" Leon struggles to hear her.

"I said it's impossible!" Sai surprises herself and Leon with her outburst. She never spared a thought about this before, but in this brief exchange, it all becomes so clear. Sai repeats herself again, this time with a more measured tone. "What you are trying to do…it's impossible."

"I don't believe that." Leon speaks as a matter of fact, not belief. He knows Sai is wrong.

"But it is," she pleads. "There are just too many things to consider. There are things out there that we don't fully know about." Something about her tone catches Leon's attention. He knows she is not speaking hypothetically. There is something other than androids that Sai is referencing. "What are you talking about?" he asks, curious.

Sai takes a deep breath, preparing herself for what she has to say next. "You never discovered what your ability was, right? Your ability to negate magic?" Leon hesitates, knowing Sai knows the answer already.

"No."

"And you don't have any memory of your parents, do you?"

"What are you getting at, Saiyonoshi?"

"I know why you're able to negate magic and why you can't remember your parents." She takes another deep breath, barely able to believe what she is about to say. "The reason you were always so drawn to Shanai Desi is not simply because she was a geneticist whose research spoke to you. It goes deeper than that, much deeper." Leon is quiet. "It's because she was your mother." This revelation is surprising for Leon and he is hesitant to believe it.

"How would that even be possible?" he asks.

"It's true," Sai assures, "but you don't remember because she wiped your memory."

"Wow," Leon laughs, "that's some real science fiction theory you've got going there. Last I checked technology like that didn't exist. How would she have done that?"

"It has nothing to do with technology, but everything to do with what she was." This is the truth Sai has been building up to, an unbelievable fact about their world. Sai stares at Leon with eyes more serious than before. "Leon, your mother was a psychic capable of altering the minds of others." Leon is floored at hearing this. Sai continues getting everything out in the open. "Your ability to disrupt magic casting is a psychic ability, so you're also a psychic..." Sai waits a moment before acknowledging what she has to say next.

"And so am I..."

· · · ● · ● ● · · ·

A few hours earlier, back in Julio's house, Sai and Ren stand flabbergasted in front of him. They can't believe what they've just heard.

"What do you mean psychic?" Ren asks the question as if she is hearing the word for the first time in her life. The floating objects in the room lower with ease. Julio Kim doesn't even look tired. Like Ren, Sai doesn't fully understand the scope of Julio's claim. Psychic? Of course she's heard the word but it meant no more in reality than the word elf.

"It's simple," Julio explains. "Zaradox is a company specializing in psychic research. Ailanne was a researcher working with them and was a psychic herself. Her son was under study because he was a Legacy, a psychic born to two psychic parents and would prove to be even more powerful."

Both Ren and Sai take a step back with Ren falling into the seat behind her. "You're kidding me," she says, "psychics are real?"

"Is it really that hard to believe?" Julio comments. "It is merely another form of nature, the same way magic users and non-users are. Psychics just aren't as well-known because they are a minority in the world currently, and various individuals have done an excellent job at keeping their existence to nothing more than rumors, similar to people talking of ghosts, aliens, and other such hard-to-believe things."

Ren holds her head in her hands, trying her best to accept everything while Sai just stares off without a word. She thought she had a handle on the world, but the last few days have proven anything but. "So, Leon is a psychic?" Ren finally suggests.

"It would be my guess." Julio confirms. "If Ailanna and Shanai are in fact the same person, then her son was most definitely a psychic." Sai snaps back to the conversation. The words have landed. She is finished with the emotions of disbelief, now is the time for progress.

"Assuming what you're saying is true," Sai inquires, "what was Ailanne able to do?"

Julio is able to answer immediately and without doubt. "She was able to alter the memories of others, or even erase them entirely." Sai and Ren glance towards each other, both understanding that the pieces are fitting.

"That...that could explain why Leon has no memories of his parents." Sai realizes. "If she wanted to keep him safe from the Zaradox Corporation by hiding him, it would make sense for her to erase his memory of her so he would never try to find her, just in case Zaradox ever tracked her down." Ren nods in agreement.

"Yes," Julio agrees, "but Zaradox did stop looking for them once word spread that she died. I'm guessing she separated from her son and erased his memory of her as an added precaution." Julio floats his tea over to his hand as he takes his seat again. Sai's seen things float before, but the idea that it's happening without magic breaks every rule of law she's spent her life learning. He sips at his cup with thoughtful reflection. "Must have been hard for her…"

"Wait," Ren says, realizing something herself, "everything Leon has been doing has been because of Shanai Desi." She turns to Sai. "Even the place we first found him was one of her labs. How did he find her if he doesn't remember that she's his mother?"

"Even if you overwrite memory," Julio explains, "there are certain instincts that still draw us to situations or people: similar to déjà vu or a feeling of familiarity to a person or place despite being unable to pinpoint where that feeling originates." Julio takes a long hard look at both Sai and Ren. "The mind may forget but the body remembers. It is the reason muscle memory exists as well. More than likely this Leon stumbled across Ailanne and her research and found an unexplainable interest in her. It's probably what led him to follow her so closely. She was a stranger but felt familiar, and it was a feeling he was unable to shake, so he tried to do his best to follow her through her research."

"This…is truly unbelievable." The waterfall of information threatens to overwhelm Sai.

"It's a theory," Julio corrects, "but one with a high probability of proving true."

"Okay," Ren says, accepting the truth they've heard, "assuming Leon is Shanai's son, and has been following her unknowingly because of his connection to her, and he is in fact a psychic, how do we stop him?" Ren turns back to Sai. "He can still disrupt your magic casting." She turns to Julio next.

"Is there a way to disrupt the powers of psychics?" she asks.

"Not with anything available here," he replies, "and to get your hands on tech like that would take quite some time. Which you seem to be lacking…" Sai goes to sit beside her sister. As for their goal of stopping Leon, they seem to have hit a dead end. "So there's no way to stop him?"

"Well," Julio offers, "you could just try to activate your magic out of his effective range of negation, but you would need to know how wide his ability can affect."

Ren turns to Sai. "I started an analysis of the disruption coming off his body from when you fought him," she explains. "Once my computer is done, we may be able to know how far his ability extends."

"That's great," Sai smiles, "then we'll have a smart way to be able to fight him!" She stands to her feet. All of this was more than she expected, but with this information she can approach him differently. "We should get back. I want to start searching for where he may be hiding and formulating our strategy to take him down!"

"Sounds good to me, baby sis," Ren agrees, excited. "Blue should be able to help us too!"

"Great!" Sai and Ren prepare to leave. They face Julio Kim, not attempting to hide their gratitude. "Thank you," they say in tandem.

"Don't mention it," he smiles.

"Still, who would have thought that psychics were actually real," Sai laughs. "This world is truly amazing."

"It is," Julio agrees. "Sometimes, when you're searching for an answer to a question, you merely have to look outside perceived realms of understanding." Sai freezes in place. She's been so focused on Leon this entire time that a simple possibility never crossed her mind...not until hearing what Julio said. Ren notices her sister's hesitancy to leave. Sai's still expression raises concern in Ren. "Sai?"

Sai slowly turns to Julio. "Mr. Kim?"

"Yes?"

"How many types of psychic abilities are there?"

"That's an unanswerable question," he says. "Similar to magic, new abilities are constantly being discovered and the documented abilities that have been recorded so far number in the hundreds."

"Are there any abilities that have to do with coming back from the dead?" It is now that Ren connects the dots. She also turns to Julio, eager for his reply.

"Reviving from the dead?" he repeats. "I can't say I've heard of an ability that does that." His response disappoints her more than she expects. She hadn't heard of psychics before today, but the chance that she had finally found the solution to her personal mystery excited her more than she realized, even if it was brief. She drops her head in defeat. Another dead end.

"What about having different personalities?" Ren blurts. Sai glances at Ren: a different question and hopefully a different answer. Ren nods and continues. "Are there any psychic abilities where alternate personalities are a side effect?"

"What is this about?" Julio questions before offering an answer.

"Me." Sai responds honestly. "It's about me."

Julio sees the look in her eyes and understands. As if purposefully leaving them in suspense, he takes another sip of his tea, then answers. "Well, there is one ability that has been known to give way to alternative personalities." He looks Sai right in her eyes. "What you're talking about is a *medium...*"

• • • • • • • • • •

Leon stares at Sai, wide-eyed. It's as if the story is just too incredible to be believed, but it's true and Sai knows it.

"A...a medium?" he questions.

"Yes," Sai answers. "Whenever I die, my body allows different spirits around me to take over. When they do, their energy slowly heals and revives my consciousness. Then, once my consciousness has fully returned, they are forced out and I'm able to regain control of my body again." Her gaze drops to her hand. "Rosa, Bill, Yuan, and the others...I'm not really immortal. They're just bringing me back so that I don't stay dead." She chuckles to herself. "I don't even think they realize they're dead."

"That's not...that's just...psychic?" Leon has a hard time accepting everything he's heard.

"Yeah," Sai agrees, "it was hard for me to accept too, but that's my point." She looks up to Leon with confident eyes. "Here you are trying to turn non-users into users when *you* aren't either yourself. You always thought you were a non-user but this entire time you were something completely different." Sai steps forward, gesturing at the world around them.

"Here was this entire other thing neither of us knew was even real. Who's to say there aren't other types of people out there we don't yet know about?" She takes another step closer to Leon. "I really do understand what you're trying to do, but it's impossible. There are too many differences out there." She takes one final step so that she is right in front of him.

"The world is not just black and white," she whispers. "Magic users, non-users, androids, psychics, there are all types of living things in the world, each with its own distinct history and experience. How do we know that psychics don't deal with just as much discrimination as non-users?" Leon is shaken, his entire understanding of the world compromised. Sai sees this and offers comfort, placing her hand on top of Leon's.

"You wanted to find a common experience that every person on the planet would have, as magic users, but there is one thing that users, non-users, androids, psychics, and every other living thing on the planet has in common already." Leon stares into Sai's eyes, wishing to know the answer.

"It's that we are all created."

This resonates. Leon shifts his gaze, lost in his own thoughts and reasoning. Sai quickly glances at her watch. She is almost out of time.

"No matter what we go through in life, at some point, we all have to be 'born,' and it is the one thing we all share. In the end, the only thing that can truly change people...is people." Her words hit home.

His entire life has been built around the idea that he could force the world to change. The very notion that he can do nothing is difficult for him to accept. "So what you're saying is that my plan is impossible? You're saying it's impossible to eliminate persecution and discrimination?" There is a sadness, a hopelessness behind his words, a hopelessness Sai will amend.

"What I'm saying is that making us all the same isn't the answer, learning more about each other is." She hasn't had her answer for long, but it's one she was able to reach because of everyone. Ren, Blue, even Leon. Each of them allowed her to find an answer to this mystery. An answer she believes in. "As long as we have differences, we can't eliminate bigotry and hatred one hundred percent, but maybe by talking and understanding each other, we can get to ninety eight." The words linger in the air. Their arguments and perspectives laid bare, they are reaching the end of their interaction. All that is left now is to choose.

"No," Leon whispers. His assertion is without hesitance or fear. The doubt he showed in the presence of her argument evaporates. "That's not good enough." He hits Sai's hand away. "What you propose is akin to doing nothing! The worst thing anyone can say is 'that's just the way the world is!' It's lazy and gives an excuse to do nothing about it! Not me! I'm doing something! I will change the world and allow us to live together in an age where hatred, bigotry, persecution, and discrimination are one hundred percent removed!" Sai instinctively steps back. She can't convince him anymore and she knows it.

"What have you ever done, Sai, you, who just realized this world wasn't perfect for everybody and lived as such?!" His voice booms, all manner of calm a memory.

"I never sai-"

"You enjoyed your life as a magic user! Did you ever once reject the privileges bestowed upon you for just being born 'better,' or did you happily take advantage of every unfair benefit allotted to you?!" Leon steps towards Sai. "What actions have you taken? All you offer are words, and your solution to the problem is more words?" Each step has the force of an army marching on a conquest. Sai slowly retreats as his anger reaches a fever pitch. This is not the same man Sai has been talking to.

"I reject your solution, and I reject your weakness! Talking may solve some problems, but it will not solve this. Your 'talking' is merely another way for you to remain apathetic towards the problem, allowing yourself to simply converse about an issue that doesn't really affect you from the safety of your privilege, never having to truly devote anything of yourself!"

It's clear to Sai. The damage is done, the pain deep rooted. There is no coming back. There are no more words to be shared. The conversation is over.

Sai backs away from him, glancing down at her watch with every step. The timer just reaches zero.

· · · ● · ● · ● · ● · · ·

Outside the mansion, at various positions throughout the woods, sit large, mounted guns. They each initialize and charge up to full power.

The guns fire laser beams at the mansion.

The lasers don't travel instantly.

They move slowly with a blue aura engulfing them.

· · · ● · ● · ● · · ·

She stops moving, prepared to hold her ground while taking note of precisely where she stands. She meets Leon's gaze with her own as he stops right in front of her face.

"Leon, please," Sai pleads one last time, "there's always another way. I want what you want. I just believe there's a better way to achieve it."

"Sai! Get away from him!" Dane kneels on the staircase, gun trained down on Leon. "Stay over there, Dane!" She shouts. Leon quickly looks towards Dane, then back at Sai. She hasn't known him long, but she knows that look.

He is never going to stop. She knows what she has to do.

"It doesn't have to end like this..." Sai whispers.

"This isn't an end," Leon whispers back, "it is a beginning. The world only changes...when you force it to..." Sai lowers her head. To Leon, the gesture appears as defeat, to Dane, as fear, but for Sai it is none of those things.

It is sadness.

"I'm sorry..."

The blue aura disappears from the lasers.

Sai drops to the ground. Multiple lasers pierce the walls around the lab from all angles. The walls remain undamaged as the lasers fire at Sai. They miss her and hit Leon. More lasers fire. He dodges away. Sai rolls across the ground quicker than ever. A beam skims over her shoulder. Clothing and flesh burn away. Dane ducks to avoid the fire but nothing is actually near him. Just as suddenly as it begins, it ends. An eerie quiet creeps through the lab. It is broken by short, dragging steps. They stop just short of Sai. When she looks up, a sizzling Leon looks down. Burns cover his body. Parts of his clothing are ignited with small fires. "What...what happened?" he asks. He kneels and falls over to the ground.

Sai lets out a sad sigh as she moves closer to him, pulling a holo-display from her wristwatch. On the display is a timer clock that has reached zero, as well as a few targeting screens showing Sai's outline where they currently are. There is also a rough outline of guns lined on the outer edges of the hologram.

"The SPMD retrieved these guns from an illegal auction earlier this month," she explains. "As long as you have the DNA of the target you want to...kill...you can set these weapons up before hand and program them when to fire."

"I didn't have your DNA," she continues, "so I used my own." She walks around the lab, showing the display to Leon the entire time. The guns shift, continuing to target her. With each step they adjust ever so slightly to aim where Sai is located.

"Since I knew I wouldn't be able to use my magic around you, before I came in here I cast a spell on the guns."

• • • ● • ● • ● • •

Sometime earlier, before Sai entered the mansion: She stands on the edge of a hill. Her hands lit in blue, she throws her orb into the air. At its apex it splits, then falls to various locations on the ground. The segments of the orb fall on each of the mounted guns set up around the mansion, engulfing them in a blue hue.

· · · ● · ● · · · ·

"Once the timer hit zero, the guns would fire." Sai shows Leon the timer again. "My spell gave me time to notice my position, make sure you were near me, and allow me to move when I realized my spell would wear off."

"You...you were setting me up?" Leon struggles to say, sounding betrayed that everything she said to him was nothing more than her attempt to get him to drop his guard.

"I didn't want to," Sai assures, "I didn't want to have to use them, but you needed to be stopped."

"Why?" Leon laughs. His laugh is interrupted by the blood he coughs up. "Because you didn't want to lose?"

"No," Sai says, shaking her head, "a lot of people died because of you...and you have to pay for that..." Dane approaches from behind Sai, lowering his gun. She turns to face him, both relieved that everything is finally over.

"Hey..." she says.

"Hey," he says back.

"Everything alright upstairs?"

"They're locking it down," he informs her, "I ran off in the direction I saw you go the moment I could, but it looks like you had everything under control."

"Yeah, sorry," she replies. "I know we said we'd do this together, but because of my plan, I had to face him alone." Dane clearly does not approve but what's done is done, so he lets it go.

"I realized. At least it worked out." No sooner are the words out of his mouth than Leon appears behind him like a ghost.

"Dane, look out!" Sai tries to warn him as fast as she can. Dane is impressive, able to pull his gun almost completely on Leon, but Leon is milliseconds quicker. Leon punches him hard in the gut. The sound of cracking ribs reverberates in the air. Blood hits the ground. Leon kicks out Dane's leg. The bones bend in directions they shouldn't and his body follows. The gun hits the floor but, as with Sai, before Dane can fall Leon grabs him by the head, wrapping his arms around it like a vise. He's going to break Dane's neck.

"Stop!" Sai extends her hand as if it's the only thing that will stay Leon's own. Leon's breath comes in bursts. His raspy and disheveled appearance is a far cry from the collected, fastidious man he once was. His disorder is only matched by his desperation. Sai raises her hands in surrender. She looks down at Dane, hoping this isn't the last few moments she'll see him breathing. "You said you only killed people as needed. You never wanted so many people to die right? I believe you." Leon pauses, his eyes unable to meet Sai's. Dane is completely unconscious from the pain. Leon's hold is the only thing keeping Dane's body up. "If you believe what you said, then there's no reason to hurt him." Leon hesitates, struggling with what he should do.

"Please, Leon...let him go..." Her voice is soft, begging. She's lost so much already. She can't lose Dane, too. Leon waits, considering her words, and for the briefest moment Sai wonders if this is what Ren was feeling all those times before. She's able to breathe again when Leon releases Dane, dropping him to the floor. Leon stands firm, burned and in pain, but firm nonetheless.

"I can't let you stop me," he says, "you know that, right?"

"I know," Sai whispers in return, "and you know I can't let you go, right?"

"I know." Resigned to what has to happen, the two stand across from each other. The lab is lonely, quiet, their breathing being the only sound. What Sai feels isn't tension, but serenity. It is a strange thing to feel in the moment, and it's followed by an even stranger thought; she wishes she could stay in this moment for just a little longer. It's impossible though. They know what must be done and they're both in agreement.

One last fight.

It's unclear who lunges first, or perhaps they both lunge at the same time, but before either of them realizes, they're fighting. They are not merely fighting for their lives, but their ideals.

Leon is slower than when he first fought Sai, gasping in pain with each of his swings. Sai, still not being the best of fighters, struggles to hit Leon with enough force to hurt him. She takes hits and so does he. Each of them would like to fight more effectively than they currently are, but neither is able. There is no form, no strategy, just random punches and kicks whenever opportunity comes.

Their blood splatters any surface around them, mixing together till the blood's owners become indiscernible. As their arena is coated more and more in red, so are their bodies, but neither fall. Leon steps back for a brief moment to look upon the girl in front of him. She is battered, bruised, and barely able to stand, but in her eyes he sees her determination, the same determination that once carried him so far. She rushes back at him. As she steps closer, her eyes lit by a fire not present before, it's as if the very wings of her resolve carry her forth and in that moment, he admires her. It is enough.

Sai's punch connects point blank in Leon's face. The force is enough to send him flying back. He hits the ground hard, landing face up, on his back. Sai falls forward. Everything she had left was put into that swing. She stops herself from hitting the ground completely, supporting herself on hands and knees. As she kneels across from Leon, he stares up at the lab ceiling above.

"I...I can't move..." His voice is low, soft, reminding Sai of the time they first met.

"Same," she whispers. The two rest, the serenity that existed before the fight returning because of their inability to continue.

"I'm sorry." Leon's words drift in the air.

"For what?" she finally asks.

"For what I did to your sister...and for what I did to you..." Silence again. As Leon lies there, he makes no attempt to move or escape. For the first time in his life, he can't fight, so he doesn't try. "I really respect you two," he smiles. "I wish I could have met you both under different circumstances...I think we would have gotten along..."

"Nah." Sai smirks. Looking at him resting there, harmless, she would have never thought this one man could have caused so much pain. "You would have liked my sister. I would have still pissed you off..."

"Perhaps..." Leon closes his eyes. "I guess I will be arrested soon."

"If all goes well," Sai retorts.

"Saiyonoshi?" She looks at him. He looks at her with a firm gaze. "Based on your experiences, I do not believe the reason for why you feel the way you do is wrong, but I do believe the way you feel in itself is." Sai just listens. "Regardless, I would like to talk about it again sometime. Do you think we could?"

"You attacked my sister, killed countless people, and even killed me once," Sai laughs quietly and concludes, "maybe..."

A smile crosses Leon's face. "Good enough for me..."

A strange feeling runs through Sai, a feeling as if she is tired, exhausted. She feels herself fading, disappearing into the darkness. It's the same as when she dies. Her head lowers and silence overtakes the room once more. After a moment, she stands and makes her way over to Dane. Leon can hear her walking, but her steps aren't the steps of someone who was unable to move seconds earlier. He turns his head in her direction.

"Saiyonoshi?" No answer. He cannot see her and he's too hurt to lift his head any further. Soon her steps change direction again. Now she approaches him. As she draws closer, Leon can tell something's changed, and he can't shake the uneasy feeling crawling up his spine. She kneels down beside him, but the first thing he sees isn't her face, but rather, Dane's gun pointed at his head.

"Saiyonoshi…" he whispers once more. She shakes her head without an answer. It's at that moment Leon realizes what's happened. His next question is a simple one.

"Who…who are you?"

"My name is Yuan."

The voice is different from Sai's, even Rosa's. This voice speaks with a tone neither calm nor sweet. There is an assuredness in it the others didn't have, but it acts as a veil for something more sinister beneath.

"You're one of her personalities…"

"Correct."

"Did…did she die?"

"No. Sai was completely fine. There was no danger to her life." She speaks matter-of-factly, but there's still something uneasy about her voice.

"Then how?" The chill in Leon's spine remains.

"No one knows this, but I can take over Sai whenever I wish."

"How is that possible?"

Dane regains consciousness behind Sai and Leon, unseen by either. He glances over to her, seeing her knelt over Leon while holding his gun. "Sai?"

"I've always been aware of what I am, and that gives me an advantage over the others," Yuan explains, "but it's only for a limited time, mind you. Her consciousness will always eventually force me back out. It is her body after all." She presses the gun to Leon's forehead.

"What are you doing?" He knows what's about to happen, but what he really wants to know is why.

"You're too dangerous," Yuan explains. "You see, I actually agree that a world of magic users sounds like heaven on earth. It's a way to finally eliminate all the non-users; however..." She cocks the gun back. "In a world of magic users, the one that can negate their abilities is God. I can't allow that."

"What makes you think I'll succeed?" Leon says quietly. "I've already lost."

"No, you haven't." Her assertion impresses him. There's no doubt in her mind. "You may have Sai fooled, but I see through you..."

"That so?" Leon closes his eyes, at peace. "I guess this is it then." Yuan's finger begins to tighten on the trigger. "Tell me something," Leon interrupts. Yuan relaxes her grip.

"What is it?" she asks.

"You're a spirit, aren't you? So you've died before, right?" Yuan's silence is her answer.

"Can you tell me...what's it like to die?"

It's a simple one, a question Yuan can understand, a question about death coming from someone about to face their own. Her face saddens as she reflects on what it means to truly be dead.

"Lonely."

She pulls the trigger.

The shot rings throughout the warehouse. Dane barely holds in a gulp as he watches in horror. Yuan stands, still holding his gun. Yuan looks at her hands and blue light dances around them.

"As I thought," she says, "you can't negate magic if you're dead." She stretches her hand out over Leon's body. A magical glyph appears underneath it. The glyph spins rapidly. As it does, Leon's body begins to decay, breaking down to muscle, bone, and eventually to dust. The glyph then disappears and the dust lightly blows away.

Dane can no longer help himself. He shrieks, grabbing Yuan's attention. When she turns to him, he stares back in disbelief, as if he's never seen her before. He's more right than he knows. "Sai, what have you done?" Yuan walks to him slowly. If her intention is to scare him, she more than accomplishes her goal. She drops the gun beside him and lowers herself down to his level.

"My name is Yuan," she explains, "not Sai." She places a hand on Dane's head the way one would a small child. "You mean a lot to Sai, so I don't want to have to kill you. So listen, Chief, and listen well. Your life depends on what I say next." His fear and confusion hold his tongue, but that's good enough of an answer for her. Yuan's face is dangerously serious. "I hear everything Sai hears and I know everything Sai knows. I can take over her body whenever I wish and she won't even know it's happening. Knowing that, I suggest you don't try to tell her or anyone she cares about what you saw tonight. If you do, I'll make sure to kill you, your relatives, and anyone close to you in the most excruciating ways I can think of." Dane's breath comes in bursts. His inability to respond was amusing at first, now Yuan simply finds it annoying. "Nod if you understand, dear." Dane nods.

"Good." Yuan smiles. "Sai's coming back now, so remember..." She raises her finger to her mouth and purses her lips.

She lowers her head and her movement stops. It's almost as if it were a game of statues, because Dane doesn't dare move either. When he does, it's an involuntary spasm at hearing his name called.

"Dane..." Sai whispers.

"S-Sai?"

She quickly turns back to where Leon was resting. He's gone. Frantic, she turns back to Dane for answers. "What happened? How'd he get away?"

Dane cannot fully understand what is happening. If not for the threat he just heard, he would want to inquire more. "You don't...remember?"

"I...I must have blacked out." She looks up at Dane. "I'm so sorry," she cries, "I figured he wouldn't be able to move. I'm so sorry." Her disappointment in herself is clear. Her energy, tone, personality: this is the Sai he knows. She lowers her face. Five minutes earlier he'd have rushed to console her, but now, he hesitates.

"It's...it's alright," he explains, touching her face. He's somehow able to stop his hand from shaking. "I don't think we have to worry about ever seeing him again."

"How can you be sure?" she asks. He looks deep into her eyes. They are ones he's seen since she was a child, but for the first time, he doesn't recognize them. There's something else behind them.

"Just a hunch," he whispers cautiously, "besides, we have to get the other thing we came here for." Sai realizes what he's referring to: the table with the vials on them.

"Ren..."

· · · ● · ● · ● · · ·

Sitting in the hospital room across from Ren, Sai counts herself lucky she's able to be there at all. Her arm may be in a sling, and she may need to be on a few pain meds for a while, or until she dies again, but for now, this is fine. She quietly looks at her sister resting peacefully in her bed. If Sai didn't know, she wouldn't think anything was wrong with Ren. Sai's gaze shifts down to her hand. She holds both vials within it, one marked A, the other B.

She leans back, letting her focus drift to the ceiling above. So much has happened. There's so much she never knew, never expected. Her eyes shift back to her sleeping sister. Dane stands off to the side, watching Sai with caution. She appears to him just as she always has: a little girl trying to find her way. Still, he knows there's more to her now and for a moment he wonders if he'll ever be able to look at her the same. Dane enters from the hallway. With his leg in a cast and his eyes more tired than ever, he hobbles on his crutches to her side. "You okay, kiddo?"

The quiet of the room is her response.

His gaze turns to the vials in her hand. As if to relieve her burden even slightly, he places his hand lightly against her own. The touch brings life into Sai's eyes and she's able to speak, albeit softly. "I didn't know anything, Dane." She breathes deeply, anything to try and make what she is going through a little easier.

"Blue, Ren, Leon...all their experiences were so different than mine. I never knew what any of them went through." Dane sits quietly beside her, not an advisor but an outlet. "Blue wondered if he deserved everything he went through. Ren told herself it was just the way the world was and there was nothing she could do about it." Tears build behind her eyes. She raises her free hand to her face in a vain attempt to catch them. "Leon felt so strongly that he devoted himself to trying to change the world no matter what." She turns to Dane, barely keeping herself together.

"He's not wrong either. Magic users will continue to be treated better in the future. The world won't change for non-users like Ren. I stopped the one person doing something about it." Her voice trails off, seemingly lost in the air before finding its way back to her throat. "Ren told me she's happy with who she is, but now I have the chance to give her a life where she never has to go through any of that again. How can I be the one to make that choice for her?!" She shouts at Dane, but he's just a body in a room. He could never give her an answer and she knows it. Still, he does his best.

"I've known you girls your entire lives and even I don't understand everything either of you go through. I don't know you as well as you know each other." A deep sigh escapes his chest. "It's tough, not being your father, but feeling at times that I so desperately want to help you as if I was." He leans forward, whispering. "You know what helps me get by, day-to-day?" Sai shakes her head.

Dane smiles. "It's the thought that no matter what happens, you girls will always have each other's backs." He stands, ready to leave Sai with one final thought. "Whatever you choose, I know it'll be what you think will make Renayaka happy." And with that he's gone, leaving Sai and Ren alone. She stares down at her sister. Lying there, Ren looks like she's sleeping peacefully, blissfully unaware of the power Sai holds in her hand. Sai rubs her fingers tenderly against Ren's cheek. Ren is her sister, her partner, and her friend. Sai will always love her.

And she prays Ren will do the same.

The two vials feel heavy in Sai's hand, heavier than any vial of liquid has any right to be. Ren has waited long enough. It is time for Sai to save her. Without a word she injects a vial into Ren's neck...

· · · ● · · ● · ● · · · ·

Day comes slowly. Sai sleeps on top of Ren's covers, snoring loudly with drool trickling from her mouth onto the sheets. She feels something flick her forehead and she jumps awake. Looking up, she sees something more beautiful than anything she could ever see in Scylarus Park.

"If I wanted to have someone drool on my leg, I'd buy a cute puppy." There she was, the sun shining through the windows, illuminating her as if her body could attract the light itself. Ren's smile is enough to warm Sai's heart, but her voice is a fine bonus. "Hey, baby sis."

Tears in her eyes, Sai squeezes Ren with all the strength she can muster, despite only having one arm to do it with. Ren doesn't fight it and squeezes Sai in return. Neither says another word, simply content to hold each other for as long as they can.

Sai eventually allows herself to let go. She makes herself comfortable on top of Ren's bed, beside her legs. Their reunion aside, it was time to supply the answer Ren needs to hear. Sai can see Ren wants her to say it, but Sai chooses to look away rather than face the uncomfortable truth. Since Sai doesn't offer it unprompted, Ren is forced to ask out loud.

"Did you get him?"

Sai considers lying, but ultimately, decides to answer truthfully. "I had him, but he got away."

"I see..."

"We were able to shut down his lab, and Dane seems convinced that we won't see him again, but I'm not so sure, and I know I let you down and-" Ren pulls Sai's head into her chest, cradling it in her arms as one would a newborn baby.

"You're safe, baby sis," Ren whispers, "and you were able to save me. We're together. That's all that matters." Sai allows herself to be held, smiling as her sister hugs her. "I just wish Blue could be here too," Ren whispers sadly. Sai pulls herself away from Ren.

"I have something to show you." Sai removes a small tablet from a bag. She swipes up a holo-display from the tablet into the air in front of them. Ren watches the floating display carefully, but it appears to be nothing more than a black screen with a blinking cursor. She turns to Sai, confused. "What is this?"

"Wait a second," Sai whispers. The cursor moves as words are typed.

Hello Renayaka...I am glad Saiyonoshi was able to save you...

Tears well up in Ren's eyes as she turns to glance at Sai. She knows. "Is this..."

Sai nods her head, giving Ren the answer she hoped for. "It is."

"How...how is this possible?" Her disbelief almost drowns her happiness.

"Before his body was destroyed he was able to upload his consciousness to your computer," Sai explains. They both recall how it took a second before the light in his eye went out.

"He was close enough to our network to place himself wirelessly into your system," Sai continues. "He helped me find the radial analysis of Leon's powers that you had started working on." Sai recalls how she was looking at Ren's files.

· · · · **·** · **·** · · ·

"What?" She studies the diagram. She floats her hand over Ren's virtual mouse, combing through the files over and over. "Oh my god, how did you do this Ren?" Sai feels herself shift from despair

to hope with each new click. "This...this is the answer." Sai can't help but smile at the genius displayed by her sister. The celebration is cut short when all the files suddenly disappear, replaced by a single black screen. Confused, Sai watches the screen cautiously until a small green, blinking light flashes on her face. She leans into the computer in utter astonishment.

Saiyonoshi...It is me...Blue...

• • • • ● • ● • • • •

Ren holds her tablet, barely able to contain her excitement. "This is incredible! He's alive!" she shouts.

"Yeah," Sai smiles. "He can only exist in anything connected to your system for now, but I've already placed an order for a new body."

"Really," Ren says, "a new body huh? He's getting some new upgrades."

"Nope," Sai laughs, "he told me he only wants one that is exactly like the one he had before. If he makes any upgrades he'll do them himself." Ren nods in agreement, unable to fully look away from Blue in her hands.

"It's good to have you back, Blue."

It is good to be back, Renayaka...

"So," Ren says, finally looking up, "where's my breakfast?"

"Huh?" Sai asks, confused.

"You normally make breakfast, and I don't care if I'm in a hospital, you skipped out on cooking a few times this week. You always put it on Blue to cover for you, but you owe me breakfast."

"Been a little busy," Sai argues back, pointing at her bandages and holding her arm, "and where's my dinner? I haven't had a nice warm meal in days!"

"Um," Ren replies, motioning to herself. "I've been in the hospital. What do you want from me?"

"Food, damnit!"

"Well, how could you wake me up and not have a single cute thing for me to squeeze? I probably would have recovered quicker if you just thought to bring a kitten and put it in my comatose hand!"

"Well, excuse me! The next time you're dying, I'll keep that in mind!"

As the girls playfully argue, Dane stands off to the side watching them interact. Their bond brings a smile to his face. He doesn't have children of his own, but standing there watching the sisters playfully tease one another, the warmth spreading in his chest convinces him otherwise. They eventually spot him at the door. Sai motions him to come in and after taking a deep breath, he does.

"Dane!" Ren yells, "what the hell? You let Sai come with you on a mission? What happened to all that yelling you did at me about 'putting her in harm's way' and stuff?" Her impression of him is actually pretty good.

"You know your sister," Dane replies, "she's a hardheaded moron that does what she wants anyway."

"Hardheaded genius is what you meant to say!" Sai laughs back.

· · · · ● · ● · · · ·

Halfway across the city, in an abandoned underground lab, thousands of tiny work droids hibernate. Above their collective "heads" a countdown timer reaches zero and the droids all light up. A door in front of them slides open. The droids pour out of the building and into the street. Inside them are tons of yellow vials labeled HSAP23.

A holo-display illuminates overhead.

Become a magic user, become ONE.

About Author

Chris is a writer from Atlanta, Georgia but currently lives in California. With a love of all things writing, he spends his time taking inspiration from the stories of video games, anime, comic books, and movies. He has two manga titles, Death of Darkness and Edge of the End, which tell two different stories from various artist teams. He is currently hard at work on his next novel in conjunction with work that further explores the world of Revysed.